The Reflection Chamber

Mirrors of the Mind: A Journey into the Supernatural

Adrian L. Harrow

Table of Contents

Chapter 1
Mirrored Beginnings

In the dimly lit therapy room of Dr. Adrian Harrow's clinic in Mireworth, the soft hum of the city beyond barely penetrated the walls. The clinic was a sanctuary, a place of healing, shadowed by rows of tall, ornate mirrors that lined its walls. These were not ordinary mirrors; they were Dr. Harrow's tools, reflecting more than just physical appearances—they peered into the psyche.

Dr. Harrow adjusted the angle of a particularly grand mirror, its surface antique and tinged with the patina of age. As his new patient, a middle-aged woman named Clara, entered, her eyes flickered momentarily towards the mirror, a flash of unease crossing her features. "Good morning, Clara," Harrow greeted warmly, guiding her to a seat facing the mirror. "Today, we're going to try something a little different," he explained, his voice a calm, reassuring timbre that seemed to soften the room's sharp edges.

As he detailed the process of his innovative mirror therapy, Clara's reflection caught her eye—her posture stiffened, then relaxed under Harrow's careful instructions. The session began with Clara recounting her recurring dreams, her voice echoing slightly in the quiet room. Dr. Harrow encouraged her to look into the mirror to observe herself as she spoke. "What do you see, Clara?" he asked gently.

As Clara described her reflection, she paused—a shadow seemed to pass behind her in the glass, though no one else was present in the room. Harrow noted this with a frown, marking it down in his journal. The phenomenon was unusual but not unprecedented in his recent sessions.

After Clara left, feeling strangely lighter yet unsettled, Dr. Harrow remained behind, his eyes fixed on the mirror. The room was silent, the kind of silence that presses against your ears. He replayed Clara's session in his mind, pondering the brief shadow that had appeared. Harrow walked over to the mirror, his reflection staring back at him—a seasoned psychiatrist yet increasingly a man grasping for understanding beyond the conventional. His therapy was groundbreaking, his results impressive, yet doubts lingered like the cool shadows at the edges of the room.

As Dr. Harrow was about to leave the room, he glanced once more at the mirror. For a heartbeat, he thought he saw another figure standing beside his reflection, its features blurred and indistinct. Blinking, he looked again, but the vision was gone. A chill ran down his spine, a rare feeling of dread that he couldn't shake off. He locked the therapy room behind him, the click of the lock unusually loud. Something was amiss, and the ripples were just beginning to spread.

Later that afternoon, as the sun cast long shadows across the cobblestone streets of Mireworth, Detective James Corbin stepped into the quietude of Dr. Harrow's clinic. His presence was a stark contrast to the tranquil ambiance, the crisp click of his shoes echoing off the polished wooden floors.

Dr. Harrow greeted him with a cautious nod, motioning towards his office. "Detective Corbin, thank you for coming on such short notice," he said, closing the door softly behind them.

Corbin settled into a chair across from Harrow, his demeanor one of professional skepticism. "Dr. Harrow," he started, his voice even, "there's been a troubling pattern emerging with your patients. You're aware of this, I assume?"

Harrow's eyes flickered with a hint of defensiveness. "Yes, Detective, I am deeply concerned about the incidents. It's why I agreed to meet so readily. What exactly has your investigation uncovered?"

"There's been a series of disturbances. Patients of yours, experiencing severe psychological episodes shortly after sessions with you," Corbin detailed, unfolding a small notebook filled with meticulous notes. "Can you explain your methods, Dr. Harrow? Specifically, this mirror therapy you've been employing?"

Harrow leaned forward, his hands clasped together. "The mirrors are a tool, Detective. They help patients confront their reflections, their true selves. It's meant to aid in breaking through denial and facilitating recovery."

"But isn't it also true that these mirrors could be causing harm? Perhaps pushing them too far?" Corbin pressed, his eyes narrowing slightly.

"It's a delicate process," Harrow admitted, his voice tinged with frustration. "But no harm is intended. These reactions... they're unexpected. I'm trying to understand it myself."

Corbin flipped through his notes. "There was one case in particular, Clara Roberts. She reported seeing shadows, hearing whispers during her sessions. Care to elaborate?"

Harrow paused, recalling the session. "Clara did mention that, but I assumed it was part of her hallucinatory experiences, a symptom of her condition."

"And yet," Corbin continued, his tone sharpening, "she was found in her apartment yesterday, in distress, claiming that her reflection was watching her, speaking to her."

"That's deeply troubling," Harrow said slowly, a frown creasing his brow. "I need to review all the sessions closely. There might be something I missed."

"Or something you unleashed," Corbin suggested bluntly. "Look, Dr. Harrow, your techniques are unconventional. I respect that innovation can be valuable, but not if it endangers people."

"I assure you, Detective, my primary concern is the well-being of my patients," Harrow replied earnestly. "Perhaps I could show you the therapy room, explain the process in more detail?"

Corbin nodded stiffly. "Lead the way, Doctor."

They moved through the hallway to the therapy room, the door swinging open to reveal the rows of ornate mirrors. Harrow gestured towards them as he explained, "Each session is carefully monitored. Patients are encouraged to talk through their reflections, to confront and reconcile with parts of themselves they've been avoiding."

Corbin peered into one of the mirrors, his reflection staring back at him. "And if these mirrors are more than just glass? If they're somehow amplifying or twisting their thoughts?"

"That's a theory worth exploring," Harrow conceded, the possibility unsettling him. "But how? These are just mirrors, after all."

"Sometimes, Doctor, the simplest explanation is not always the correct one," Corbin remarked, turning back to face Harrow. "I'll be keeping a close eye on this, Dr. Harrow. For now, I suggest you do the same with your mirrors."

As Detective Corbin left, Harrow remained in the room, the weight of the detective's words settling around him like the dusk outside. He approached one of the mirrors, his reflection somber in the fading light. The doubts that Clara had expressed echoed in his mind, mixing with the detective's suspicions and his own growing fears.

Was it possible that the mirrors, his chosen instruments of healing, could indeed be reflecting something dark, something he had not intended? The room grew darker, the only light now coming from the setting sun outside, casting long shadows that seemed to flicker and whisper just beyond the edge of sight. Harrow watched, and for a moment, thought he saw a shadow move where no one stood.

The clinic's waiting room was silent except for the soft murmur of the rain against the window panes. Dr. Adrian Harrow sat across from Elena Markham, his clinic's consultant on folklore and the supernatural. The space between them was filled with open books and scattered papers, their contents dealing with ancient myths surrounding mirrors.

"Elena, this is all fascinating, and terrifying, to be honest," Harrow began, tapping a finger on a page illustrating an old mirror said to trap spirits. "These legends, could they really be related to what's happening with my patients?"

Elena, her eyes thoughtful as she scanned the texts, nodded slowly. "It's not unheard of, Adrian. Mirrors have been at the center of supernatural beliefs for centuries. They're considered conduits in many cultures—gateways to another realm or as traps for souls."

"But these are just ordinary mirrors," Harrow protested, though his voice carried a hint of doubt.

"Are they?" Elena countered gently. "Or perhaps they've become something more under the right conditions? Think about it, your therapy intensifies emotional states, right? What if it's not just about the psyche? What if these emotional states are affecting something more... elemental?"

Harrow considered this, his brow furrowed. "So, you're suggesting that the mirrors might be reacting to psychological energies? Becoming a sort of catalyst?"

"Exactly," Elena affirmed, her gaze intense. "And whatever is happening, it's not just psychological. Adrian, there have been cases, records of anomalies similar to yours where mirrors are involved. You need to consider the possibility that you might be dealing with something... supernatural."

"Supernatural," Harrow repeated, the word foreign on his lips. "I'm a scientist, Elena. I deal with the mind, with tangible things."

"And yet here you are, dealing with shadows and whispers that don't belong in the realm of the tangible," Elena pointed out, her voice soft but firm.

Harrow sighed, running a hand through his hair. "Okay, let's theorize that you're right. What do we do? How do we handle something like this?"

"There are ways," Elena said, flipping through a book to a section marked with old, yellowed bookmarks. "Rituals, specific conditions, certain symbols that can cleanse or bind. It's not science, Adrian, but it might be necessary."

Harrow looked skeptical but intrigued. "And you believe this could work? That we could actually 'cleanse' a mirror?"

"It's worked before, according to these texts. But it's more about containment, prevention. Adrian, if these mirrors are acting as gateways or traps, we need to ensure they do no further harm," Elena explained, her hands gesturing towards the books spread between them.

"Prevention, right," Harrow mused. "Okay, how do we start? What's the first step in this... cleansing process?"

"First, we need to understand exactly what we're dealing with. We need to observe, record, and interact carefully with these mirrors. See if the phenomena can be reliably reproduced," Elena suggested, her voice taking on a tone of professional detachment.

Harrow nodded, feeling the weight of responsibility settle on his shoulders. "And I'll need to speak to the patients involved, observe them outside of the therapy sessions. Maybe there's a pattern we haven't noticed."

"That's a good start," Elena agreed, her expression easing into one of supportive camaraderie. "I'll compile a list of protective measures we can take—symbols, materials that might help shield us from any negative effects."

"As much as this goes against my better judgment, I trust your expertise, Elena. Let's proceed carefully," Harrow decided, his decision firm despite his lingering doubts.

Elena smiled slightly, her confidence reassuring. "We'll handle this, Adrian. Whatever it is, we'll deal with it together."

As the storm outside grew heavier, casting a symphony of rain against the clinic, Harrow and Elena continued their planning, surrounded by ancient lore and modern fear. Unseen by them, a faint shimmer passed over one of the mirrors in the hallway outside, like a shadow flitting across the glass, unnoticed yet palpably present.

Late into the night, the clinic was cloaked in a thick silence, broken only by the low dialogue between Dr. Adrian Harrow and Detective James Corbin, who had returned with more questions and an undeniable curiosity about the unfolding events.

"Dr. Harrow, when we spoke earlier, you didn't mention anything about these... supernatural theories," Corbin noted, his tone mixing skepticism with a reluctant interest as they stood in the dimly lit hallway outside the therapy room.

Harrow, feeling the weight of each word, replied, "Detective, until today, I hadn't given much credence to those theories myself. But things are happening here that I can't explain through conventional psychology."

"So, you're telling me that you believe your mirrors are what? Haunted? Portals?" Corbin asked, arching an eyebrow as he glanced towards the closed door of the therapy room.

"It sounds absurd when you say it out loud," Harrow admitted, shifting uncomfortably. "But yes, something along those lines. Elena has been helping me understand the potential... historical and mythological aspects of it."

"Elena Markham, the folklore expert?" Corbin clarified, crossing his arms. "And she thinks what's happening here has a historical precedent?"

"She does. There are legends and records of mirrors being more than just reflective surfaces. They're sometimes believed to capture or release spirits, based on the conditions around them," Harrow explained, his gaze fixed on the door as if expecting it to burst open.

"And these conditions—are they present here?" Corbin pressed, his detective instincts peaking.

"Possibly. The emotional intensity of the therapy, the specific type of mirrors... It could be creating a perfect storm," Harrow reasoned, his voice a mix of scientific curiosity and creeping dread.

Corbin sighed, rubbing the back of his neck. "Look, Dr. Harrow, I deal in facts, evidence... tangible things. This is out of my usual scope. But," he paused, looking Harrow in the eye, "I've seen enough in my time to know that sometimes, the world is stranger than it seems."

"Exactly," Harrow responded, grateful for the opening. "And I think we need to investigate this fully, scientifically, but with an open mind. Perhaps monitor the room, the mirrors, during sessions."

"You want surveillance? On mirrors?" Corbin asked, his tone a mix of incredulity and intrigue.

"Yes. Cameras, audio... anything that might help us catch whatever is happening," Harrow suggested, his determination firming.

Corbin nodded slowly. "Okay. I can arrange for discreet surveillance. It's... unorthodox, but if it helps get to the bottom of this, then we'll do it."

"Thank you, Detective. I appreciate your willingness to consider... unconventional possibilities," Harrow said, offering a small, tense smile.

"Just don't make me regret it, Doctor," Corbin replied, a half-smile appearing on his face as he turned to leave. "I'll be in touch about the setup. Keep me informed of anything out of the ordinary."

"I will. And Detective? Thank you," Harrow called after him, feeling a mix of relief and anxiety as he turned back towards the therapy room.

Left alone in the quiet of the hallway, Harrow approached the therapy room door, his hand hesitating on the knob. He took a deep breath and entered, the room bathed in moonlight streaming through a small window. The mirrors, usually so still and silent, seemed to pulse with a life of their own. Harrow walked slowly to the central mirror, staring into his own reflection. The face staring back at him was familiar, yet it held a trace of something else—a flicker of motion in the corner, a subtle distortion that wasn't there before.

Harrow stepped back, his heart racing as he scribbled a note to remind himself to discuss the surveillance setup with Elena in the morning. As he left the room, the faint echo of his footsteps mingled with the distant rumble of thunder, leaving an eerie resonance lingering in the air.

Chapter 2
Shattered Reflections

The early morning light had barely begun to filter through the gauzy curtains of Dr. Adrian Harrow's office when the sharp ring of the telephone shattered the pre-dawn calm. The urgent news on the other end was grim: another patient, following a session involving the mirrors, had been found in a state of profound distress at her home, surrounded by fragments of what used to be her own living room mirror.

Harrow arrived at the scene with a heavy heart, his mind racing with implications. The living room was a tapestry of chaos—cushions upturned, books scattered like fallen leaves, and in the center of it all, the shattered mirror. Each shard seemed to echo a silent scream, a frozen cascade of terror that had burst forth from its once-whole structure.

Detective James Corbin was already there, his expression a mixture of concern and curiosity. They exchanged a brief nod; words were unnecessary—the scene spoke volumes. Harrow knelt beside the largest fragment of glass, its surface smeared with the remnants of a silvery, ghostly film. He reached out, hesitated, and then withdrew his hand, a chill running down his spine as if the fragment had whispered a warning.

As forensic technicians moved methodically around the room, Harrow stood and surveyed the chaos. His eyes were drawn to a small, framed photograph that had fallen face-down near the fireplace. Picking it up, he brushed off the glass dust. It was an image of the patient, smiling, captured in a moment of evident joy. The stark contrast between the image and the current reality was jarring.

Turning to Corbin, who was watching the technicians, Harrow finally spoke, his voice low. "Any idea what triggered this?" he asked, though he felt he already knew the answer.

Corbin shook his head, his face grim. "It's unclear, but it seems to follow the pattern—reflection, fragmentation, fear. It's like these mirrors are not just reflecting images, but fears, deep-seated emotions."

Harrow nodded slowly, his mind racing with the implications. The reflections in the mirrors weren't just passive; they were interactive, dynamic, almost sentient. He pondered the possibility that whatever phenomenon they were dealing with, it was not just triggered by the presence of the patient but was somehow responsive to them.

The sun rose higher, casting light that seemed to cleave through the shadows of the room, throwing sharp edges and angles into stark relief. Harrow stepped over to the window, looking out at the city awakening below. The normalcy of the scene outside was at odds with the storm of thoughts raging in his mind.

He needed to find a pattern, a clue, anything that might help make sense of these incidents. Were they purely psychological, triggered by the patients' subconscious fears reflected back at them? Or was there truly something more arcane at work, something rooted in the myths and legends that Elena had spoken of?

As he pondered these questions, Harrow felt a growing sense of duty to unravel this mystery, not just for his professional integrity, but for the safety of his patients. The reflection technique, designed to heal, was revealing depths and dangers he had never imagined. The line between science and myth was blurring, and Harrow found himself standing at the precipice, looking into an abyss that looked back into him.

Resolving to delve deeper into both the scientific and the supernatural, Harrow knew the path ahead would be fraught with challenges. But the journey was necessary, not just to restore peace to his clinic, but to protect and possibly save lives. With each broken mirror, the urgency grew, and with it, Harrow's determination to find answers—or at least, to find the right questions. As he left the patient's house, the shattered reflections behind him seemed to whisper of dark secrets yet to be uncovered, secrets that Harrow was now bound to chase.

Back at the clinic, Dr. Adrian Harrow convened a meeting with Elena Markham and Detective James Corbin in his office, the walls lined with books that seemed to absorb the tension in the air.

"Thank you both for coming on such short notice," Harrow began, his voice heavy with concern. "We need to address the escalating incidents related to the mirror therapy sessions."

Elena leaned forward, her expression serious. "Adrian, the patterns you're seeing—are they all specifically tied to the sessions involving the mirrors?"

"Yes," Harrow confirmed. "Every incident has occurred shortly after a session. It's undeniable now that there's a connection."

Corbin, who had been flipping through his notes, looked up. "Have you considered halting these sessions, Dr. Harrow? Until we understand what's actually happening?"

"I have, and I might have to do just that," Harrow admitted, his hands clasped tightly together. "But I'm also concerned about stopping abruptly. There might be consequences to that as well."

Elena nodded thoughtfully. "It's like we're dealing with something that's been awakened, and we don't fully understand its nature or how to safely interact with it."

Corbin rubbed his chin, his skepticism mingling with concern. "What exactly do you think is happening during these sessions? What are these... effects?"

Harrow sighed, searching for words that sounded rational. "It's as if the mirrors are reflecting more than just light. They're reflecting emotions, fears... perhaps even more ephemeral aspects of the psyche."

"And you believe this is what's causing the disturbances?" Corbin pressed, trying to keep up with the conversation that edged towards the unbelievable.

"It's the most plausible explanation we have right now," Elena interjected. "There are historical precedents for this, cases where objects believed to be ordinary turned out to be catalysts for paranormal activity due to their historical or emotional significance."

"So, we're saying these mirrors might be... haunted? Or cursed?" Corbin asked, his tone incredulous but curious.

"Not in the traditional sense," Elena explained. "But they could be acting as conduits or amplifiers for latent psychic energies or emotions, possibly due to their composition or their history."

Corbin leaned back, processing the information. "This is outside my usual field, but I'm here to help. What do you need from the police, Dr. Harrow?"

"Surveillance and security," Harrow responded quickly. "We need to monitor the rooms where these mirrors are installed, see if we can catch any unusual occurrences on camera."

"That can be arranged," Corbin nodded. "I'll have cameras set up discreetly and ensure someone is monitoring them during sessions."

"And what about the historical research?" Harrow turned to Elena. "Can you delve deeper into the origins of these mirrors? Perhaps understanding their past might help us handle their present."

"I'll start immediately," Elena assured him. "There might be records, sales receipts, previous owners—anything that could tell us more about where these mirrors came from and why they might be behaving this way."

As the meeting concluded, the trio stood, a silent agreement hanging between them that the path ahead would be fraught with uncertainty. They each felt the gravity of their task—an intersection of science, history, and the supernatural that none had anticipated when they first embarked on their respective careers.

Harrow escorted his colleagues to the door, his mind already racing ahead to the next steps. As Elena and Corbin left, he turned back to his office, where the setting sun cast long shadows across the floor. The room felt different now, charged with a new purpose and a new urgency, as if the very air was waiting to see what would happen next.

Dr. Adrian Harrow sat alone in the dimly lit therapy room, the silent witnesses—his mirrors—surrounding him like somber spectators to his deep contemplation. The faint hum of the newly installed surveillance cameras was a stark reminder of the strange turn his scientific pursuits had taken. The air felt thick with the weight of unanswered questions as he reviewed the notes from his previous sessions, each line a breadcrumb on the path to understanding.

Elena Markham knocked softly before entering, her presence bringing a slight shift in the room's atmosphere. "Adrian, any revelations while I was out digging through the archives?" she asked, settling into the chair across from him.

"Not yet," Harrow replied, his voice tinged with frustration. "It's like looking for a pattern in chaos. But your findings could be the key. Anything on the mirrors' origins?"

Elena laid out a stack of old documents and photos on the table between them. "A bit, yes. It seems these mirrors were part of an estate sale about a decade ago. Before that, they belonged to a family known for their eclectic and extensive art collection. There's a history there, perhaps even the kind we're concerned about."

Harrow leaned forward, intrigued. "Do these documents mention anything specific about the mirrors? Any... unusual events or properties noted?"

"Not explicitly," Elena admitted, her eyes scanning the pages. "But I did find a reference to the family acquiring them under unusual circumstances. They were apparently part of an older collection from Europe, rumored to be cursed. It's vague, though—mostly hearsay and speculation."

"That's more than we had yesterday," Harrow mused, his mind racing with possibilities. "We need to trace this back to Europe then. See if there's a deeper history that was never documented properly."

Elena nodded, her expression serious. "I agree. Meanwhile, I suggest we conduct a few controlled experiments with the mirrors. If there's any truth to these rumors, we might be able to observe something under the right conditions."

Harrow considered this, his scientific curiosity piqued despite the circumstances. "What kind of experiments did you have in mind?"

"Simple at first," Elena proposed. "Observational studies, recording what happens when different subjects interact with the mirrors. We could vary the light, the room's setup, the subject's state of mind. See if anything triggers a noticeable effect."

"Sounds like a plan," Harrow agreed, a flicker of hope stirring within him. "Let's set it up for tomorrow. We'll start with observations and work our way up to more interactive experiments."

As they discussed the logistics, the setting sun cast a golden glow through the window, bathing the mirrors in a soft light that seemed to temporarily soften their ominous presence. The room took on a less foreboding air, a brief visual respite from the gravity of their discussions.

After Elena left to prepare for the next day's tasks, Harrow stayed behind, his gaze lingering on the largest mirror. He approached it slowly, a mixture of apprehension and determination in his steps. Placing his hand on the cool glass, he whispered a question into the reflective surface, half-expecting an answer.

Nothing happened, and yet the silence felt like a response of its own. Harrow stepped back, a thoughtful frown creasing his brow as he turned off the lights and left the room. The mirrors remained silent, holding their secrets a little longer, reflecting nothing but the empty room and the fading light as the door clicked shut behind him.

The following morning, the therapy room was prepped like a stage for a pivotal experiment. Cameras and microphones were positioned strategically around the space, capturing every angle of the ornate mirrors that lined the walls. Dr. Adrian Harrow and Elena Markham reviewed the setup, ensuring that everything was in place for the observational study they had planned.

"Are you sure about this, Adrian?" Elena asked as she checked the focus on one of the cameras. "We're stepping into relatively uncharted territory here."

Harrow nodded, his expression resolute. "It's necessary, Elena. We need to understand what we're dealing with, scientifically. If these mirrors have properties beyond the ordinary, it's our responsibility to uncover them."

Elena adjusted the microphone near the central mirror. "Okay, let's start with ambient light observations. We'll see if the reflections change under different lighting conditions."

As Harrow took notes, they varied the lighting in the room, dimming the lights gradually until only a single, soft spotlight illuminated the main mirror. They observed silently, watching for any abnormalities in the reflection.

"Anything?" Harrow finally broke the silence.

Elena, who had been staring intently at the mirror, shook her head. "Nothing out of the ordinary. Let's move on to introducing subjects."

They called in a volunteer, a staff member from the clinic who had agreed to participate in the study. As the volunteer sat in front of the mirror, Elena instructed him, "Just relax and look at your reflection. Tell us if you notice anything unusual."

The volunteer nodded, his gaze fixed on the mirror. Minutes ticked by, with Harrow and Elena watching closely, recording his every reaction.

"It feels a bit colder," the volunteer remarked after a while, a slight shiver in his voice.

"Temperature drop?" Harrow quickly noted it down, then checked the thermometer they had set up. "There's a slight decrease. Could be a draft, though."

"Let's not rule anything out," Elena suggested, her eyes never leaving the mirror. "Now, please describe what you see in the mirror, any details that feel off."

"It's just my reflection... but it seems like there's a shadow or smudge on the glass. It's not on my face but beside it," the volunteer reported, leaning closer, curiosity piqued.

Elena and Harrow exchanged a look. "Noted," Harrow said, writing it down. "Does the shadow move with you if you move?"

The volunteer shifted in his seat, watching closely. "No, it stays in the same spot. That's odd."

"Indeed, it is," Elena murmured, moving to adjust the light once more. "Let's document the position and shape of the shadow."

After several more minutes of observation and note-taking, they concluded the session. The volunteer left, and Harrow turned to Elena, a mixture of excitement and concern in his eyes. "We've got something here. An anomaly worth exploring further."

"Agreed," Elena replied, her mind already racing with hypotheses. "We should review the footage, see if the cameras caught the shadow. And perhaps we can replicate this with other volunteers, see if there's a pattern."

Harrow nodded, feeling a surge of both trepidation and anticipation. "Let's prepare for a series of sessions this week. Different times of day, different lighting, different subjects. We need to be thorough."

As they turned off the equipment and left the room, the shadow remained, imperceptible to the naked eye but captured by the vigilant lenses of the cameras. It was a small, indistinct anomaly, yet it held the potential to unravel the mysteries hiding within the glass, waiting silently for the observers to discover its secrets.

Chapter 3
Into the Past

In the dusty, somber confines of the Mireworth University library, Dr. Adrian Harrow and Elena Markham poured over ancient texts and manuscripts, their quest for understanding leading them to the depths of occult knowledge that lay forgotten in the archives. The room was dimly lit, the only sounds were the rustle of pages and the soft, rhythmic tapping of Elena's pen against her notebook.

"Here," Elena said, her voice hushed as she handed a heavy, leather-bound book to Harrow. "This might have something on the properties of mirrors used in rituals."

Harrow opened the book carefully, the pages yellowed and fragile. "It says here that mirrors were often believed to be windows to other worlds, and in some cultures, they were used to trap or communicate with spirits. It's fascinating and unsettling in equal measure."

Elena leaned closer, peering over his shoulder. "Does it mention anything about mirrors acquiring... properties? Say, from events or emotions around them?"

Harrow scanned the text, his finger tracing the ancient ink. "Yes, actually. There's a passage about mirrors absorbing the essence of their surroundings, becoming more than just reflective surfaces. It suggests that rituals were sometimes performed to cleanse or bind them."

"That lines up with what we've been experiencing," Elena noted, her mind racing with the implications. "These mirrors in your clinic could have absorbed emotional residues, if we're to believe this."

"Do we?" Harrow asked, looking up at her with a skeptical expression. "Do we really believe that an object can absorb emotions, energy like that?"

"It's not about belief in the conventional sense, Adrian," Elena responded thoughtfully. "It's about understanding possibilities outside our current scientific framework. We've seen enough to question the conventional, haven't we?"

Harrow nodded slowly, conceding the point. "Alright, so let's say the mirrors at the clinic have become... charged in some way. How do we cleanse them? Is there a ritual specific to this?"

Elena flipped a few pages, her eyes scanning quickly. "Here, there's a section on purification rituals for objects believed to harbor spirits or energies. It involves salt, herbs, and... oh, this is interesting... a full moon."

"A full moon," Harrow echoed, his tone a mix of intrigue and incredulity.

"It's symbolic, tied to renewal and clarity," Elena explained. "But for our purposes, it's the details of the ritual that might be more pertinent. We could adapt these practices, use them to try and neutralize whatever is happening with the mirrors."

Harrow considered this, his scientific mind wrestling with the esoteric nature of the solution. "And if it doesn't work?"

"Then we keep looking for answers," Elena stated resolutely. "But first, we document everything we do, maintain our scientific approach as much as possible."

"Agreed," Harrow said as he closed the book, dust particles swirling in the air, caught in a shaft of light from the nearby window. "Let's plan this ritual. We need to prepare carefully, understand each component and its purpose."

As they gathered their notes and prepared to leave, the weight of their task felt palpable, pressing upon them with a severity that matched the musty, book-laden air of the library. Yet, there was a spark between them, a shared drive to pierce the veil of mystery surrounding the mirrors, driven by a convergence of ancient knowledge and modern necessity. They left the library with a sense of purpose, the old texts under Harrow's arm feeling lighter than the burden of uncertainty that lay ahead.

The clinic after hours held a silence so deep it seemed to echo through the empty halls, a stark contrast to the bustling daytime. In this quiet, Dr. Adrian Harrow and Elena Markham set about preparing for the ritual they hoped would cleanse the mirrors. The therapy room, usually a place of introspection and healing, was transformed into a ceremonial space, the air thick with anticipation and the faint scent of sage.

Elena laid out the materials they had gathered: salt, which she poured into a circle around the central mirror, and bundles of dried herbs tied with string. The full moon was two nights away, and they planned to use its light, believed to purify and renew. She explained the symbolism of each item to Harrow, who took meticulous notes, his skepticism tempered by a growing curiosity about the potential of these ancient practices.

"Salt is often used as a barrier in folklore, to protect and to bind," Elena said as she carefully positioned the last of the salt. "It's supposed to prevent anything harmful from crossing."

Harrow nodded, his gaze fixed on the circle of white grains. "And the herbs?"

"They're for purification, to cleanse any negative energies," she replied, lighting the end of a bundle and letting the smoke drift gently around the room. "Different cultures use different herbs, but sage is one of the most common for these purposes."

As they worked, Harrow felt a shift in the atmosphere. Whether it was the actual items they were placing or simply the intent behind their actions, the room seemed to pulse with a new energy. The mirrors, once mere reflective surfaces, now took on a more ominous presence, as if waiting for the ritual to challenge their hidden depths.

Once the preparations were complete, they stepped back to review the setup. Harrow's mind, usually so grounded in the tangible and the scientific, found itself grappling with the reality of what they were about to undertake. The blend of Elena's knowledge of folklore with his own experiences created a bridge between two worlds, one he had never planned to cross.

"We'll need to be very precise with the ritual," Elena reminded him, checking the alignment of the herbs and the salt. "Everything has to be done just right, according to the traditions we're drawing from."

Harrow, looking around the room, felt a mix of apprehension and a faint, uncharacteristic thrill. "This is outside anything I've ever done," he admitted. "But if it can help... if it can really do something about the mirrors, then it's worth it."

"Exactly," Elena agreed, her expression serious but her eyes alight with a scholar's passion for the unknown. "We're venturing into uncharted territory, but we're doing it with as much preparation and knowledge as we can gather."

They finished their preparations in silence, each lost in their own thoughts about the coming night of the full moon. As they left the therapy room, the door closing softly behind them, the salt circle glinted in the dim light, a stark white line against the dark floor. The herbs' smoke lingered, a fragrant reminder of the ritual to come, blending the ancient with the modern in an uneasy truce.

Outside, the clinic was quiet, the city sounds muffled by the walls, but inside, the preparation had stirred something that felt like the beginning of an answer, or perhaps more questions. As they walked down the hallway, the echoes of their steps seemed to carry a weight, a resonance with the past that they were about to invoke, under the light of the moon that had witnessed countless such rituals before.

Under the clear night sky, with the full moon casting a silvery glow, Dr. Adrian Harrow and Elena Markham stood ready outside the clinic, the chill of the night air wrapping around them like a cloak. The therapy room, visible through the window, glowed faintly with the light of several candles placed in a precise arrangement around the room.

"Are you ready for this?" Harrow asked, looking over to Elena with a mixture of anticipation and anxiety.

"As ready as we can be," she responded, clutching a small, leather-bound book of rituals. "Remember, every step needs to be performed exactly as we planned. The alignment with the moon, the circle of salt, the invocation—everything is crucial."

Harrow nodded, taking a deep breath to steady his nerves. "Let's begin then. You lead, I'll follow your cues."

They entered the therapy room, stepping carefully over the threshold while avoiding the salt circle. Elena directed Harrow to stand to one side of the circle while she positioned herself on the opposite side. She opened the book to a marked page, her finger tracing the lines of an ancient invocation.

"First, we light the sage again, to cleanse the space as we start," she instructed, handing Harrow the smoldering bundle. He took it, waving the sage around the perimeter of the salt circle, the herbal smoke twisting and curling in the moonlight streaming through the window.

"Now, repeat after me," Elena said, her voice taking on a solemn tone as she began the invocation. "Spirits of the mirror, we call upon thee."

"Spirits of the mirror, we call upon thee," Harrow echoed, his voice steady.

"To the forces that bind, we offer release," Elena continued, her eyes fixed on the text.

"To the forces that bind, we offer release," Harrow repeated.

"Accept this offering, return to peace," Elena said, closing her eyes briefly.

"Accept this offering, return to peace," Harrow recited.

Elena then closed the book and placed it gently on the floor beside her. "Now, we pour the salt water around the outside of the salt circle, to reinforce the boundary and seal the ritual space," she explained, handing Harrow a small bowl filled with water mixed with salt.

Carefully, Harrow walked around the circle, pouring the saltwater slowly, his hand steady despite the surreal nature of the actions. The moonlight seemed to intensify, bathing the room in a spectral light, making the mirrors shimmer ominously.

"Finally, we ask for closure and peace," Elena stated, her voice a whisper now. "With this circle complete, let no spirit or shadow remain trapped. Be released and be at peace."

"With this circle complete, let no spirit or shadow remain trapped. Be released and be at peace," Harrow repeated solemnly, feeling a sudden drop in temperature, a sign, perhaps, of the ritual taking effect.

Elena nodded, a signal that the formal part of the ritual was done. "It's finished. We've done all we can. Now, we wait and watch."

They stepped back, observing the mirrors. The air felt charged, a static hum that raised the hairs on Harrow's arms. They watched in silence, the only sound the soft flicker of candle flames.

After a long moment, Elena spoke, "Do you feel that? The room—it feels lighter."

Harrow, peering intently at the mirrors, realized that the oppressive feeling that once hung over the room like a pall seemed to have dissipated. "It does. Whether it's the power of suggestion or the ritual, something feels different."

"We'll need to monitor the room over the next few days, keep a close eye on any changes or lack thereof," Elena suggested, already thinking ahead to the implications of their actions tonight.

"Agreed," Harrow said, feeling a cautious relief. "Let's hope we've truly brought some peace to this place."

As they extinguished the candles and prepared to leave the room, the moonlight remained, a silent witness to the night's events, its light streaming through the window undimmed. The shadows that once danced at the edges of the mirrors seemed to have retreated, leaving behind only the reflections they were meant to hold.

The following morning, Dr. Adrian Harrow and Elena Markham met in his office, the early sunlight filtering softly through the blinds, contrasting sharply with the intensity of the previous night's ritual. They sat opposite each other, each holding a cup of coffee, the steam rising gently.

"Have you noticed any changes since last night?" Harrow asked, his eyes searching Elena's for any sign of confirmation.

Elena set her cup down, her brow furrowed in thought. "It's too soon to say definitively. The atmosphere felt lighter when we left, but whether that's a lasting change or just a temporary effect, we'll need more time to evaluate."

Harrow nodded, sipping his coffee slowly. "I agree. The real test will be observing the patients' reactions during their sessions. Have you scheduled any follow-ups?"

"Yes, I've arranged for a few of the patients who experienced disturbances to come in later this week. We'll see if there's any recurrence of their previous experiences," Elena replied, tapping her fingers against her notebook.

"That will be the true measure," Harrow acknowledged. "If the ritual did have an effect, we should see a reduction, or hopefully, an elimination of the anomalies."

Elena leaned back in her chair, her expression thoughtful. "Adrian, what if the changes aren't as clear-cut as we hope? What if there's only a partial reduction in the phenomena?"

Harrow considered this, his eyes narrowing slightly. "Then we go back to the drawing board. We'll need to consider other variables that might be influencing the results. It might not just be the mirrors but something more intrinsic to the patients or the environment."

"That's a valid point," Elena agreed, her mind already racing through possible scenarios. "We should also keep an eye on any external factors that could be influencing the outcomes. Anything from environmental stressors to changes in the patients' personal lives."

"Absolutely," Harrow said, his tone firm. "Let's document everything meticulously. We need as much data as we can gather to make informed decisions moving forward."

Elena nodded, her gaze drifting to the window where the morning light was growing stronger. "I'll start compiling a detailed observation schedule. We'll monitor the therapy sessions, the environmental conditions in the room, even the times of day when the sessions are held. Everything could be relevant."

Harrow smiled slightly, appreciative of Elena's thoroughness. "Your attention to detail is invaluable, Elena. This situation... it's stretching the boundaries of my usual practice."

"It's a challenge, but one we're meeting head-on," Elena said, returning his smile. "Whatever the outcome, we're learning, adapting. That's key in any scientific endeavor."

Harrow's smile widened a bit. "Scientific and, perhaps, a bit beyond the scientific," he mused, glancing at his notes from the ritual. "I never thought I'd see the day when I'd be conducting a ritual in the clinic."

Elena chuckled. "Life is strange, Adrian. It often leads us down paths we never expected to take."

As their meeting drew to a close, they both felt a renewed sense of purpose. The challenges they faced were daunting, but the path they were on was illuminated by their shared commitment to uncovering the truth, whatever it might be.

They left the office together, stepping into the bustling corridor of the clinic. The world outside continued unabated, oblivious to the small mysteries being unraveled within the clinic's walls. Harrow and Elena parted ways at the door, each moving back into their routines, the shadows of the previous night lingering just out of sight, waiting to reveal their secrets.

Chapter 4
Reflections of Doubt

Detective James Corbin stood in the middle of the therapy room, his eyes scanning the array of mirrors that adorned the walls. Dr. Adrian Harrow had arranged to meet him there, hoping to gain a better understanding of the therapy methods that might be linked to the mysterious incidents.

"You believe these can help people confront their innermost fears?" Corbin asked, skepticism lacing his voice.

Dr. Harrow nodded, explaining the psychological principles behind his methods. "Yes, Detective. The mirrors aren't just reflective surfaces; they're tools that help patients see themselves more clearly, to confront what they usually avoid or deny."

Corbin, hands clasped behind his back, walked slowly around the room. "And these incidents... the disturbances you've called me about... you think there's something about the mirrors that's causing them?"

"It's one theory," Harrow admitted, his voice betraying a hint of doubt. "We're exploring all possibilities, but yes, there seems to be a connection between the mirror sessions and the... occurrences."

"And what exactly are these occurrences?" Corbin probed, stopping to peer into one of the mirrors, his reflection staring back at him.

"Patients have reported seeing distortions in their reflections, feeling presences, hearing whispers," Harrow explained, watching the detective's reaction closely.

"Presences? Whispers?" Corbin turned to face Harrow, his brow furrowed. "That sounds more like a psychological break than anything else."

Harrow sighed. "Normally, I would agree. But the consistency of reports, from patients with no prior history of hallucinations, suggests something else might be at play."

Corbin resumed his slow pace around the room. "And you've brought in Ms. Markham to help? The folklore expert?"

"Yes, her expertise has been invaluable," Harrow confirmed. "She's helping us understand the historical and cultural context of mirrors, which might give us insight into these... phenomena."

Corbin shook his head slightly, clearly struggling with the concept. "Mirrors with historical powers... It's a bit out there, Harrow."

"I understand how it sounds," Harrow conceded, walking alongside the detective. "But I've seen enough to believe that we need to consider all angles, even the less conventional ones."

"And these rituals you mentioned," Corbin said, stopping to face Harrow directly. "You seriously believe that performing some sort of... ceremony around these mirrors can change what's happening?"

Harrow met his gaze steadily. "We're considering that possibility, yes. If there's even a chance it could help, I have to try it."

Corbin nodded slowly, processing the information. "Well, I'll say this: I've seen a lot in my time, and I've learned there's often more to things than meets the eye. I'll keep an open mind, but I'm here for facts, Harrow. Anything concrete you find, I want to know."

"Understood, Detective," Harrow replied, appreciating the man's openness. "And thank you for keeping an open mind."

"As long as you keep looking for logical explanations too," Corbin said, offering a slight smile. "Keep me posted, Doctor. This is your field, but remember, it's my case now too."

As Corbin left the room, Harrow felt a mixture of relief and apprehension. The detective's involvement added a new layer of complexity to the situation. He glanced back at the mirrors, their surfaces quiet and inscrutable, keeping their secrets for now. Harrow knew that the answers might lie hidden in the reflections, waiting for the right moment to reveal themselves.

Back at the clinic, another session ended with the air feeling charged, the room colder. Detective Corbin's unexpected visit added tension, mingling with the lingering smell of sage left from the ritual. Dr. Adrian Harrow paced the length of the therapy room, his thoughts as tumultuous as the storm clouds gathering outside the window. Each step he took was a physical manifestation of his inner turmoil, echoing softly off the clinic walls.

Elena Markham arrived shortly after, her expression reflecting a mix of concern and curiosity. "Any changes since the ritual?" she inquired, her voice low, as if afraid to stir the quiet.

Harrow stopped pacing and turned to her, his face drawn with fatigue. "It's hard to say definitively. The room feels different, emptier somehow, but whether that's due to the ritual or just my perception, I can't be sure."

Elena nodded thoughtfully, her eyes scanning the mirrors. "Perception or not, any change is worth noting. Have the patients reported anything unusual today?"

"Not as of yet," Harrow replied, his gaze following hers to the mirrors. "The day is still young, and the real test will be during the sessions themselves. We'll have to observe closely."

As they talked, a patient arrived for her scheduled session. Harrow and Elena paused their discussion to focus on the task at hand. The woman seemed tense, her eyes darting nervously towards the mirrors as she entered the room. Harrow greeted her warmly, trying to ease her anxiety, but the atmosphere in the room remained thick with unspoken questions.

Throughout the session, Harrow observed the woman carefully, noting every flinch, every hesitant glance she cast toward the mirror. The session unfolded without incident, yet the tension never fully dissipated. The mirrors remained silent observers, reflecting nothing out of the ordinary today.

After the patient left, Harrow and Elena reviewed the session's audio recordings. "No disturbances, no anomalies captured," Harrow noted, a trace of relief in his voice. "Perhaps the ritual had some effect after all?"

"Or perhaps today just wasn't the day for them," Elena suggested pragmatically. "We can't draw too many conclusions from a single, uneventful session."

Harrow acknowledged her point with a nod. "True. Consistency will be key. We'll need to keep monitoring the sessions, keep looking for any patterns or triggers that might have been overlooked."

The day wore on, the sky outside darkening as the promised storm began to make itself known. Rain tapped against the windows, a rhythmic sound that seemed almost in sync with the ticking of the clock on the wall. Time, it seemed, was moving both too quickly and too slowly, each second laden with potential.

As evening approached, Harrow prepared to close the clinic. The day's sessions had provided no new insights, leaving him with a mix of frustration and cautious optimism. Maybe the mirrors had settled. Maybe the disturbances were over. Or maybe, he thought as he turned off the lights, the quiet was just the calm before another storm.

Elena left with a promise to continue her research into the mirrors' origins, hopeful that historical records might yet reveal something useful. Harrow watched her go, her figure gradually disappearing into the rain-soaked evening. He locked the clinic door behind him, the sound echoing in the empty hallway.

Outside, the city was a blur of wet streets and hurried people. Harrow stood under the awning, watching the rain fall, the droplets reflecting the neon lights of the city in countless tiny flashes. The world moved on, oblivious to the small mysteries harbored within the walls of his clinic. Yet those mysteries lingered, hanging in the air like the humidity before a storm, waiting for the right moment to manifest.

In the dimly lit interior of Dr. Adrian Harrow's office, the shadows seemed to play on the walls as he and Elena Markham discussed the latest developments. The rain had ceased, leaving a silence that filled the room with a weighty presence.

"Adrian, the historical research is proving more fruitful than expected," Elena began, her laptop open to a document filled with ancient script. "I've traced the mirrors back to a collector in Prague, early 20th century. He was known for his fascination with occult artifacts."

Harrow leaned forward, intrigued. "Prague? That's significant, isn't it? The city has a rich history of mystical lore and alchemy."

"Yes, exactly," Elena confirmed. "And there's more. This collector, Gustav Malinovsky, was reputed to have held séances in his home, using various artifacts to supposedly bridge the world of the living and the dead. The mirrors were part of his collection."

"A séance," Harrow mused aloud. "That could explain a residual... presence, for lack of a better word. If the mirrors were used in such rituals, they might well have absorbed something of those events."

"It's a strong possibility," Elena agreed. "The question now is, what do we do with this information? How can we use it to help your patients?"

Harrow rubbed his temples, feeling the gravity of the situation. "We need to consider all our options. If these mirrors are indeed... contaminated, for lack of a better term, we may need to remove them from the clinic."

"But if we remove them, what then?" Elena asked, her brow furrowed. "Do we destroy them? And if we do, are we certain that will neutralize whatever influence they might have?"

"I'm not sure," Harrow admitted. "But perhaps destruction isn't our only option. If we can understand the nature of their influence, maybe we can find a way to cleanse them more thoroughly, using more targeted rituals."

Elena nodded thoughtfully. "I could look into specific cleansing rituals. There are several traditions that deal with purifying objects that are believed to hold spiritual energies. It might require some experimentation, but it's worth exploring."

"That sounds like a sensible next step," Harrow agreed. "Meanwhile, I'll keep a close eye on the therapy sessions. Any sign of disturbances, and we'll have to accelerate our decision."

"Let's hope it doesn't come to that," Elena said quietly. "But if it does, we'll be prepared to take whatever steps are necessary."

As they wrapped up their meeting, Harrow felt a mix of apprehension and resolve. The path forward was unclear, fraught with as many questions as answers, but the determination to protect his patients gave him the courage to face whatever lay ahead.

Elena packed up her notes and laptop, ready to dive deeper into her research. "I'll send you anything I find immediately," she promised as she stood to leave.

"Thank you, Elena. Your help has been invaluable," Harrow said, genuinely grateful. "I don't know how I would manage this without your expertise."

With a reassuring smile, Elena left the office, her silhouette merging with the shadows of the hallway. Harrow sat back in his chair, the soft creak of the leather seeming loud in the quiet room. The evening stretched before him, filled with research and reflection.

Outside, the clinic was silent, the echoes of the day's conversations lingering in the empty rooms. Harrow's thoughts were a jumble of history, mystery, and the very real concerns of his practice. The night ahead promised little sleep as he pondered the revelations of the day and the actions they might necessitate.

That evening, Detective James Corbin arrived at the clinic with an unexpected development that required Dr. Adrian Harrow's immediate attention. The clinic's therapy room, once a sanctuary for healing, now felt more like a command center, with notes and diagrams scattered across the main table.

"Dr. Harrow, we've had a breakthrough of sorts on the background checks of the mirrors," Corbin began, his voice indicating he bore news of significant weight.

Harrow, looking up from his notes, replied, "A breakthrough? What have you found?"

"It appears that one of the mirrors, the one reported in most of the disturbances, was part of an estate that had numerous items with... let's just say, a questionable history," Corbin disclosed, handing Harrow a file filled with police reports and auction house records.

Harrow skimmed through the documents quickly. "Questionable how?"

"Some of these items were retrieved from sites known for cult activities. This mirror, in particular, was linked to an incident in the '90s where it was supposedly at the center of a ritual gone wrong," Corbin explained, watching Harrow's reaction closely.

"That's... unsettling," Harrow admitted, feeling a chill despite the room's warmth. "This could explain some of the phenomena we've been experiencing."

"Yes, it might. And it raises serious questions about the safety of keeping these items in your clinic," Corbin pointed out, his concern evident.

"I agree. It might be prudent to remove this particular mirror from use, at least until we can be certain of its effects," Harrow concluded, feeling a mix of relief and anxiety at the prospect.

"Do you think that will be enough to stop the disturbances?" Corbin asked, skepticism threading through his voice.

"It's a start. But honestly, I think we need to consider more drastic measures," Harrow suggested, pondering the implications of their findings.

"Such as?" Corbin prodded, keen on understanding Harrow's perspective.

"Perhaps removing all the mirrors from the therapy sessions for a time, or even permanently if necessary. We could also intensify our research into decontaminating them, maybe even consult with more experts in this...unusual field," Harrow proposed, the weight of each option bearing down on him.

"That sounds like a plan. I'll support you in whatever action you decide to take," Corbin affirmed, his role as an investigator merging with that of an ally in this strange situation.

"Thank you, Detective. Your help has been invaluable," Harrow said, genuinely appreciative of the detective's open-minded approach.

As Corbin prepared to leave, Harrow walked him to the door. "I'll keep you updated on any changes, and I'll start making arrangements for the mirrors first thing tomorrow."

"Good. I'll look forward to hearing about any progress," Corbin replied, stepping into the cool evening air.

Left alone in the now-quiet clinic, Harrow felt a sense of determination settling in. The path forward was fraught with unknowns, but the decision to confront the mystery head-on provided a clear directive. He returned to the therapy room, his gaze lingering on the mirrors that lined its walls. They no longer seemed mere objects, but bearers of hidden stories and potential threats. The evening closed around him, the shadows in the room deepening as he considered his next steps, the quiet punctuated only by the soft ticking of the clock and the distant sounds of the city at night.

Chapter 5
The Mirror's Edge

That night, in Elena's home, surrounded by her collection of ornate mirrors, they delved deeper into the lore of an entity known as "Mirrormask." As Harrow caught his reflection in one of the mirrors, he saw a shadow flicker behind him. Shaken, he finally began to grasp the gravity of their discovery.

"Something was watching, waiting," Harrow murmured, turning to face Elena with a mix of fear and determination in his eyes.

Elena, seated across a table strewn with ancient books and manuscripts, looked up with a solemn nod. "It's not just a legend, Adrian. This Mirrormask, if that's what we're dealing with, it's been here, influencing events more than we dared to assume."

Harrow paced the room slowly, his reflection passing through the mirrors around them with each step. "And the mirrors, the ones from your clinic—they could actually be gateways? Holding back something like Mirrormask?"

"It seems likely," Elena replied, her voice steady despite the chilling implications. "These mirrors aren't just reflecting images but could be portals, trapping or releasing...whatever Mirrormask really is."

"But why? Why my clinic? Why now?" Harrow asked, stopping to face one of the mirrors, his expression fraught with confusion and concern.

Elena sighed, her gaze thoughtful. "It could be the mirrors themselves. They were gathered from different sources, each with its own history. When brought together, their combined energies might have triggered something... awakened it."

Harrow rubbed his forehead, trying to process the enormity of the situation. "So, what do we do? How do we stop it?"

"We need to understand more about these mirrors and Mirrormask," Elena suggested, her fingers brushing over a particularly old tome. "We start by tracing back each mirror's history, and we also need to look deeper into this entity's origins. There might be a way to sever the connection."

"Okay, let's outline a plan," Harrow said, regaining some of his composure as he sat down across from Elena. "First, we isolate the mirrors in the clinic, prevent any further interactions. Second, we gather all the information we can find about Mirrormask and similar entities. And third, we need more expertise—this is beyond anything I've ever dealt with."

"I agree," Elena replied, opening her laptop to begin compiling a list of contacts and experts in occult phenomena. "I also think we should talk to Marcus Eldridge again. He might know more about the mirrors, especially if any were part of his collection before."

"Right," Harrow nodded. "I'll arrange a meeting with him first thing tomorrow. Meanwhile, could you start pulling together all the historical data on the mirrors? Anything you find could be crucial."

Elena started typing, her focus absolute. "I'm on it. And Adrian, we should also consider conducting some controlled experiments. If we can observe the entity's interactions with the mirrors under safe conditions, we might learn how to counteract it."

Harrow considered this, the scientist in him intrigued by the challenge. "That sounds like a solid addition to our plan. Let's make sure we proceed carefully, though. We can't afford any mistakes."

As they worked into the early hours, the room filled with the soft glow of the laptop screen and the dim light from a desk lamp, casting long shadows across the walls. The mirrors around them seemed almost to watch, silent observers to the urgent, whispered strategizing.

Finally, as dawn began to break, casting pale light into the room, Harrow and Elena agreed to take a short break. "We'll reconvene in a few hours," Harrow said, standing and stretching his tired muscles.

"Agreed," Elena replied, her eyes weary but resolute. "We're getting closer, Adrian. I can feel it."

As Harrow left Elena's home, the city was waking up around him, unaware of the battle being waged in quiet rooms against unseen foes. The morning light was a stark contrast to the night's dark revelations, but it offered a semblance of hope, a reminder that after every night, no matter how dark, the sun would rise.

Morning light spilled across the cluttered surface of Dr. Adrian Harrow's desk, illuminating the myriad of papers and old texts that lay scattered like the pieces of a particularly perplexing puzzle. He had been up most of the night, his mind tirelessly weaving through the complex tapestry of information that might lead to an understanding of the entity known as Mirrormask.

Marcus Eldridge, a collector of obscure artifacts and an occasional consultant on matters of the paranormal, arrived mid-morning, his presence filling the small office. Harrow greeted him, his expression a mixture of fatigue and urgency.

"Marcus, thank you for coming on such short notice," Harrow began, motioning towards the seat across from him.

"Of course, Adrian," Marcus replied, his voice deep and resonant, his eyes quickly taking in the chaotic state of the office. "I understand we're dealing with something quite out of the ordinary?"

"Yes, exactly," Harrow confirmed, sliding a couple of photographs of the mirrors across the desk. "These mirrors are part of the problem. We suspect they might be acting as portals, or at least as amplifiers for something we believe to be tied to an entity known as Mirrormask."

Marcus leaned forward, his interest piqued as he examined the photographs. "Mirrormask, you say? I recall that name from a series of lectures on esoteric mythologies. It's often depicted as a shadow entity, one that exists between reflections and reality."

"That matches our findings," Harrow noted, tapping his fingers on the desk. "Do you know of any way to counteract or contain such an entity?"

"The lore is vague, but it suggests the use of specific symbols or materials known to ward off evil. Silver, for instance, has been mentioned as a reflective metal that can disrupt or contain malevolent entities," Marcus explained, his tone suggesting a blend of skepticism and fascination.

Harrow jotted down notes. "Silver, then. We might try incorporating that into our strategy. And the symbols?"

"I can provide you with some references to ancient texts that might contain the symbols you need. However, their use must be precise," Marcus warned, his brow furrowing with the weight of his knowledge.

"Precision won't be a problem," Harrow assured him, his mind already racing with potential applications. "Anything else you can suggest?"

"Only that you proceed with caution, Adrian," Marcus replied, standing to leave. "These forces, if not properly managed, can be far more dangerous than you might anticipate."

"Thank you, Marcus. Your insights have been invaluable," Harrow said, rising to shake his hand.

As Marcus left, Harrow sat back down, his eyes lingering on the photographs of the mirrors. He felt a mixture of anticipation and dread at the path that lay ahead. There was much to do, and the stakes were high.

He spent the remainder of the morning compiling a detailed list of the materials and symbols Marcus had mentioned, interspersed with calls to Elena to update her on their new direction. Their conversation was brief but intense, each exchange sharpening their focus and refining their approach.

By the time he paused for lunch, Harrow felt a cautious optimism. The network of allies and the accumulation of knowledge they were building gave him hope that they might indeed find a way to confront Mirrormask and perhaps restore safety and normalcy to his clinic.

As he stepped out of his office to clear his head, the clinic was quiet, the usual hustle of patients and staff subdued by the gravity of the ongoing investigation. The quiet hum of the building seemed to echo his thoughts—a constant reminder of the unseen forces at play, just beyond the veil of the ordinary world.

The clinic was unusually silent as Dr. Adrian Harrow prepared for a significant experiment. Alongside Elena, they carefully laid out sheets of polished silver around one of the suspect mirrors, based on Marcus Eldridge's advice. The soft gleam of the metal cast eerie reflections on the walls, creating a tapestry of light and shadows that flickered with the subtle movements in the room.

"Are you sure this will work?" Harrow asked, looking skeptically at the arrangements. "Silver to disrupt or contain the entity—it sounds like something out of a medieval text."

"It's all we have based on historical precedents," Elena replied, her voice steady despite the uncertainty. "And Marcus seemed quite confident in his recommendations."

Harrow nodded, his gaze fixed on the mirror. "Okay, let's go through the plan once more. We expose the mirror to the silver, observe any changes, and document everything. If anything unusual occurs—"

"We shut down immediately and reevaluate," Elena finished for him, checking the video equipment set up to record the experiment. "I'm ready if you are."

"Let's begin then," Harrow decided, his voice firm as he reached for the light switch to dim the room further, enhancing the effect of the silver's reflection.

As the lights dimmed, the two stood back and observed. For a moment, nothing happened. The mirror reflected the silver's gleam dully, the room bathed in an almost ethereal light. Then, slowly, a shadow appeared at the edge of the mirror's surface, creeping along the frame like smoke.

"Do you see that?" Harrow whispered, his voice a mix of excitement and apprehension.

"Yes, I see it," Elena confirmed, her eyes not leaving the mirror. "It's reacting. Keep watching."

The shadow grew denser, swirling within the mirror's confines as if testing the boundaries set by the silver. Harrow and Elena exchanged a look of silent agreement to continue observing.

Minutes passed, the tension in the room building as the shadow seemed to pulse against the invisible barrier. Then, as quickly as it had appeared, it receded, the mirror's surface returning to normal.

"It's pulling back," Elena noted, relief evident in her voice. "The silver might be working. It's containing it, at least for now."

Harrow exhaled deeply, the stress of the moment catching up with him. "Let's keep the setup overnight. Monitor any changes and check the recordings in the morning."

"Agreed," Elena said as she made notes on a clipboard. "We'll need to analyze the footage, see if we can learn anything more about its behavior, its reactions to the silver."

As they prepared to leave the room, Harrow paused, looking back at the mirror. "We might be on to something, Elena. A real way to combat this."

Elena nodded, her expression one of cautious hope. "It's a breakthrough, Adrian. Let's just hope it holds."

They left the room, the door closing softly behind them. The silver lay still around the mirror, a silent sentinel in the dim light. The clinic settled around them, the quiet more profound in the wake of the experiment.

Walking down the hallway, Harrow felt a mixture of relief and the heavy burden of responsibility. The night would be long, the waiting difficult, but the first signs of success brought a glimmer of hope that they might yet find a way to resolve the mystery of the Mirrormask and protect those who came to his clinic seeking solace, not spectral encounters.

The next morning, Dr. Adrian Harrow and Elena Markham convened in the clinic's main office to review the overnight footage from the experiment. The room was quiet, save for the soft hum of the computer as it played back the recordings.

"Look there," Elena pointed at the screen where the shadow had first appeared against the gleam of the silver. "See how it reacts? It's almost as if it's testing the boundaries the silver sets."

Harrow nodded, his eyes fixed on the movements within the mirror. "It's fascinating and terrifying in equal measure. The silver does seem to contain it, at least temporarily. What do you make of the fluctuations here?"

"It could be a response to the silver itself. Maybe it's not just a physical barrier but has some sort of psychological or spectral effect on Mirrormask," Elena theorized, pausing the video and zooming in on the area of fluctuation.

"That would align with the folklore Marcus mentioned," Harrow mused. "Silver disrupting evil spirits or entities. Perhaps it interferes with its ability to manifest or exert influence."

"Exactly. And if that's the case, we might be able to use silver more strategically," Elena suggested, her mind racing with possibilities. "Not just as a barrier, but integrated into the therapy sessions themselves, in a controlled manner."

Harrow considered this, tapping his pen against the notepad in front of him. "Integrating silver into the sessions... It's unorthodox, but given what we're facing, it might be necessary. We should start small, perhaps a test session with minimal exposure, and see how it interacts."

"I agree. A controlled environment will give us more data and maybe help us understand how to use silver effectively against Mirrormask," Elena said, making notes on her laptop.

"Do you think we should involve Marcus again? His insight was invaluable," Harrow asked, already considering the logistics of such a collaboration.

"Definitely," Elena replied quickly. "His understanding of occult objects could help us refine our approach. Plus, he might know of other materials or symbols that could enhance the silver's effect."

"Good point. I'll reach out to him today," Harrow said, feeling a plan beginning to form. "In the meantime, let's set up a preliminary test. We'll need a volunteer from the staff who understands the situation and is willing to participate."

"I'll handle that," Elena offered. "I think Janet might be a good candidate. She's shown interest in the research aspect and understands the risks involved."

"Excellent," Harrow said, standing to stretch his legs. "And what about the mirrors? Should we continue using the same one, or try different ones?"

"Let's stick with the same mirror for now," Elena decided. "It's already shown a significant response, and changing variables might complicate our results."

"Agreed," Harrow concluded, his tone resolute. "We're making progress, Elena. Real progress. It's a bit unorthodox, but it's necessary."

Elena nodded, a slight smile breaking through her otherwise serious demeanor. "It's certainly one for the history books. Let's just hope the next chapter is about how we resolved it."

As they finalized their plans for the upcoming test, the clinic around them began to stir with the day's activities. Patients and staff moved through the halls, unaware of the groundbreaking experiments being planned in their midst. Harrow and Elena's conversation marked a turning point, setting the stage for a deeper exploration into the unknown.

With a renewed sense of purpose, Harrow watched Elena as she prepared to leave the office to arrange their next steps. The challenge they faced was daunting, but the path forward was clearer now than it had ever been.

Chapter 6
Fragmented Truths

In the subdued light of the therapy room now modified for their experiment, Dr. Adrian Harrow and Elena Markham prepared the space meticulously. Sheets of polished silver lined the walls, reflecting a soft, eerie glow that seemed to pulse with a life of its own. In the center, the same mirror that had shown the most significant reactions sat, its surface clean and deceptively tranquil.

"Are we ready to begin?" Elena asked, checking the placement of the video cameras, which were positioned to capture every angle of the mirror and the surrounding area.

"I think so," Harrow replied, reviewing the checklist in his hand. "Janet is prepped and understands the protocol?"

"Yes, she's ready. She understands that she needs to signal immediately if she feels anything out of the ordinary," Elena confirmed, her voice steady despite the underlying tension.

Janet, a clinical assistant well-versed in the day's unique procedures, took her seat in front of the mirror. Her expression was calm, but her hands betrayed a slight nervousness as she adjusted her chair.

"Remember, just interact as you normally would during a session," Harrow instructed her, his voice reassuring. "We're looking for any signs of fluctuation in the mirror's behavior, anything at all that deviates from the norm."

Janet nodded, taking a deep breath as she settled her gaze on her own reflection. "I'm ready," she announced, her voice barely above a whisper.

As the experiment commenced, Harrow and Elena observed from behind a protective screen of silver. Minutes ticked by with only the soft hum of the equipment filling the room. The mirror initially reflected only Janet's anxious face and the silver-lined walls.

Then, subtly at first, the air around the mirror seemed to shimmer, a visual distortion that grew gradually more pronounced. "Elena, do you see that?" Harrow whispered, pointing towards the phenomenon.

"Yes, I see it," Elena replied, her focus intense as she took notes. "It's starting. Look at the edges of the mirror."

The silver appeared to react, its surface rippling as if in response to the mirror's fluctuations. Janet remained still, her eyes locked on the shifting image before her.

"I feel... cold," Janet spoke up, her voice a mix of fascination and fear. "There's a chill, right here."

"Note that," Harrow said to Elena, who was already recording the observation. "It could be a sign of the entity trying to manifest or interact."

As they watched, the temperature in the room dropped noticeably, a cold that seemed to emanate from the mirror itself. Yet, the silver barriers held, their glow steady and seemingly protective.

After several minutes, the activity around the mirror began to subside. The visual distortions lessened and the room's temperature slowly returned to normal.

"Let's end here," Harrow decided, his voice low. "We don't want to push too far in one session."

Elena nodded in agreement. "We have enough to analyze for today."

As Janet rose from her chair, she looked slightly dazed but unharmed. "Did you get what you needed?" she asked, wrapping her arms around herself as though to shake off the residual cold.

"We did, thank you," Harrow reassured her, his concern for her well-being apparent. "You did excellently. We'll review the findings and plan our next steps accordingly."

With the session concluded, Harrow and Elena collected the recordings and other data. The room felt different now, the weight of their tentative victory hanging in the air. They had witnessed the protective power of silver against whatever resided within the mirror, a discovery that opened new avenues of research and potential defense.

As they left the therapy room, locking the door behind them, the silver-lined walls continued to reflect the dim light, silent guardians against the unseen.

In the quiet confines of his office, Dr. Adrian Harrow pored over the recordings from the silver trial with a meticulous eye. The footage showed the subtle changes in the air around the mirror, each frame potentially significant to understanding the phenomenon they faced. His notepad was filled with observations and timestamps, an attempt to decode the visual puzzle laid out before him.

Elena Markham, sitting across from him, was equally absorbed in cross-referencing the experimental data with historical accounts of similar phenomena. Her books were open to pages marked with colorful tabs, the ancient texts whispering secrets from ages past. She occasionally glanced up at the screen, her eyes sharp, searching for correlations between their findings and the documented lore.

The room was heavy with concentration, the only sounds being the occasional shuffle of paper and the low hum of the computer. Every now and then, Harrow would pause the footage, leaning back in his chair, his mind racing through the implications of what they observed. The chill that Janet had reported, caught clearly by the thermal cameras, suggested an interaction between the physical environment and whatever entity might be present.

Elena finally broke the silence. "This fluctuation here," she pointed at a particular timestamp where the air around the mirror seemed to pulse, "it's consistent with a containment breach. The silver reacted, but there was still some sort of... leakage."

Harrow nodded slowly, marking the moment in his notes. "It means the silver isn't a perfect barrier. It's more like a filter, maybe slowing or dampening whatever is trying to get through."

They continued their analysis, noting each minor anomaly. The work was tedious but necessary, a slow piecing together of a complex supernatural puzzle. Harrow felt the weight of their task; each piece of data was a step towards safety or disaster, a delicate balance they had to maintain.

Late into the afternoon, as the sunlight began to fade, casting long shadows across the room, they compiled a list of modifications for their next experiment. They planned to adjust the placement of the silver, increase the density of the barriers, and introduce a variable—a different mirror, to test if the phenomena were linked to specific items or were a general property of all mirrors in the clinic.

Harrow stretched, his muscles stiff from hours of sitting. "We're making progress," he said, more to himself than to Elena. "It's slow, but it's there."

Elena closed one of her books with a soft thud. "Progress in dealing with the paranormal is rarely straightforward or fast. We're charting unknown territory here."

As the day turned into evening, they organized their findings and prepared the report on the day's experiment. The clinic was quiet, the usual daytime bustle replaced by an evening calm. Harrow looked around his office, at the books, the scattered papers, the flickering screen, and felt a mix of foreboding and resolve.

They were on the edge of a breakthrough, he could feel it. Each experiment, each hour spent in analysis, brought them closer to understanding and hopefully controlling the forces they had unwittingly unleashed. The weight of responsibility was heavy on his shoulders, but the pursuit of knowledge and safety for his patients spurred him on.

With a final review of their notes, Harrow and Elena set their plan for the next day, each step carefully calculated. The experiment would be risky, but it was a calculated risk, one they had to take to push forward. As Elena left, Harrow turned off his office lights, the room settling into darkness. The challenges of the day were many, but the potential for discovery kept him tethered to the cause, ready to face whatever the next day might bring.

The clinic seemed unusually quiet, as if holding its breath, while Dr. Adrian Harrow and Elena Markham prepared for a more ambitious phase of their experiment. With the lessons from the previous trials fresh in their minds, they had redesigned the setup in the therapy room, reinforcing the silver barriers and introducing a new mirror, older and reportedly more active historically, to test the consistency of the phenomena.

In the cool, shadowed environment of the room, the array of silver now formed a nearly complete enclosure around the new mirror. The meticulous arrangement reflected not just the physical light but also the heavy expectations of the experiment. Harrow checked each element personally, ensuring that every reflective surface was positioned with precision, creating a lattice of potential energy containment.

Elena, meanwhile, calibrated the monitoring equipment, her movements precise and practiced. Sensors to measure temperature fluctuations, electromagnetic fields, and spectral imaging were arrayed around the room, each one feeding data back to a bank of monitors outside the experimental zone.

As the final preparations were made, Harrow stepped back to review the setup. "Do you think this will hold?" he asked Elena, a trace of apprehension in his voice.

"It's our best configuration yet," she responded confidently, her eyes scanning the silver-lined room. "If there are any weaknesses in our approach, we'll see them today."

With everything in place, they initiated the experiment, retreating behind the safety of the observation window. The room was dimly lit by a series of soft lights that cast long shadows across the silver and mirrors, creating a play of light that seemed almost alive.

The first few minutes passed without incident. The sensors remained quiet, the readouts steady. But as the time stretched on, a palpable tension built up, pressing against the calm. Then, without warning, a drop in temperature was registered by the sensors, a sudden chill that made Harrow and Elena exchange a quick, knowing look.

The monitors showed a slight distortion in the air around the mirror, a visual echo that seemed to dance across the silver surfaces. This time, however, the silver held strong, the eerie movements contained within the grid they had created.

Elena recorded every detail, her notes meticulous. "The containment is working," she whispered, her voice barely audible over the hum of the equipment. "But the strength of the response is stronger than before."

Harrow nodded, his gaze fixed on the screens. "It's reacting to the silver, maybe even being provoked by it. We need to monitor closely, see if it escalates."

The experiment continued, the minutes ticking by heavily. The room's atmosphere grew thicker, the shadows deeper. The silver barriers shimmered under the strain of whatever pressed against them from the other side. Despite this, the enhancements appeared to hold, the phenomena not breaking past the boundaries they had reinforced.

As the session drew to a close, Harrow felt a mixture of relief and unease. "We're holding it back, but for how long?" he pondered aloud, his voice reflecting his deep-seated concerns.

"We improve and adapt," Elena replied, her tone resolute. "Each trial gives us more data, helps us refine our approach."

With the experiment concluded for the day, they powered down the equipment and secured the room, the silver still gleaming faintly in the dim light. As they left, the weight of their findings hung between them, a silent acknowledgment of the challenges that lay ahead.

The clinic settled into the evening, the day's trials leaving a residue of spectral unease. Harrow walked through the quiet hallways, his mind busy with plans for further reinforcement and research. Each step was a reminder of the journey still before them, the silver their shield against the shadows they sought to understand and contain.

As dusk settled, the clinic's atmosphere felt charged, a silent storm brewing within its walls. Dr. Adrian Harrow and Elena Markham convened in his office, surrounded by the scattered evidence of their relentless research into the phenomena associated with the mirrors.

"We've managed to contain it so far, but today's results were unsettling," Harrow began, reviewing the day's data displayed across his laptop screen. "The activity was more intense, even with the enhanced silver barriers."

Elena, looking over the spectral images captured during the experiment, nodded in agreement. "It's adapting, or at least responding more aggressively to our measures. We might need to think about additional strategies, perhaps even different materials or more complex symbols."

Harrow rubbed his temples, feeling the weight of each decision. "Marcus mentioned gold as another potential protective element. It's historically been used in conjunction with silver for purification and protection rites."

"Do you think we should integrate it into the experiment?" Elena asked, her eyes scanning a text on ancient alchemical defenses.

"It might be worth a try," Harrow replied thoughtfully. "Gold and silver together could create a stronger barrier. We'll need to test the theory, of course."

Elena closed the book she had been consulting and looked directly at Harrow. "I'll start sourcing high-purity gold leaf. We can apply it in strategic spots around the mirrors and observe any changes in the entity's behavior."

Harrow nodded his approval and then sighed, a deep, weary sound. "There's also the matter of the clinic's day-to-day operations. We've been so focused on this crisis that I'm concerned about the impact on our patients."

"We've been careful not to let this affect them directly," Elena reassured him. "But you're right, we need to maintain a balance. Perhaps we can schedule the experiments after hours, minimize any disruption."

"That's a good plan," Harrow agreed, his mind already turning to logistics. "We need to keep this under wraps as much as possible until we understand how to fully control or eliminate the threat."

The conversation shifted to planning the next steps. Details were hashed out, schedules rearranged, resources allocated. The room was filled with a sense of urgent purpose, the critical nature of their work never more apparent.

As they wrapped up their meeting, Harrow stood and stretched, his body stiff from hours of tension. "Thanks, Elena. I don't know how I would manage this without your expertise."

Elena smiled, gathering her notes. "We're in this together, Adrian. We'll see it through to the end."

With a plan in place, they left the office, the corridor's lights flickering slightly as they passed, a reminder of the unseen forces still at play within the clinic. Harrow felt a resolve settling in his chest, the determination to protect his patients and his practice from whatever darkness lurked behind the glass.

The night closed in around the clinic, the shadows deepening as Harrow locked his office door. The challenges they faced were daunting, but the path forward, though shrouded in uncertainty, was marked by the steady light of their combined resolve.

Chapter 7
Echoes of the Past

Dr. Adrian Harrow stood in the now-familiar confines of the therapy room, his gaze fixed on the new additions to the setup. Small sheets of gold leaf had been carefully placed alongside the silver that lined the walls, each shimmer of metal adding to the room's strange, luminescent quality. Elena Markham was at his side, adjusting the positioning of one of the cameras to ensure every angle was covered for their next experiment.

"Are you sure this combination will be more effective?" Harrow asked, his voice tinged with both hope and skepticism.

Elena nodded, her hands steady as she secured the camera. "According to the texts we've studied, gold has been used to amplify the properties of silver in numerous protective rituals. It's supposed to enhance the barrier function, especially against more... persistent entities."

Harrow considered this, watching as the soft light played over the gilded surfaces. "And if this doesn't work?"

"Then we go back, review, and try again. We're in uncharted territory, Adrian. Every test is a step forward, even if it doesn't give us the results we expect," Elena responded, her determination clear.

They finalized the preparations and retreated behind the protective glass that now shielded the observation area. Janet, once again their volunteer, took her place in front of the mirror. Her familiarity with the procedure was evident in her calm, collected demeanor.

"Janet, remember, any sign of discomfort or anything unusual, you let us know immediately," Harrow instructed through the intercom.

"Understood, Dr. Harrow," Janet's voice replied, steady and a bit resolute through the speaker.

As the experiment commenced, Harrow and Elena watched intently. The previous sessions had prepared them for unusual occurrences, but the addition of gold was a variable they could only hope would prove beneficial.

Minutes ticked by without incident. The mirror reflected Janet's image back at her, overlaid with the subtle glitter of gold and silver. Then, without warning, the temperature in the room dropped sharply—an anomaly they were now familiar with.

"It's reacting," Elena noted, her eyes fixed on the temperature readout. "But look, the fluctuation is less severe this time."

Harrow observed, noting the mild distortion around the edges of the mirror that quickly stabilized. "The gold, it might be helping. The reaction is there, but it's not escalating."

"Seems like it," Elena agreed, making quick notes on her clipboard. "The containment is holding more effectively. This is good, very good."

The experiment continued, and the entity, whatever it was, seemed less able to affect its surroundings than before. The session ended with no further anomalies, and Janet reported feeling none of the oppressive sensations that had accompanied previous tests.

"This is a significant improvement," Harrow said as they debriefed Janet, who nodded in agreement.

"We're making progress," Elena added, a smile of relief crossing her features. "The combination of silver and gold may be the key to fully containing the entity."

As they reviewed the footage and data from the session, their conversation turned towards the next steps. "We should replicate this test, see if the results are consistent. If they are, we might consider permanently integrating gold into the therapy room's design," Harrow suggested.

"That sounds like a prudent approach," Elena replied. "I'll start arranging for the materials needed for further testing."

The clinic was quiet as the evening approached, the day's successes a rare but welcome change. Harrow and Elena left the therapy room, locking it behind them with a sense of cautious optimism. The golden and silver reflections on the walls seemed to promise more than just safety; they hinted at a solution that might soon be within their grasp.

Later that week, Dr. Adrian Harrow and Elena Markham gathered in the clinic's conference room, spread with notes and laptops open to graphs and data analysis software. The walls around them were adorned with whiteboards filled with formulae and procedural diagrams—a testament to their intensive investigation.

"Let's review the data from our last three sessions," Elena began, clicking through a series of charts. "It appears that the addition of gold not only stabilized the silver's containment properties but also significantly reduced the frequency and intensity of the anomalies."

"Yes, the results are promising," Harrow agreed, peering over his glasses at the screen. "But are we seeing any long-term effects on the mirrors themselves? Any signs of degradation or alteration in their properties?"

"Not so far," Elena replied, switching to another document. "The mirrors remain structurally and functionally intact. I've been monitoring their physical and spectral properties daily. There's been no change that would indicate damage or alteration."

"That's good news," Harrow said, leaning back in his chair. "So, incorporating gold into the setup has been effective and safe. The real question now is, how do we apply this solution broadly? Can we adapt it for regular use in all therapy sessions, or is it too specialized?"

Elena considered this for a moment. "I think it's feasible to adapt it, but we need to consider the practical aspects. Installing silver and gold linings in all therapy rooms could be costly and might alter the therapeutic ambiance we strive for."

"True," Harrow acknowledged, tapping his pen against the table. "Perhaps we could design a more discrete integration. Use the metals in key locations within the room—places less visible to patients but still effective in containing and suppressing the entity."

"That's a viable approach," Elena noted, jotting down some ideas. "We could use decorative elements or fixtures that incorporate these metals. It would maintain the room's aesthetic while providing the necessary protection."

"Exactly," Harrow said, nodding enthusiastically. "And we should continue testing. Maybe introduce a few more variables to ensure we're covering all possible scenarios. We don't want any surprises down the road."

"Agreed," Elena said. "I'll set up a schedule for ongoing tests. We should also consider writing up our findings for a case study. This could be valuable information for the wider psychological and paranormal research communities."

Harrow smiled, a mix of pride and relief evident on his face. "It's been quite the journey, hasn't it? From not believing to... well, integrating gold and silver into therapy rooms to counteract paranormal entities."

"It's not the usual career path for psychologists, that's for sure," Elena chuckled. "But it's groundbreaking work. We're really onto something here, Adrian."

"As groundbreaking as it is, we need to stay grounded," Harrow added, his tone becoming serious again. "Our primary goal has always been the safety and well-being of our patients. This solution needs to enhance that, not complicate it."

"You're right," Elena agreed, closing her laptop. "Let's proceed carefully, with our patients' best interests at heart."

As they wrapped up their meeting, the pair felt a renewed sense of purpose. The challenge they had faced was turning into an opportunity not only to advance their own understanding but to potentially pioneer a new approach to therapy environments.

Walking out of the conference room, Harrow paused to glance back at the whiteboards, filled with data and diagrams. They weren't just symbols and numbers; they were a sign of progress, of a battle being won, slowly but surely. The evening light faded into the clinic, casting long shadows that somehow seemed less ominous now.

Dr. Adrian Harrow and Elena Markham were seated at a large table in the clinic's research library, surrounded by architectural plans and design proposals. They were in the midst of planning how to incorporate their newfound defensive strategies into the clinic's infrastructure without disrupting the therapeutic environment.

"Here's the proposed design for the new therapy rooms," Elena said, spreading out a blueprint across the table. "The gold and silver elements are integrated into the trim and ceiling details. It's subtle, but should be effective based on our experiments."

Adrian leaned forward, examining the designs closely. "I like the subtlety. It's important that these changes don't make the rooms feel less welcoming or more clinical. Have you run these by the design team for feasibility and cost?"

"Yes, they believe it's doable," Elena confirmed. "The cost is higher than standard materials, but considering the benefits, it seems justified. We'll need to adjust our budget, maybe phase the renovations to spread out the expenses."

"That makes sense," Adrian nodded. "How about the existing rooms? Retrofitting them might be more challenging."

Elena flipped to another page showing a retrofit plan. "For the existing rooms, we're looking at adding moldings and replacing some fixtures with those containing the metals. It's less invasive and can be done relatively quickly."

"Good," Adrian said, still scanning the plans. "What about patient and staff reactions? Have we considered how we're going to explain these changes?"

"That's a good point," Elena acknowledged. "We need a communication plan. Perhaps framing it as an upgrade to enhance the therapeutic environment, which isn't far from the truth. We can highlight the aesthetic improvements without going into too much detail about their functional purposes."

Adrian smiled slightly. "A bit of transparency mixed with discretion. I think that's wise. We don't want to alarm anyone, nor do we want to attract undue attention to the more unconventional aspects of our work here."

"Exactly," Elena agreed. "I'll draft some communication guidelines and run them by you. We'll need to train our staff too, so they're prepared to answer questions in line with the guidelines."

"That's going to be crucial," Adrian said, tapping his finger on the table thoughtfully. "Support from our staff will make this transition smoother. Maybe include a staff briefing session as part of the rollout plan?"

"Will do," Elena replied, making a note. "I'll organize a series of briefings before we start the work. It'll help to address any concerns early on and ensure everyone is on the same page."

As they continued to discuss the logistics, the room was filled with a sense of proactive energy. They were no longer merely reacting to a mysterious threat but were taking thoughtful steps to safeguard the clinic's future.

Adrian looked around the library, at the stacks of research that had brought them to this point, and felt a surge of professional pride. "We've come a long way, Elena. This is going to be a significant chapter in the clinic's history."

Elena nodded, her expression one of determined satisfaction. "Indeed. It's about securing our future and continuing to provide a safe space for healing. Let's make sure we do this right."

With the meeting drawing to a close, they gathered their materials, ready to take the next steps. The late afternoon light filtered through the windows, casting long shadows across the room, a reminder of the time passing and the work still ahead.

Stepping out into the corridor, Adrian and Elena shared a look of mutual resolve. The clinic was quiet at this hour, the hustle of the day settling down, mirroring their transition from planning to action.

The following weeks at the clinic were marked by a whirlwind of activity. Dr. Adrian Harrow and Elena Markham oversaw the renovation of the therapy rooms, transforming them with subtle yet effective modifications. The clinic buzzed with the sound of construction during off-hours, the work meticulously scheduled to avoid disrupting therapy sessions.

Carpenters and decorators, briefed thoroughly on the purpose behind their unusual materials, worked diligently to incorporate the silver and gold into the decorative aspects of each room. The new designs were elegant, the precious metals finely worked into crown moldings and light fixtures, their presence almost imperceptible unless one knew exactly what to look for.

Adrian occasionally visited the rooms under renovation, observing the progress and ensuring that the implementations met their specifications. "How's the fitting going over here?" he asked one afternoon, watching a craftsman apply gold leaf to a section of crown molding.

"Very well, Dr. Harrow," the craftsman replied, his hands steady as he worked. "This material is a bit more delicate than what we're used to, but it's coming together nicely."

"Excellent," Adrian nodded, pleased with the craftsmanship. "It's crucial that it not only functions well but looks good too. We don't want anything to feel out of place."

Indeed, the aesthetics of the therapy rooms were preserved, their calming colors and soft lighting complemented by the new, subtly shimmering additions. Patients commented on the fresh look, appreciating the refurbishments without being aware of their deeper significance.

Elena, meanwhile, managed the project's logistics, coordinating with suppliers and the design team. She updated Adrian regularly, ensuring that every detail adhered to their planned timeline and budget. "We're on track with Phase One," she reported during one of their weekly meetings. "The first set of rooms should be ready by next week."

"That's great to hear," Adrian responded, relief and satisfaction in his voice. "Once they're done, we should start monitoring the effects immediately. I'm curious to see if there will be any noticeable changes in the atmosphere or if it will enhance the therapeutic process."

"Agreed," Elena said, closing her laptop. "I've arranged for discreet sensors to be installed that will monitor environmental variables. We'll have data on everything from air quality to ambient electromagnetic fields."

As the renovations neared completion, the clinic began to regain its usual rhythm. The last of the construction tools were cleared away, and the newly transformed therapy rooms stood ready to welcome patients into a subtly safer environment.

On the day the first renovated room was reopened, Adrian stood at the doorway, observing. The morning light streamed through the window, reflecting softly off the golden accents. It was a small victory, perhaps, but a significant one in their ongoing battle against unseen forces.

"Looks good, doesn't it?" Elena joined him, her eyes taking in the room.

"It does," Adrian agreed, a hint of pride in his tone. "It's more than just aesthetics now. It's about providing safety, peace of mind, and healing— all underlined by the strength of silver and gold."

As they watched a patient enter the room, settle into the comfortable chair, and look around with a relaxed smile, both Adrian and Elena felt a profound sense of accomplishment. They had turned a crisis into an opportunity, enhancing their clinic's environment in ways no one could visibly detect but which held deep significance.

The clinic closed that evening with the new rooms fully integrated into its daily operations. Adrian and Elena left feeling that they had not only fortified the physical space but had also strengthened their resolve and commitment to their patients' well-being. The battle with Mirrormask, though largely invisible, had imbued them with a new level of understanding and capability, ready for whatever challenges might next arise.

Chapter 8
Breaking Point

In the newly renovated therapy room, bathed in the gentle light filtering through the gilded curtains, Dr. Adrian Harrow and Elena Markham met to discuss the initial feedback since the room's reopening. They sat across from each other, each with a folder of notes and a laptop, the air filled with a sense of cautious optimism.

"How have the sessions been going since we introduced the new elements?" Adrian began, his tone hopeful yet measured.

Elena flipped open her laptop, her eyes scanning the compiled data. "So far, the feedback has been overwhelmingly positive. Patients feel the rooms are more welcoming and serene. Interestingly, none of them have reported any of the previous... disturbances."

"That's excellent news," Adrian replied, relief evident in his voice. "It suggests that the silver and gold integration isn't just aesthetically pleasing but also functionally effective."

"Yes, and the environmental readings have been stable," Elena added, pulling up some graphs on her screen. "No unusual fluctuations since the renovation. It seems we've not only contained the entity but also stabilized the ambient energy of the rooms."

Adrian nodded, his mind processing the implications. "Do you think this will hold long-term? Should we prepare for any potential resurgence?"

"It's possible we may see some activity in the future," Elena considered, her tone realistic. "These entities, if that's what we're dealing with, can be unpredictable. However, the current setup appears robust. I'd suggest regular monitoring and perhaps a quarterly review of the environmental data."

"That sounds prudent," Adrian agreed. "Keeping ahead of any changes will ensure we maintain a safe and therapeutic environment. What about the staff? How have they adapted to the changes?"

"They've been great, actually," Elena responded, a smile crossing her features. "They appreciate the new design and understand the deeper reasons behind it without needing too much detail. It's made them feel more involved in the clinic's mission, more secure."

"Good to hear," Adrian said, feeling a swell of pride for his team. "And the additional training?"

"It's gone very well. The training sessions have helped them feel equipped to handle questions from patients and to act if they notice anything unusual," Elena explained.

"Excellent," Adrian mused, leaning back in his chair. "This whole process has been a remarkable journey—from uncertainty and risk to innovation and enhancement. It's a testament to our ability to adapt and respond to extraordinary challenges."

"It really is," Elena agreed, her eyes reflecting a shared sentiment. "And our research has contributed to a broader understanding, not just here, but potentially for the entire therapeutic community."

"We should consider publishing our findings," Adrian suggested, thinking of the wider implications. "It could help others who might be facing similar issues. There's a lot we've learned about environmental psychology and paranormal intervention."

"I've started drafting an article on the subject," Elena revealed, her enthusiasm palpable. "With your input, we could create a comprehensive case study."

"That's a fantastic idea," Adrian said, nodding vigorously. "Let's do it. It could be groundbreaking, literally and figuratively."

As they concluded their meeting, they both felt a sense of accomplishment and a renewed commitment to their work. The challenges they had faced had not only tested their resolve but had also deepened their understanding of their practice and its possibilities.

Leaving the therapy room, they felt reassured by the sound of calm conversations and the quiet workings of the clinic around them. The sun was setting, casting long shadows through the hallways, but the light within the clinic was steady and warm, a beacon of their continued dedication and care.

The clinic had settled into a new routine, the integration of gold and silver into the therapy rooms no longer a novel change but a standard feature. Dr. Adrian Harrow found himself walking the quiet halls of his clinic late one evening, reflecting on the transformation that had taken place. Each room, now shimmering subtly with the integration of protective metals, held a tranquil air, promising safety and healing.

In the stillness, Adrian paused outside one of the newly renovated rooms, peering through the glass pane in the door. The room was empty, the soft lighting casting gentle patterns on the lush carpet below. It was here that many patients had found relief, not just from their personal ailments but from the unexplained disturbances that had once marred the clinic's comforting atmosphere.

Earlier that day, Adrian had met with Elena Markham to discuss the ongoing monitoring of the rooms. "The sensors have shown nothing out of the ordinary," she had reported, her voice filled with cautious relief. "It seems the disturbances have been fully contained."

"That's reassuring," Adrian had replied, though a part of him remained vigilant. The mystery of what they had encountered lingered in his mind, a reminder of the unknown forces that could exist just beyond the veil of normalcy.

As he continued his walk, his thoughts turned to the paper he and Elena were preparing. It was to be a detailed account of their experiences and findings, a document that could potentially help others in the psychological and paranormal research communities understand and perhaps even prevent similar occurrences.

The quiet of the clinic was a stark contrast to the tumultuous period they had just endured. It allowed Adrian a moment to think about the future, about how the clinic could further its mission not only to heal but also to explore the boundaries of human experience and understanding.

He stopped by his office to pick up some notes he had left on his desk, his eyes catching a photo of the clinic staff taken at their last holiday party. The smiles on their faces were a testament to their resilience and dedication, qualities that had been crucial over the past months. Adrian felt a surge of gratitude for his team, whose support had been unwavering.

Locking his office behind him, he made his way back through the dimly lit hallways to the exit. The night was quiet, the only sounds being his footsteps and the distant hum of the city. As he stepped outside, the cool air greeted him, a refreshing change from the controlled climate of the clinic.

Adrian took a deep breath, allowing the calm of the evening to wash over him. The challenges they had faced had brought change, growth, and ultimately, a deeper understanding of the mysterious interplay between the physical and the metaphysical.

As he walked to his car, parked under a streetlight that cast long shadows on the pavement, he thought about the next steps, the upcoming challenges, and the possibilities that lay ahead. The clinic was more than a place of healing now; it had become a ground for pioneering research into the realms of human experience that were often left unexplored.

Driving away, the clinic receded in his rearview mirror, its windows reflecting the last light of the streetlamps. Adrian felt a quiet confidence in the path ahead, armed with knowledge and an ever-present curiosity, ready to face whatever mysteries might next emerge from the shadows.

In the cozy, book-lined conference room of the clinic, Dr. Adrian Harrow and Elena Markham were deep in discussion, surrounded by open laptops and stacks of research papers. They were finalizing their paper, a comprehensive analysis of the phenomena they had encountered and the solutions they had implemented.

"Adrian, do you think we've covered the theoretical implications thoroughly?" Elena asked, scanning through the document on her laptop. "It's crucial that we contextualize our findings within the broader field of paranormal and psychological research."

Adrian, who was reviewing a section of the paper, looked up thoughtfully. "I believe we have, but perhaps we should emphasize the interdisciplinary approach more. It's not often that psychological therapy intersects so directly with elements that some might consider... well, supernatural."

"That's a good point," Elena agreed, typing a note to herself. "We should highlight how our work can bridge these often disparate fields. It's about broadening the perspectives within both domains."

Adrian nodded and then pointed to a graph on his screen. "Also, look at this data from the environmental sensors during the trials. We should discuss how the changes in electromagnetic fields could correlate with paranormal theories about energy manipulation."

"Yes, that will definitely strengthen our case," Elena said, pulling up corresponding data on her computer. "I'll integrate that into the section on environmental dynamics. It will show how physical changes in the room's atmosphere could potentially interact with psychological states."

"Exactly," Adrian replied, pleased. "And speaking of psychological states, we should also elaborate on the feedback from our patients. The improvements in their therapy outcomes since the renovations have been significant."

"I've got all the patient feedback summarized here," Elena said, showing him a chart on her laptop. "There's a noticeable decrease in anxiety levels and an improvement in overall session effectiveness. It's quite compelling."

Adrian leaned closer to look at the chart. "That's excellent. Include that right after the technical explanation of the room modifications. It will help ground our findings in practical outcomes."

"Do you think we should include personal reflections? Maybe a section on our own experiences and observations throughout the process?" Elena suggested, her eyes reflecting a hint of excitement about the idea.

"That would add a unique dimension to the paper," Adrian mused. "It's not just about the data, but about the human element, the lived experience of tackling something as unconventional as this."

"Great, I'll draft something," Elena said, her fingers poised over the keyboard. "It might also help other practitioners feel more prepared if they ever encounter something similar."

As they worked, the conversation flowed freely, their collaboration seamless. They discussed each section of the paper, ensuring it was both scientifically robust and accessible to readers from multiple disciplines.

"This could really make a splash in both the psychological and paranormal research communities," Adrian said with a hint of pride. "I think we've managed to strike the right balance between rigorous data and engaging narrative."

"I think so too," Elena agreed, her smile reflecting a sense of accomplishment. "It's almost ready to submit. Just a few more tweaks and a final proofread."

"Let's aim to submit by the end of this week," Adrian suggested, feeling a surge of anticipation about sharing their work with the world. "Who knows how many are out there facing mysteries of their own, waiting for a sign that they're not alone in their experiences?"

"Absolutely," Elena said, her enthusiasm matching his. "It's not just about what we've discovered, but about what we can inspire in others."

Their meeting continued into the evening, the room bathed in the warm glow of the desk lamp, as they put the finishing touches on their paper. With each sentence refined and each paragraph polished, they were not only documenting a significant chapter in their clinic's history but also paving the way for future explorations into the unknown.

The day Dr. Adrian Harrow and Elena Markham submitted their comprehensive paper on their clinic's paranormal and psychological interventions was marked with a subdued celebration in Adrian's office. They had sent off their findings to a respected interdisciplinary journal, and now, leaning back in their chairs, they allowed themselves a moment of quiet satisfaction.

"It's out of our hands now," Adrian said, gazing at the confirmation email on his screen. "It feels a bit like sending a child off to college."

"It does," Elena agreed, her smile reflecting a mix of relief and anticipation. "But I think we've done everything we can to ensure it makes an impact."

Their conversation shifted to what might come next. They discussed potential responses from the academic community and how they might address questions or criticisms that could arise.

"I expect there might be some skepticism," Adrian mused, his fingers tapping on the desk. "Our findings do challenge some conventional boundaries between psychology and the paranormal."

"That's true," Elena replied, her expression contemplative. "But the data is solid, and our methodologies were rigorous. We're prepared to defend our work."

As the clinic resumed its usual rhythm, Adrian and Elena found themselves monitoring the incoming responses. Early feedback from peers they had shared preprints with was encouraging—curiosity mixed with commendable caution, a sign that their work was stirring the interest they had hoped for.

In the following weeks, Adrian often walked through the therapy rooms, observing the seamless integration of the gold and silver elements into the therapeutic environment. The rooms were not only sanctuaries of mental health recovery but also testaments to the clinic's resilience and innovation in face of the unknown.

Patient feedback continued to be overwhelmingly positive, with many expressing a newfound sense of security and calm during their sessions. This feedback was meticulously collected by Elena, who believed ongoing documentation was key to understanding the long-term impact of their interventions.

"Have you seen the latest patient satisfaction surveys?" Elena asked Adrian one afternoon as they reviewed the ongoing data collection.

"I have," Adrian replied, looking over the graphs she had prepared. "It's remarkable. Not only are we seeing a decrease in reported disturbances, but overall therapy effectiveness seems to have improved as well."

"It's an added validation of our efforts," Elena noted, satisfaction evident in her tone. "It seems that creating a physically and psychologically secure environment does enhance therapeutic outcomes."

Their research had indeed sparked a broader dialogue, with inquiries and invitations to speak at conferences beginning to come in. The implications of their work were far-reaching, prompting discussions on how environmental factors could be more deeply integrated into therapeutic practices for both traditional and unconventional challenges.

As they prepared for a presentation at an upcoming conference, Adrian and Elena refined their talking points, eager to share their insights and learn from others who might offer new perspectives or similar experiences.

"We're not just sharing our findings; we're inviting a conversation," Adrian remarked during one of their preparation sessions.

"And that's how progress is made," Elena added, her eyes bright with the excitement of academic exchange. "By challenging, questioning, and, most importantly, opening up to new ideas."

With the conference on the horizon, they finalized their visual aids and checked their data sets, ensuring every detail was ready for scrutiny. The clinic was quiet as they left for the evening, the weight of their forthcoming presentation a fresh challenge to their seasoned minds.

Driving home, Adrian reflected on the journey they had embarked upon. What had started as a crisis had transformed into a catalyst for growth and innovation, influencing not just their own practices but potentially those of the broader therapeutic community. As the city lights passed by, he felt a profound connection to his work, knowing that each step forward was a part of a larger, ongoing exploration into the human mind and the mysteries that sometimes surround it.

Chapter 9
Through the Looking Glass

The day of the conference dawned bright and clear, a sharp contrast to the complex, often shadowy subject matter Dr. Adrian Harrow and Elena Markham were prepared to discuss. The large conference center was bustling with activity, attendees from various disciplines mingling in the sprawling lobby, their badges flickering in the morning light.

Adrian and Elena arrived early, their presentation materials neatly packed in sleek, professional folders. They navigated through the crowd, exchanging brief nods and smiles with familiar faces and colleagues eager to hear about their pioneering work. The atmosphere was charged with intellectual curiosity, the air humming with snippets of conversations about new research findings and innovative practices.

Upon reaching the designated hall for their session, they set up their materials. The room slowly filled with an assortment of psychologists, therapists, paranormal researchers, and a few skeptically inclined academics, all taking their seats in anticipation of the presentation.

As the last few attendees filed in, Adrian stepped up to the podium. His heart was steady, his years of experience grounding him despite the groundbreaking nature of their research. He started by outlining the unusual phenomena they had encountered at the clinic, the integration of precious metals into the therapeutic environment, and the surprisingly positive effects these changes had brought about.

Elena then took over, delving deeper into the technical aspects of their findings. She discussed the environmental modifications, the specific properties of silver and gold, and their implications for both psychological and paranormal interventions. Her part of the presentation was rich with data, each slide meticulously detailed, showing graphs, feedback summaries, and even a few anonymized case studies.

The room was attentive, the audience captivated by the novelty and rigor of the presentation. Questions were saved for the end, as was customary, but Adrian could see the gears turning in the minds of many attendees, their expressions ranging from intrigued to critically thoughtful.

As the presentation drew to a close, Adrian wrapped up with a few reflections on the potential for future research and the importance of interdisciplinary approaches when dealing with phenomena that do not neatly fit into traditional scientific frameworks. He emphasized the need for openness in scientific inquiry, particularly when faced with the unknown.

The applause at the end of their session was gratifying, a solid recognition of their hard work and the thought-provoking nature of their study. As the audience began to disperse, several peers approached the podium, eager to discuss further or to ask detailed questions not covered during the Q&A.

Adrian and Elena handled the inquiries with expertise and patience, providing thoughtful answers that often led to broader discussions about the implications of their work. The interest was evident, and many expressed a desire to visit the clinic to see the modifications firsthand or to discuss potential collaborative research.

After the session, as the conference continued with other presentations and workshops, Adrian and Elena decided to attend a few themselves. They participated actively, drawing connections between their own work and the subjects discussed in other sessions, enriching their understanding and broadening their network.

The day was long and filled with intellectual stimulation, leaving them both energized and exhausted in equal measure. By the time the evening keynote address came around, they were ready to relax and absorb rather than present and defend.

As they left the conference hall that evening, the sunset painted the sky in hues of orange and purple, a beautiful close to an invigorating day. The success of their presentation had not only validated their hard work but had also opened new avenues for future exploration and collaboration. The ride back to their hotel was quiet, each lost in thoughts of what had been achieved and what might come next. The road ahead was promising, filled with potential and the certainty of further discovery.

The second day of the conference featured specialized workshops, and Dr. Adrian Harrow and Elena Markham found themselves at a roundtable discussion titled "Integrating Novel Methods in Therapeutic Practices." The room was set up to facilitate an open exchange, with experts from various fields seated around a large oval table.

As the session started, the moderator, a renowned psychologist known for her work in integrative therapy techniques, addressed the group. "Today, we're here to explore how unconventional methods can be effectively incorporated into our practices. Dr. Harrow, perhaps you could start us off by summarizing how your clinic has adopted such methods?"

Adrian nodded, clearing his throat slightly. "Certainly. Our clinic has recently integrated specific metals—silver and gold—into our therapy environments, based on their historically documented protective qualities. This was in response to unexplained disturbances that seemed to affect the therapeutic process."

"That's quite fascinating," a neuroscientist across the table chimed in. "Were these metals chosen based on cultural histories, or was there a scientific basis for their selection as well?"

"The choice was initially guided by historical and cultural records," Elena interjected. "However, we also conducted controlled experiments to scientifically validate their effectiveness. We've seen a measurable improvement in both the environmental stability of our therapy rooms and in patient outcomes."

A clinical psychologist next to her leaned forward, intrigued. "What kind of improvements in patient outcomes are we talking about? Can you provide specific examples?"

Elena responded, "Certainly. We've noted a significant decrease in anxiety levels during sessions and an increase in patient satisfaction. Moreover, the disturbances we previously encountered have not recurred since we implemented these changes."

An expert in environmental psychology, who had been listening intently, added, "This is a compelling intersection of environmental psychology and therapeutic practice. How do you ensure these changes are perceived positively by your patients and not as something esoteric?"

Adrian smiled, acknowledging the concern. "That's an excellent point. We've been very careful in how we introduce these changes. Everything is framed within the context of enhancing therapeutic comfort and effectiveness. The aesthetics of the metals are integrated in a subtle way that aligns with our clinic's overall design philosophy."

A researcher specializing in alternative therapies spoke up, "Have you considered the placebo effect in your evaluations? How do you differentiate the results from potential placebo responses?"

"That's part of why we maintain rigorous scientific protocols," Adrian explained. "We control for placebo effects through blinded studies and detailed environmental monitoring. This helps us ensure that the changes we observe are due to the interventions themselves, not placebo responses."

As the discussion unfolded, more questions were asked, ranging from the specifics of the environmental monitoring to ethical considerations in introducing such novel interventions. Adrian and Elena provided detailed responses, drawing on their extensive preparation and the data they had collected.

The workshop concluded with the group expressing a keen interest in visiting the clinic to see the modifications firsthand and discussing potential collaborative studies. The moderator thanked Adrian and Elena, noting, "Your work is pushing the boundaries of what we understand about therapeutic environments. It's an important reminder of how interdisciplinary approaches can lead to significant advancements in mental health treatment."

As the participants dispersed, Adrian and Elena exchanged a look of satisfaction. The engagement from their peers not only reinforced the value of their work but also opened up new pathways for future exploration and collaboration.

They left the workshop room energized, ready to attend other sessions, each bringing new insights that they could potentially integrate into their ongoing work. The dialogue from the roundtable reverberated in their minds, a symphony of possibilities that could shape the future of therapeutic practice.

In a quieter corner of the bustling conference venue, Dr. Adrian Harrow and Elena Markham engaged in a deep conversation with Dr. Lisa Mendez, an expert in environmental psychology they had met during one of the sessions. They discussed the potential for collaborative research, their coffee cups steaming gently on the table between them.

"Dr. Mendez, your insight into environmental factors and their psychological impacts is quite aligned with what we're trying to accomplish at our clinic," Adrian began, eager to explore the possibilities.

"Please, call me Lisa," she responded with a smile. "I was quite intrigued by your presentation yesterday. The use of metals like silver and gold to enhance therapeutic environments— it's quite innovative. How do you see our collaboration taking shape?"

Elena leaned forward, her enthusiasm evident. "We were thinking about a joint study, perhaps. One that could combine our practical findings with your theoretical frameworks. We've seen the effects firsthand, but we're interested in diving deeper into the why and how."

"That sounds fascinating," Lisa replied, her interest piqued. "Especially if we could measure how these environmental modifications influence therapy outcomes over a longer period. We could use a variety of psychological assessments and environmental sensors."

"Exactly," Adrian agreed. "And perhaps your expertise could help us refine our monitoring techniques. We're especially interested in more subtle environmental changes that could be affecting therapy sessions."

"I'd love to get involved with that," Lisa said, her mind already racing with ideas. "We could apply some advanced statistical models to analyze the data. It might give us insights into patterns we haven't yet considered."

Elena nodded, "We'd also appreciate your perspective on how to communicate these changes to a broader audience. Ensuring that our research is understood and accessible is crucial for its application in everyday clinical practices."

"That's an important aspect," Lisa acknowledged. "Educating the community about why these changes are beneficial and how they work could really help in reducing any skepticism or misconceptions."

Adrian sipped his coffee, thinking through the logistics. "What about funding? Collaborative grants might be available for this kind of innovative project. We could look into joint applications to cover the costs of a comprehensive study."

"I have some contacts at the National Health Institute that might be interested in this sort of interdisciplinary research," Lisa suggested. "A preliminary proposal outlining our aims and preliminary data could open some doors."

"That would be fantastic," Elena responded, her optimism growing. "We could draft a proposal over the next few weeks. Adrian, perhaps we could host a meeting at our clinic? It would give Lisa a chance to see our setup firsthand."

"I'd like that," Lisa said. "Seeing your work in action would definitely help in shaping the research proposal."

As their meeting drew to a close, they exchanged contact information and agreed to start outlining a project plan. The collaboration felt like a natural step forward, blending their innovative approaches with rigorous academic analysis.

Leaving the table, Adrian felt a renewed sense of purpose. The conference had not only reinforced their own work but had opened up new avenues for growth and discovery. Walking back through the conference hall, the chatter and noise around them seemed less like a distraction and more like the hum of a world teeming with possibilities.

Their conversation continued as they walked, discussing potential timelines and the next steps needed to bring their collaborative project to fruition. The future was uncertain, but it was brimming with potential, ready to be shaped by their continued efforts and newfound partnerships.

After the conference, Dr. Adrian Harrow and Elena Markham returned to the clinic invigorated and full of ideas. They were determined to translate the enthusiastic discussions and potential collaborations from the conference into tangible action. The clinic, with its calm and welcoming atmosphere, felt even more like a groundbreaker in the intersection of traditional and innovative therapeutic practices.

In Adrian's office, the two sat across from each other at the large oak desk that was now scattered with notes and a large calendar. They were deep in the process of scheduling the necessary steps for their upcoming collaborative project with Dr. Lisa Mendez.

"We need to ensure that we have everything lined up for Lisa's visit next month," Adrian was saying, marking the calendar. "I want her to see the clinic in full operation, including a live demonstration of how the therapy rooms function with the new modifications."

"That's a good plan," Elena agreed. "I'll arrange for a couple of our therapists to be available for demonstrations. We should also prepare a presentation on the initial data we've collected since the renovations."

Adrian nodded in approval. "And let's not forget to include a tour of the monitoring equipment and the data processing center. It's important for her to understand the full scope of our operations."

"Absolutely," Elena replied, jotting down another note. "I'll coordinate with the IT department to ensure they're ready to show off our setup. They've been instrumental in integrating the environmental sensors and ensuring we capture accurate data."

The discussion then turned to the specifics of the research proposal they planned to draft with Lisa. "We need to outline our primary objectives clearly," Adrian said thoughtfully. "It's not just about validating the use of metals in therapeutic settings but also understanding the underlying mechanisms at play."

Elena was quick to add, "And we should emphasize the potential for broader applications. If we can demonstrate effectiveness here, there's no reason why these methods couldn't be adapted for use in other therapeutic environments."

"That's an excellent point," Adrian said, his mind already racing with possibilities. "Let's make sure to frame our research questions around both practical outcomes and theoretical advancements."

As they wrapped up their meeting, they reviewed their checklist: finalize the agenda for Lisa's visit, prepare the data presentation, coordinate with the IT department, and begin drafting the research proposal. Each task was assigned a deadline, ensuring that nothing was overlooked.

Leaving Adrian's office, Elena felt a mixture of excitement and responsibility. The clinic was on the verge of pioneering something truly groundbreaking, and the next few months would be crucial in shaping the future of their practice.

Adrian, too, felt the weight and thrill of the coming challenges. As he walked Elena to the door, he said, "This is going to be a significant undertaking, but I can't think of anyone I'd rather have by my side for this journey."

"Likewise, Adrian," Elena responded with a smile. "We're making history here, one step at a time."

As the door closed behind her, Adrian turned back to his desk, his gaze falling on the scattered papers and the glowing computer screen. Outside, the clinic carried on its nightly routine, a beacon of care and innovation. Inside, the plans being laid were poised to propel them into new realms of understanding and influence.

Adrian's last thoughts before turning off the lights were of the future, filled with the promise of discovery and the satisfaction of making a meaningful impact, not just within the walls of his clinic, but across the broader landscape of mental health care.

Chapter 10
The Gathering Storm

Dr. Lisa Mendez arrived at the clinic on a bright spring morning, her eyes wide with curiosity as she stepped through the doors. Dr. Adrian Harrow and Elena Markham were there to greet her, their faces alight with the anticipation of sharing their work and discussing the future.

"Lisa, welcome to our clinic!" Adrian extended his hand warmly. "We're thrilled to have you here."

"Thank you, Adrian. I've been looking forward to this visit," Lisa replied, shaking his hand. "I'm eager to see how you've implemented the changes we discussed at the conference."

Elena chimed in, "We have quite a bit to show you. Shall we start with a tour of the therapy rooms? We've scheduled demonstrations of the new environments."

"That sounds perfect," Lisa responded, her professional curiosity piqued.

As they walked through the clinic, Adrian and Elena pointed out the subtle yet significant modifications. The first stop was one of the newly renovated therapy rooms. "Here you can see how we integrated the silver and gold into the room's design," Elena explained, gesturing towards the elegantly inlaid patterns on the walls and ceiling.

Lisa examined the designs closely. "It's beautifully done," she remarked. "It's so seamlessly integrated that one might not even know it's there for any reason other than aesthetics."

"That was the goal," Adrian said. "We wanted to enhance the therapeutic atmosphere without making it feel clinical or intimidating."

Lisa nodded appreciatively. "And what have the patient reactions been?"

"Overwhelmingly positive," Elena answered. "We've seen a noticeable improvement in the comfort levels reported by our patients, and the disturbances we were concerned about have not recurred."

As they moved to the next room, Lisa asked, "Could you tell me more about the environmental monitoring you've implemented?"

"Of course," Adrian replied, leading the way to a small control room filled with monitors. "We track everything from temperature fluctuations to electromagnetic fields. The data helps us ensure that the environment remains stable and conducive to therapy."

Lisa looked at the screens displaying real-time data. "This is impressive. The level of detail could really provide a lot of insights into how physical environments impact psychological therapy."

"We think so," Elena agreed. "And we're just scratching the surface. We believe there's much more to learn from this data."

They then sat down in Adrian's office to discuss the potential collaborative research in more depth. "We're particularly interested in exploring how these environmental factors could be influencing therapy outcomes," Adrian explained.

Lisa was quick to see the potential. "There's a real opportunity here to bridge environmental psychology and clinical practice in ways that haven't been done before. What do you need from me to get this collaboration off the ground?"

"We'd appreciate your expertise in designing the study, especially in developing the methodologies for data collection and analysis," Elena said.

"And we'd love your input on our draft proposal for funding," Adrian added. "Your insights would be invaluable."

Lisa nodded, her mind already racing with ideas. "I think we could put together a very strong proposal. Your preliminary data is compelling, and with a rigorous study design, we could really explore the implications of your findings."

"Exactly what we were hoping for," Adrian smiled. "Let's set up regular meetings to start outlining the project in detail."

As Lisa prepared to leave, she turned to both Adrian and Elena. "I'm genuinely excited about what we're starting here. What you've achieved is remarkable, and I believe it's just the beginning."

With that, they parted ways, Lisa heading out with notes in hand and a schedule of upcoming meetings, while Adrian and Elena returned to their day, energized by the promising new direction their work was taking. The clinic, once just a place for healing, was becoming a hub of innovation and research, pushing the boundaries of what was possible in therapeutic practice.

Back in Dr. Adrian Harrow's office, he and Elena Markham sat across from each other, their laptops open and documents spread out between them. They were ready to dive deep into drafting the research proposal with Dr. Lisa Mendez, who joined them via a video conference.

"Alright, Lisa, let's get started on this proposal," Adrian began, his tone businesslike yet tinged with excitement. "We've outlined the main objectives based on our last discussion. Shall we go through them one by one to ensure everything aligns?"

"Sounds good," Lisa responded from the screen, her image clear and focused. "Why don't we start with the primary research question? We need to define it precisely to guide the scope of our study."

Elena nodded, scrolling through a document on her laptop. "We propose to investigate how the integration of specific environmental enhancements—namely, silver and gold—impacts therapeutic outcomes. We need to determine whether these elements can consistently create a more stable and effective therapeutic environment."

Lisa considered this for a moment. "That's a solid start. We should also consider exploring secondary questions, such as the potential psychological mechanisms at play. How do these changes affect the patient's perception and interaction with the therapy environment?"

"That's an excellent point," Adrian agreed. "It ties directly into the broader implications of environmental psychology. We should also include a methodology section that explains how we'll measure these interactions and perceptions."

"Yes, and let's not forget to outline our data collection methods," Elena added. "We'll need detailed information on the environmental sensors and psychological assessments we plan to use."

Lisa was already typing notes on her end. "For the methodology, we should include a mixed-methods approach. Quantitative data from the sensors and qualitative data from patient interviews could provide a comprehensive view."

"Agreed," Adrian said. "Now, moving on to the significance of the research. It's crucial that we convey the potential impact of our findings."

Elena chimed in, "This research could significantly alter how therapeutic environments are designed. It has the potential to enhance clinical practices and patient outcomes on a wide scale."

Lisa nodded, "Exactly, and let's make sure we address the innovative aspects of our approach. We're bridging gaps between traditional psychological methods and environmental studies, which is relatively unexplored territory."

"As for the budget," Adrian shifted the topic slightly, "we need to be realistic but also ensure we have enough resources to cover all aspects of the research, including unforeseen expenses."

Lisa suggested, "Include detailed budgeting for the materials—silver and gold aren't cheap, plus the costs for additional sensors and possibly even hiring a dedicated research assistant."

Elena was quick to add, "We should also factor in costs for publishing and potentially presenting our findings at conferences. Spreading the word is just as important as the research itself."

"That's a comprehensive outlook," Lisa concluded. "Once we finalize this draft, I can start reaching out to my contacts for potential funding. I believe there's a lot of interest in innovative mental health research right now."

"Thank you, Lisa," Adrian said, gratitude evident in his voice. "Your expertise and network could really make a difference here."

As the meeting drew to a close, they reviewed their action items and set a date for their next discussion. With a few clicks, the virtual connection was ended, and Adrian and Elena leaned back in their chairs, both feeling the weight and potential of what they were undertaking.

With the conversation still fresh, they spent the next few hours refining the proposal, driven by a shared vision of improving therapeutic environments and, ultimately, patient care. The clinic was quiet around them, a stark contrast to the flurry of ideas and plans that filled Adrian's office.

In the weeks that followed, Dr. Adrian Harrow and Elena Markham found themselves deep in the minutiae of their research proposal. The clinic, always a hub of activity, seemed to hum with a heightened sense of purpose as they worked to finalize the document that could potentially set a new standard in therapeutic environment design.

Adrian spent long hours in his office, his desk littered with research papers, draft sections of the proposal, and his trusty old laptop. The screen glowed late into the evening, casting a soft light that reflected off the framed degrees hanging on the walls. Each paragraph he crafted was meticulously sourced, ensuring that every claim was backed by robust data and precedent.

Elena, meanwhile, was just as absorbed in coordinating the practical aspects of the proposal. She liaised with the clinic's financial team to budget accurately for the project, accounting for everything from material costs to the potential need for additional staffing. Her spreadsheets were detailed and comprehensive, leaving no stone unturned in planning for a well-resourced study.

Together, they met regularly to discuss their progress and integrate their sections of the proposal into a cohesive whole. "How are we looking on the methodology section?" Adrian would ask, poring over the documents Elena handed him.

"We're solid," Elena would confirm, pointing to the charts and tables that outlined their planned measurements and assessments. "I've included a timeline for each phase of the study, ensuring we have ample time for data collection and analysis."

Their discussions often stretched into the late hours, fueled by coffee and the shared excitement of pioneering something new. Each meeting ended with a review of what they had achieved and what still needed to be done. "We're getting there," Adrian would say, a note of satisfaction in his voice despite the fatigue that shadowed his eyes.

As the proposal neared completion, they scheduled a final review session to go through the document line by line. The clinic's quiet conference room was the setting for this critical meeting, where they scrutinized every word and comma, ensuring clarity and precision.

The conversation during this session was sparse, focused intensely on the task at hand. "Do you think this paragraph clearly explains the theoretical framework?" Elena asked, her finger tracing the lines of text.

"It does, but let's add a sentence about how this framework is supported by recent studies in both psychology and environmental sciences," Adrian suggested, his eyes scanning the referenced articles laid out before him.

Once satisfied with the draft, they prepared to send it off to Dr. Lisa Mendez for her final input. The email, drafted with careful consideration, was concise yet thorough. "Lisa, we've incorporated all the elements we discussed and are looking forward to your expert feedback before submission," Elena typed, her hands steady on the keyboard.

With the proposal sent, a quiet tension settled over them. They had done all they could for now. The clinic continued to operate around them, oblivious to the potential changes that hinged on the success of this proposal.

Leaving the conference room, Adrian and Elena felt a mix of relief and anticipation. They walked through the corridors of the clinic, past the therapy rooms that were the heart of their study, each step a reminder of the journey they had embarked on together. The evening light faded into dusk, casting long shadows that stretched down the hallways, mirroring the elongating reach of their research efforts into the future.

Several days after sending the draft to Dr. Lisa Mendez, Dr. Adrian Harrow and Elena Markham convened in Adrian's office to review her feedback. The email from Lisa was open on Adrian's laptop, her comments detailed and constructive.

"Lisa has given us quite a bit to think about," Adrian remarked as he scrolled through the email. "She suggests we clarify the scope of the environmental modifications. Apparently, it wasn't clear whether we're applying these changes clinic-wide or just in selected therapy rooms."

"That's a good point," Elena agreed, leaning in to read the email over Adrian's shoulder. "We should specify that the initial study will focus on three therapy rooms that have been retrofitted, to control our variables more effectively."

Adrian nodded and began typing the revision into the document. "She also mentioned that our section on the psychological assessments could use more detail. We need to better explain how these assessments align with our overall research objectives."

Elena thought for a moment, then said, "Let's add a table that outlines each assessment tool we plan to use, including what specific data we expect to gather from each and how this data will contribute to our understanding of the environmental impact."

"Excellent idea," Adrian replied, making a note to include this addition. "Lisa also thinks we should strengthen our argument for the interdisciplinary approach by citing more studies that have successfully integrated environmental psychology into therapeutic practices."

"I'll pull up some recent studies and work those references in," Elena offered, opening her laptop to begin the search. "This will reinforce the innovative aspect of our proposal and show that we're building on an established foundation."

As they worked, the conversation shifted to the potential outcomes of their study. "Assuming we secure the funding, what are your thoughts on the long-term implications of our research?" Adrian asked, genuinely interested in Elena's perspective.

Elena paused, considering. "If our findings confirm that these environmental enhancements can significantly improve therapeutic outcomes, it could revolutionize the way therapy environments are designed. It might even set a new standard for clinical settings beyond mental health facilities."

"That's an exciting prospect," Adrian said, his voice filled with enthusiasm. "It underlines the importance of making sure every element of this proposal is as strong as possible."

They spent the next couple of hours revising the proposal, integrating Lisa's feedback, and refining their arguments. With each change, the document became more robust, reflecting a deep understanding of the subject matter and a clear vision for the future.

Finally, Adrian leaned back in his chair, reading through the revised proposal with a satisfied smile. "I think we've addressed all of Lisa's points effectively. How do you feel about it?"

Elena, who had been reviewing the changes alongside Adrian, nodded her approval. "It's thorough, compelling, and it sounds like us—ambitious but grounded in solid research."

"Let's send it back to Lisa for one last look before we submit it," Adrian suggested, already drafting the email. "Her final nod will give us the confidence that we're ready to move forward."

As they wrapped up their work for the day, the clinic began to quiet down, the hustle of the daytime giving way to the peaceful stillness of the evening. Adrian and Elena, feeling accomplished and hopeful, stepped out of the office into the cool night air, ready to face whatever challenges and opportunities awaited them in the unfolding future of their groundbreaking work.

Chapter 11
The Ritual Begins

Dr. Adrian Harrow and Elena Markham sat across from each other in Adrian's office, a space that had become their strategic hub over the past few months. They were surrounded by notes and laptops, the air thick with anticipation as they awaited the final response from the funding committee regarding their research proposal.

Elena, always the more visibly anxious of the two, tapped her pen against her notebook. "What if they want more revisions? Or worse, what if they don't see the potential impact of our work?"

Adrian, ever the calming presence, smiled reassuringly. "We've done everything we could to present a strong, compelling case. Lisa's final feedback was incredibly positive, and she's been through this many times. I think we stand a good chance."

Just then, Adrian's email pinged, and he quickly clicked to open the new message. Both leaned in, holding their breath as Adrian read aloud, "Dear Dr. Harrow and Ms. Markham, we are pleased to inform you..."

Elena let out a sigh of relief, her smile spreading. "They approved it?"

"They did!" Adrian exclaimed, his relief palpable. "Not only that, but they're fully funding our proposed budget. They believe our project could be a cornerstone for future research in therapeutic environmental design."

"That's incredible!" Elena beamed. "This means we can move forward with everything we've planned—the enhanced monitoring, the expanded patient studies, even the conferences to share our findings."

"Yes, and we need to start planning immediately," Adrian said, already shifting into project management mode. "First, we need to finalize the contracts for the additional sensors and get them installed in the therapy rooms."

Elena nodded, her mind racing with logistics. "I'll handle that. I'll also start drafting the schedule for patient enrollment. We need to ensure we have a diverse group to strengthen the validity of our study."

"And I'll reach out to the university's research department for assistance with data analysis," Adrian added. "With the complexity of data we expect to collect, having their expertise will be invaluable."

"Should we schedule weekly meetings with Lisa to keep her in the loop and get her input on the study's progress?" Elena suggested, knowing how crucial Lisa's insights had been so far.

"Absolutely," Adrian agreed. "Her perspective will be crucial, especially when we begin interpreting the data. Plus, her experience with these kinds of studies can help us navigate any challenges that come up."

As they continued to outline their immediate next steps, there was a knock at the door. It was Janet, their clinic manager. "I heard the news," she said, stepping into the room with a smile. "Congratulations to both of you. How can the rest of the team help get things started?"

"Thank you, Janet," Adrian replied. "Actually, could you help us coordinate with the IT department? We need to ensure the new sensors are integrated smoothly with our current system."

"Of course, I'll set up a meeting with IT first thing tomorrow," Janet responded, jotting down a note. "Anything else you need?"

"For now, that's it," Elena answered. "But there will be more as we get deeper into the project. We'll keep everyone updated."

As Janet left the office, Adrian and Elena looked at each other, a mix of excitement and the weight of responsibility settling over them. They had the green light they had hoped for, and now the real work would begin.

"We're doing this, Elena," Adrian said, a wide smile spreading across his face. "It's really happening."

"It is," Elena replied, her own smile matching his. "And it's going to be amazing."

As they wrapped up their meeting, the sun began to set outside, casting long shadows across the clinic. The journey ahead would be demanding, but they were ready to take it on, armed with determination and the support of their team. They stepped out of the office together, ready to advance not just their careers, but the field of therapeutic environmental design.

In the following weeks, Dr. Adrian Harrow and Elena Markham worked tirelessly to set up the infrastructure for their groundbreaking study. The clinic was a hive of activity, with contractors and clinic staff moving in and out of therapy rooms, installing the new environmental sensors and ensuring that everything was calibrated correctly.

One afternoon, in a recently upgraded therapy room, Adrian and Elena met with the IT lead, Marcus, to discuss the integration of the new technology.

"Marcus, how's the setup going? Are we on track with the sensor integration?" Adrian asked, looking around at the newly installed devices.

"We're mostly on schedule," Marcus replied, tapping through screens on his tablet. "The sensors are all installed, and we're finalizing the software integration. There's been a bit of a challenge syncing the new data with our existing systems, but we should have it sorted out by the end of the week."

"That's good to hear," Elena said, her tone a mix of relief and anticipation. "We need the data collection to be seamless. The integrity of our study depends on the accuracy and reliability of these measurements."

Marcus nodded in agreement. "Absolutely. I understand the stakes. We're doing everything we can to ensure the system is robust."

Adrian, satisfied with the progress, shifted the topic. "Once we have the technology squared away, we'll need to train the therapists on how to explain the new setup to patients. It's crucial they understand how to handle any questions or concerns that might arise."

Elena added, "I've drafted some talking points and a FAQ sheet for our therapists. It covers why the sensors are there, what they measure, and reassures them that their privacy is still our top priority."

"That sounds perfect, Elena," Adrian responded, pleased with her foresight. "Could you organize a training session for next week? It would be great to have everyone briefed before we start enrolling patients into the study."

"Will do," Elena confirmed, making a note on her digital pad. "I'll coordinate with Janet to schedule it."

The discussion then turned to the upcoming patient enrollment. "We've already received some interest from existing patients who are curious about the study," Elena shared. "We need to ensure that our enrollment process is clear and that we obtain all the necessary consents."

Adrian nodded thoughtfully. "Yes, the consent forms need to be thorough. Let's go over them again to make sure they cover all aspects of the study, especially the data collection and privacy sections."

"I'll review them tonight and circulate a draft for feedback," Elena promised. "Also, we should consider how we'll manage and store all the data we collect. Security and privacy need to be our top priorities."

Marcus chimed in, "I recommend setting up a separate secure server for this study. It would help isolate and protect the data."

"That's a good suggestion," Adrian agreed. "Let's look into that. Can you get us some options and cost estimates?"

"Of course, I'll have that information to you by tomorrow," Marcus replied, typing a reminder into his tablet.

As the meeting concluded, they all felt a renewed sense of purpose. The setup phase was always challenging, but it was also a testament to their commitment to advancing therapeutic practices.

Adrian and Elena left the room, discussing the next steps. The clinic was quieter now, the evening light casting long shadows through the hallways. They were on the cusp of something significant, each day bringing them closer to unlocking new understanding in the interplay between environment and mental health. The complexity of the task was daunting, but the potential to create lasting impact in the field of psychology was a powerful motivator.

In the weeks following the setup and training sessions, Dr. Adrian Harrow and Elena Markham began the patient enrollment process for their groundbreaking study. They had chosen a quiet morning to review the initial list of participants and discuss the preliminary data collection strategy.

As they sat in Adrian's office, the morning light streamed through the blinds, casting a warm glow over the documents and laptops spread across the desk. Adrian, reviewing a list on his laptop, spoke first. "We have twenty patients enrolled so far, which is a good start. How do you feel about the diversity of our participant group?"

Elena, looking over her own notes, replied, "It's fairly representative, though I think we could use more diversity in terms of age. The younger demographic is underrepresented. Perhaps we can reach out to local colleges or community centers?"

"That's a good idea," Adrian nodded. "We want to ensure our findings are applicable across a broader spectrum. I'll draft a letter to a few local institutions today."

As they continued to sift through their preparations, the discussion shifted to the initial setup of data collection, which was crucial for the integrity of their study. "How are the new sensors performing? Are we getting the type of data we expected?" Adrian asked, concern threading his voice.

"The sensors are functioning well," Elena assured him. "The initial data is quite interesting. We're seeing some variability in environmental factors like light and sound levels, which seem to correlate with patient stress markers."

Adrian perked up at this. "That's exactly the kind of insight we were hoping to find. It could suggest that subtle environmental changes have more of an impact on therapeutic outcomes than we previously thought."

"Indeed," Elena agreed, tapping a graph on her tablet. "I think once we have more data, we can start to analyze patterns. It might also be useful to adjust our data collection frequency to capture more nuanced changes during sessions."

"That might require additional calibration of the sensors," Adrian pondered aloud. "Let's make sure the IT team is on board with that adjustment."

Elena nodded, making a note. "I'll schedule a meeting with Marcus from IT for tomorrow. We need to ensure the changes won't disrupt the ongoing sessions or the integrity of the data we've already collected."

The conversation then turned to the feedback from the therapists, who were on the front lines of the study, interacting directly with the patients and the new environment. "Have there been any comments from the team on the ground?" Adrian inquired, always keen to ensure the staff felt supported.

"Overall, the feedback has been positive," Elena responded. "The therapists appreciate the enhanced environment and have noticed that patients seem more at ease. However, one therapist mentioned that some patients were curious about the sensors. We might need to revisit how we're communicating the purpose of these devices to ensure patients feel comfortable."

"That's an important point," Adrian agreed. "Let's include a brief Q&A sheet in our waiting areas and perhaps a digital version on our website. Transparency is key to maintaining trust."

As their meeting concluded, they reviewed their action list: enhancing participant diversity, recalibrating data collection tools, updating IT requirements, and improving patient communication. These tasks were critical to the ongoing success of their study.

Stepping out of the office, Adrian and Elena felt a mix of anticipation and responsibility. The clinic had become not just a place of healing but a dynamic research facility, each day bringing them closer to new discoveries about the interplay between environment and mental health. The initial data was promising, and the path ahead, while complex, was rich with potential.

As the study progressed, Dr. Adrian Harrow and Elena Markham dedicated several weeks to a meticulous examination of the data being collected. The clinic, always a place of innovation and healing, had transformed into a pioneering research facility, with the latest session data promising insights into the subtle interplay between environment and therapy outcomes.

In Adrian's office, walls lined with charts and graphs, the two researchers poured over the latest batch of data. Each point represented a fragment of understanding, a piece of the puzzle they were painstakingly assembling. The air was thick with concentration, the only sounds the quiet hum of the computer and the occasional rustle of papers.

Adrian, eyes narrowed in focus, examined a complex graph displaying patient stress markers against environmental variables. "Look at this spike in stress levels here," he pointed out, tracing the line with his finger. "It correlates directly with a dip in room temperature. It's fascinating how sensitive the responses are to such subtle changes."

Elena, reviewing a spreadsheet on her laptop, nodded in agreement. "It reinforces our hypothesis about environmental impacts on therapeutic efficacy. We should consider adjusting the thermostat settings to test if maintaining a consistent temperature could moderate stress markers more effectively."

Their analysis wasn't confined to environmental data alone. Patient feedback forms were also a critical component of their research, offering qualitative insights that enriched the quantitative data. Elena summarized the latest feedback, "Several patients noted feeling unusually calm in the therapy sessions. They're attributing it to the ambiance, but it's the changes we've made that are influencing their experience."

"That subjective feedback is invaluable," Adrian said, making a note. "It gives context to the data we're collecting. We need to ensure this is integrated into our final analysis."

As they delved deeper into the data, patterns began to emerge, some expected and some surprising. The integration of environmental sensors had provided a wealth of information, but interpreting that data required careful thought and expertise. Adrian and Elena often stayed late, discussing potential implications and refining their methodology.

The work was demanding, but moments of breakthrough invigorated their resolve. One evening, while cross-referencing data sets, Elena made a significant connection between light levels and patient anxiety. "Adrian, when you see this—during sessions with increased natural light exposure, there's a marked decrease in reported anxiety."

"That could be a key finding," Adrian responded with excitement. "We should look into controlled light exposure as a potential therapeutic tool."

The weeks passed in a blur of data, discussions, and discovery. The clinic staff, accustomed to the study's demands, supported the research by meticulously following the new protocols and providing feedback on their observations.

The research had begun to draw interest from the broader medical and psychological community. Preliminary findings, shared at small seminars and symposiums, garnered positive reactions and constructive criticism, which Adrian and Elena welcomed as essential for refining their study.

One late afternoon, as the sun cast long shadows across the office, Adrian and Elena prepared for another presentation, this time to a panel of potential investors and clinic stakeholders. The data was compelling, the implications profound, and their presentation detailed the groundbreaking nature of their work.

As they gathered their notes and prepared to step into the meeting, the clinic's halls quiet except for the soft buzz of anticipation, Adrian and Elena shared a look of quiet confidence. They were on the brink of changing not just practices within their clinic but potentially setting new standards for therapeutic environments worldwide. With each step they took towards the conference room, they carried with them not just data, but a vision for the future of therapy.

Chapter 12
Unseen Forces

As the clinic buzzed with the promising outcomes of their research, Dr. Adrian Harrow and Elena Markham began planning the next phase of their project, one that extended beyond the confines of their facility. The morning light streamed through Adrian's office window, casting a hopeful glow as they prepared for a significant meeting with potential collaborators from other clinics and institutions.

Adrian reviewed the agenda on his laptop, his expression focused yet tinged with excitement. "We need to ensure our data is compelling. This meeting could determine how broadly we can implement our findings."

Elena, organizing the printed charts and graphs on the desk, nodded in agreement. "The visual aids are ready, and I think they clearly demonstrate the positive impact of our environmental modifications. The before and after therapy outcomes are particularly striking."

Their conversation was briefly interrupted by a knock at the door. Janet, the clinic manager, entered with a fresh batch of feedback forms from recent therapy sessions. "These just came in," she said, handing over the documents. "It looks like the positive trends are continuing."

"That's great to hear," Adrian replied, scanning the forms. "This ongoing improvement will bolster our case today."

As Janet left, Elena glanced at the clock. "We should head to the conference room soon. The representatives will be arriving in half an hour."

Adrian closed his laptop. "Let's go through our main talking points once more. I want to make sure we're clear on how we can scale this project effectively."

In the conference room, a large screen displayed a slideshow of the clinic's journey, from the initial disturbances to the innovative interventions and their results. Adrian and Elena rehearsed their presentation, discussing each slide and the data it represented.

"We should emphasize the scalability of our approach," Elena suggested. "These modifications can be adapted to different environments, not just therapy clinics but potentially hospitals, schools, and even corporate settings."

"Absolutely," Adrian agreed. "And we need to address potential challenges. It's important to acknowledge that while the results are promising, scaling up will require careful consideration of each new environment's unique characteristics."

The discussion was a blend of strategy and anticipation. They analyzed potential questions and formulated clear, concise responses. As the time for the meeting approached, Adrian looked over the room setup one last time, ensuring that every detail was in place to facilitate a productive dialogue.

As the first of their guests arrived, Adrian and Elena greeted each attendee with warm handshakes and a brief overview of what they hoped to achieve in the meeting. The room filled quickly, a buzz of professional curiosity filling the air.

Once everyone was seated, Adrian opened the meeting. "Thank you all for joining us today. We're here to discuss a pioneering approach to enhancing therapeutic environments—an approach that has yielded significant improvements in patient outcomes at our clinic."

Elena took over to delve deeper into the specifics. "Our data shows not just anecdotal improvement but statistically significant changes in therapy effectiveness, correlated directly with our environmental enhancements."

The presentation was interactive, with Adrian and Elena encouraging questions and fostering a dialogue about each point they made. The representatives were engaged, asking insightful questions and expressing interest in how they might participate in expanding the research.

As the meeting progressed, it was clear that the interest in their work was robust and that the potential for collaboration was vast. Adrian and Elena responded to each query with data-backed answers, demonstrating not only the efficacy of their approach but also their commitment to a rigorous, data-driven expansion.

The session extended beyond the scheduled time, a testament to the depth of discussion and the enthusiasm of all involved. As the representatives left, many stayed behind to exchange contact information and express their eagerness to take the next steps.

Adrian and Elena, left alone in the conference room, shared a look of satisfaction and relief. The groundwork was laid for a broader application of their findings, and the potential for making a lasting impact in the field was within reach. They gathered their materials, the room quieting down as they prepared to return to their regular duties, buoyed by the success of the morning and the promising path that lay ahead.

Following the productive initial meeting, Dr. Adrian Harrow and Elena Markham spent the next few weeks deepening their collaborations with other institutions interested in implementing their environmental enhancements. The clinic served as a model, and now Adrian sat in his office, preparing for a series of video conferences with potential partners.

Elena knocked gently and entered, carrying a stack of follow-up reports. "Here are the updates from the other clinics that started testing our modifications. It looks promising, but there are variations in how well the changes are being received."

Adrian nodded, taking the reports. "Let's go through these together. It's crucial we understand the different contexts these clinics operate in. What works here might need adjustment elsewhere."

As they reviewed the data, the phone rang. Adrian answered it on speaker—it was Dr. Lisa Mendez, calling in for a scheduled update. "Adrian, Elena, how are things progressing with the expanded trials?"

"We're just reviewing the latest feedback," Adrian responded. "It's mostly positive, though there are some challenges with integration in clinics with different patient demographics and architectural styles."

"That's to be expected," Lisa replied thoughtfully. "Perhaps we need to consider a more flexible framework for implementing these changes. One that allows for customization based on specific environmental and demographic factors."

Elena chimed in, "That's a good idea, Lisa. We could develop a set of guidelines that can be adapted. For instance, the use of materials could vary, but the principles of their placement and integration remain consistent."

"I like that approach," Lisa said. "It maintains the integrity of the research while providing necessary flexibility. How about we draft a preliminary guide and review it together?"

"We'll get started on that right away," Adrian confirmed, making a note. "Also, we've scheduled demonstrations for these clinics next month. It might help to have you join, Lisa, to provide further insight into the research background."

"I'd be happy to," Lisa agreed. "Just send me the dates, and I'll make sure I'm available."

After the call, Adrian and Elena focused on preparing for the upcoming demonstrations. They outlined the key points to highlight and discussed how to address potential questions about scalability and cost-effectiveness.

"Do you think we should prepare a more detailed cost-benefit analysis for these presentations?" Elena suggested. "It might help some of the more hesitant clinics see the value."

"Absolutely," Adrian agreed. "If we can show that the initial investment results in measurable improvements in patient outcomes and therapist satisfaction, it would make a compelling argument."

The rest of the day was spent in detailed planning and discussions. They reviewed architectural plans, adjusted schedules, and refined their presentation slides. Each task was handled with a careful consideration of its potential impact.

As evening approached, Adrian and Elena wrapped up their preparations. They stepped out of the office, feeling cautiously optimistic about the coming weeks. The clinic corridors were quiet, with the evening shift change just beginning. The soft sounds of the clinic settling for the night were a stark contrast to the day's busy undertakings.

The possibility of their model becoming a standard in therapeutic environments was closer than ever, and while the path ahead was filled with challenges, it was also ripe with potential. They left the building discussing the next day's agenda, ready to continue pushing the boundaries of what was possible in therapeutic care.

The following weeks were a whirlwind of activity for Dr. Adrian Harrow and Elena Markham as they traveled to various clinics to conduct demonstrations of their therapeutic environment enhancements. Each clinic offered a new audience, a fresh set of eyes, and a unique set of challenges and questions.

At one such clinic, a modern facility located in the heart of a bustling city, Adrian prepared the demonstration room while Elena gathered the attending therapists and clinic directors in the adjacent conference room. The walls of the demonstration room had been subtly lined with silver and gold accents, similar to their own clinic's setup.

As the group entered, Adrian began the demonstration. "Thank you for joining us today. What you see here is similar to what we have implemented at our clinic. The key elements are the strategically placed silver and gold enhancements, which, as our research shows, significantly improve the therapeutic environment."

A clinic director, a middle-aged woman with a keen eye, observed the room thoughtfully. "It looks very welcoming," she commented. "But how do you measure the impact of these enhancements? What kind of data can you show us?"

Elena, ready with a tablet in hand, displayed graphs and charts. "Here you can see the before and after. We've tracked various metrics, including patient stress levels, session effectiveness, and overall environment quality. All have shown marked improvements."

Another therapist, younger and somewhat skeptical, chimed in. "How do patients react to knowing they're being monitored in this way? Does that not skew the data somewhat?"

"That's a valid concern," Adrian acknowledged. "We make sure patients are fully aware of the monitoring, which is non-invasive. We've actually found that most patients feel reassured by the measures, knowing that we are actively seeking to improve their therapy experience."

As the demonstration concluded, the group discussed practical matters such as cost, maintenance, and integration into existing practices. Elena handled these questions with ease, explaining, "The initial setup cost is balanced by the long-term benefits. Reduced patient dropout rates, better therapy outcomes, and increased therapist satisfaction all contribute to a positive return on investment."

Adrian added, "Plus, we offer ongoing support for clinics that adopt this model. It's not just about installing these enhancements but ensuring they work effectively within your specific environment."

The clinic staff seemed impressed, and many stayed behind to ask more detailed questions or to discuss potential customization options for their rooms. Adrian and Elena provided detailed responses, emphasizing flexibility and support.

As they left the clinic, the feedback was encouraging. "I think they saw the potential," Elena said, as they walked back to their rental car. "Especially once they could visualize the data and hear about the long-term benefits."

Adrian nodded in agreement as he drove them away from the clinic. "Each demonstration helps us refine our pitch and understand the concerns clinics have. It's invaluable."

The road ahead was busy with more demonstrations and discussions planned, but each successful visit added momentum to their project's rollout. As they traveled, the impact of their work became more evident, not just in improved metrics but in the conversations they sparked about the future of therapeutic environments.

By the time they returned to their hotel that evening, both were tired but fulfilled. They knew they were not just selling an idea but were advocating for a shift in how therapeutic environments are conceived and utilized—a shift that could redefine the field. As they reviewed the day's notes and planned for the next demonstration, the potential for widespread impact became increasingly tangible, driving them forward with renewed purpose.

After several successful demonstrations, Dr. Adrian Harrow and Elena Markham sat in a quaint café near one of the clinics they had visited, reflecting on the progress they had made. The aroma of coffee filled the air, mixing with the hum of midday chatter. They were joined by Dr. Lisa Mendez, who had flown in to assist with some of the more technical aspects of their presentations.

"Lisa, your presence these last few sessions has really deepened the discussions, especially around the data analysis," Adrian began, stirring his coffee. "It seems like having an expert in environmental psychology on hand is really resonating with the clinic staff."

Lisa smiled, accepting the compliment gracefully. "I'm glad to hear that. It's fascinating to see different clinics react to the data. There's a genuine interest in how these subtle environmental changes can drive big improvements in therapy outcomes."

Elena nodded, her eyes scanning through notes on her tablet. "I think what's really striking for them is seeing the tangible benefits, not just theoretical ones. For instance, the decrease in patient anxiety levels and the positive feedback from therapists—it makes it all more relatable."

Adrian looked thoughtful. "That's true. Speaking of feedback, have either of you thought more about how we can enhance our follow-up with clinics that decide to implement our model? I think ongoing support will be crucial."

"That's a good point," Lisa responded. "We should consider setting up a dedicated support system. Maybe a hotline or a scheduled monthly check-in via video conference to address any issues they encounter."

"I like that," Elena said, typing a note. "A structured support system would not only help with any teething problems but also reinforce their commitment to the new setup. We could also use those sessions to gather data on long-term outcomes."

Lisa agreed, adding, "And perhaps we could develop a training module for their staff. It could be a blend of online tutorials and live sessions, focusing on how to best utilize and maintain the enhancements."

"That would definitely add value," Adrian acknowledged, his mind already considering potential costs and resources needed. "We could pilot the training module with a few local clinics first, refine it, and then roll it out more broadly."

Elena looked up from her tablet, a new idea forming. "What about a yearly symposium? We could invite all the participating clinics to share their experiences, learn from each other, and discuss improvements."

"An excellent idea," Lisa said with enthusiasm. "It would not only build a community around this innovative approach but also keep the momentum going. Plus, it could generate more interest from other clinics and institutions."

Adrian smiled, pleased with the collaborative spirit at the table. "Let's sketch out a plan for these initiatives. We could include potential funding sources for them in our next grant application."

As their meeting continued, the trio detailed out each idea, assigning tasks and setting timelines. They were determined to ensure that the transition for clinics adopting their model was as smooth as possible and that ongoing support was robust and effective.

Leaving the café later, Adrian, Elena, and Lisa felt invigorated by the productive discussion. The path forward was becoming clearer, and the potential impact of their work seemed ever more significant. They stepped out into the afternoon sun, each filled with a renewed sense of purpose and anticipation for the next steps in their project. The road ahead was promising, and they were ready to meet its challenges together.

Chapter 13
The Breach

In a spacious conference room, adorned with the latest digital presentation technology, Dr. Adrian Harrow, Elena Markham, and Dr. Lisa Mendez were gathered around a large oval table. They were joined by a select group of potential investors and collaborators who were keen on understanding and possibly supporting the expansion of the clinic's innovative therapeutic environment model.

Adrian initiated the meeting with a warm welcome. "Thank you all for joining us today. We're here to discuss potential partnerships and funding opportunities that could help us expand our project not just nationally, but internationally."

Lisa, who had been pivotal in refining the data analysis, took the lead on presenting the findings. "Our research has consistently shown significant improvements in patient outcomes through the integration of environmental psychology principles into therapy settings. These include reduced anxiety levels and higher satisfaction rates among patients and staff."

Elena continued, "We've successfully implemented these changes in several clinics, and the feedback has been overwhelmingly positive. Today, we want to explore how we can bring this model to a wider audience and what role you could play in that expansion."

A potential investor, Mr. Thompson, leaned forward, intrigued. "Could you elaborate on what this expansion might look like? Are we talking about new clinics, training programs, or something else?"

Adrian answered, "All of the above, Mr. Thompson. We envision establishing new clinics with these enhancements as standard features. Additionally, we plan to offer training programs for existing clinics that wish to adopt our model."

Dr. Mendez added, "There's also potential for academic collaboration. We aim to study the long-term effects of our environmental modifications across different cultures and climates, which would provide invaluable data for the global medical community."

Another collaborator, Dr. Singh, chimed in, "What kind of support are you looking for from us specifically? Financial, logistical, research?"

Elena responded, "Primarily financial, but also expertise in scaling health initiatives. Logistical support, particularly in terms of international regulations and standards, would also be crucial."

Mr. Thompson nodded thoughtfully. "What about the technology involved? Is there proprietary technology that needs further development?"

Lisa replied, "Yes, we've developed proprietary sensor systems and data analytics platforms that monitor and analyze environmental factors in real-time. Further development and scaling of this technology are key components of our expansion plan."

Dr. Singh looked pleased. "I can see the potential for significant impact here. However, what guarantees can you offer that the model is as effective universally? Different regions have different environmental and cultural dynamics."

"That's a valid concern," Adrian admitted. "Which is why part of our expansion includes localized pilot studies to adapt and fine-tune the model to specific regional needs before a full rollout."

Elena jumped back in, "We're committed to a rigorous, data-driven approach, ensuring each step of our expansion is backed by solid research and clear outcomes."

The conversation moved on to specifics of potential funding amounts, timelines for initial pilot studies, and the structure of the collaborative efforts. Each participant had the opportunity to ask detailed questions, and Adrian, Elena, and Lisa provided comprehensive answers, emphasizing transparency and the project's potential for high impact.

As the meeting drew to a close, there was a sense of excitement about the possibilities. Handshakes were exchanged, and there were promises of follow-up meetings to further refine the details.

"We look forward to working with all of you," Adrian concluded, his voice reflecting both gratitude and anticipation. "Together, we can redefine therapeutic environments globally."

The group disbanded, leaving Adrian, Elena, and Lisa to gather their materials. The initial steps toward a significant expansion were in motion, and the path ahead, while challenging, held the promise of substantial global impact. They left the conference room energized, ready to tackle the extensive planning and coordination that lay ahead.

In the weeks following the pivotal meeting, Dr. Adrian Harrow, Elena Markham, and Dr. Lisa Mendez were immersed in the foundational work required to take their project to a global stage. Their clinic, once a simple therapeutic center, was evolving into the command center for what was quickly becoming an international initiative.

Adrian spent his days liaising with international health regulators and potential partners abroad. His office was strewn with legal pads filled with notes, his computer screen always split between emails and complex regulatory documents. Each conversation he had was aimed at navigating the intricate landscape of international health care standards, ensuring their model would be compliant and adaptable across borders.

Elena, meanwhile, focused on the logistical aspects of their expansion. Her desk was covered with project timelines, supply chain lists, and contact details for potential suppliers. She coordinated closely with architects and interior designers to create blueprint adaptations of their therapeutic environments that could be implemented in various international settings. Her discussions with suppliers were detailed, ensuring that the materials used in their setups—particularly the silver and gold enhancements—met both quality and ethical sourcing standards.

One afternoon, Adrian and Elena convened in his office to discuss their progress and align their strategies.

"We're making good strides in understanding the regulatory requirements," Adrian shared, flipping through a stack of documents. "But we need to make sure that every adaptation of our model meets not only health standards but also cultural sensitivities."

Elena nodded, adding, "I've been in touch with suppliers who can provide us with the necessary materials at scale. However, the challenge remains to keep the costs manageable without compromising on the quality that's central to the effectiveness of our environments."

They agreed that a key part of their strategy would be to establish partnerships with local firms in each new market. These partnerships would help navigate local regulations and cultural nuances more effectively.

Lisa joined them via video call to discuss the research component. "The pilot studies we're planning will be crucial," she said. "They will not only validate our model in diverse settings but also allow us to refine it in real-time based on immediate feedback."

Adrian responded, "Absolutely, Lisa. We're considering a phased rollout for these pilot studies, starting in environments most similar to ours and gradually expanding to more diverse settings."

As they ended the call, they set their sights on finalizing the initial pilot locations. The task was daunting, involving numerous factors from geographical diversity to local mental health needs assessment.

The rest of their day was spent in a series of back-to-back meetings with the project management team, outlining the phases of the rollout and establishing a comprehensive risk management framework. They discussed each potential risk, from supply chain disruptions to potential resistance from local health practitioners unfamiliar with their approach.

By the end of the day, Adrian and Elena had a clearer picture of the path forward. They had established a structured plan, set clear goals for each phase of the project, and built a robust framework to manage the risks involved.

Leaving the office that evening, the weight of their responsibilities was palpable, but so was their confidence in the plan they had put together. As they locked up the clinic, the setting sun cast long shadows across the parking lot, symbolizing the growing reach of their work. Tomorrow, they would continue laying the groundwork, each step bringing them closer to realizing their vision of transforming therapeutic environments around the world.

Dr. Adrian Harrow and Elena Markham sat in a small, well-lit meeting room, papers and digital devices spread out before them. Today, they were joined by a consultant specializing in international project management, Mr. Harvey Fields, to refine the strategies for their upcoming international pilot programs.

"Thank you for joining us, Harvey," Adrian began, his tone appreciative. "We value your expertise in rolling out projects like ours on an international scale."

"Happy to help," Harvey responded, adjusting his glasses. "I've reviewed the materials you sent over, and I must say, I'm impressed with the scope of your project. However, there are a few areas where we could tighten the strategy to ensure success."

Elena leaned forward, eager to dive into the details. "Could you elaborate on those areas? We want to make sure we've considered everything."

"Firstly, your timeline for the initial rollouts seems quite aggressive," Harvey noted, tapping on his tablet to bring up a Gantt chart. "Considering the complexities of dealing with multiple international regulations and the need for local adaptations, I recommend extending the timeline to allow for more comprehensive local market analyses."

"That makes sense," Adrian conceded, making a note. "We want to ensure that each pilot is fully prepared to address local needs without rushing the process."

"Exactly," Harvey agreed. "Another point is the integration of local health professionals early in the process. Have you established contacts with local clinics or health authorities who can champion your project in each region?"

"We've started discussions with some potential partners," Elena replied. "But we haven't formalized any agreements yet. We're still assessing which partners would be the best fit for our objectives."

"It's critical to have local champions," Harvey emphasized. "They can provide insights into the local healthcare landscape and help navigate bureaucratic hurdles, which can be quite substantial, depending on the region."

"Right, we'll prioritize finalizing those partnerships," Adrian said, recognizing the importance of local buy-in. "Now, about the training for these local teams—how detailed should we go in the initial phases?"

"In-depth training is crucial," Harvey advised. "You need to ensure that the local teams not only understand how to implement the changes but also fully grasp the underlying principles. This will help them troubleshoot issues and adapt the protocols as needed without constant oversight."

"That aligns with our approach to training so far," Elena added. "We've developed comprehensive training materials, but we can expand them to include more case studies and interactive modules."

"Good," Harvey nodded. "And on the topic of materials, let's talk about supply chains. Have you secured multiple suppliers for your materials to avoid any disruptions?"

"We have a primary supplier but having backups is a point well taken," Adrian admitted. "We'll identify and vet additional suppliers to ensure we have continuity."

"As for monitoring and evaluation," Harvey continued, "how do you plan to collect and analyze the data from these diverse settings?"

Elena responded, "We're setting up a centralized data management system that all pilot sites can feed into. This allows us to monitor progress in real time and compare data across different regions."

"That's excellent," Harvey affirmed. "Real-time data will enable you to make adjustments quickly and effectively, which is often necessary in the early stages of a project like this."

As the meeting drew to a close, they reviewed their updated action list: extending the timeline, strengthening local partnerships, enhancing training programs, securing backup suppliers, and refining the data management system.

"Thank you, Harvey, for your invaluable insights," Adrian said as they stood to leave the room. "With your guidance, I feel we're much better equipped to make this a success."

"It's my pleasure," Harvey replied, shaking their hands. "I look forward to seeing your project succeed on a global scale."

Elena and Adrian left the meeting room, their minds buzzing with the productive discussion and the clear steps laid out before them. As they walked back to their offices, the challenges ahead seemed more surmountable, guided by the detailed roadmap they had crafted together.

The final weeks leading up to the launch of the international pilot programs were bustling with activity for Dr. Adrian Harrow and Elena Markham. Their clinic had become a nerve center for operations, with each room occasionally serving as a makeshift command post for different aspects of the project.

As the launch date approached, Adrian found himself reviewing the final checklist with Elena in his office, which was littered with folders and coffee cups. Their focus was unwavering, each item on the list critical to the seamless execution of the pilot programs.

"Have all the training materials been dispatched to the pilot sites?" Adrian asked, marking items off the list.

"Yes, they were sent last week, and I've confirmed receipt with each site coordinator," Elena replied, her laptop open to a complex spreadsheet tracking these details. "They're scheduled to begin training their staff next Monday."

"Excellent," Adrian noted. He glanced over at the large world map pinned to the wall, dotted with pins marking each pilot location. "What about the backup suppliers? Have all contracts been finalized?"

"They have," Elena confirmed, pulling up an email confirmation on her screen. "I pushed for expedited processing to ensure we have everything in place well before we potentially need to tap into those resources."

Their conversation was brief, each point discussed a testament to the months of planning that had brought them to this moment. They were on the brink of seeing their model tested on a global scale, a thought that was both exhilarating and nerve-wracking.

After ensuring the operational aspects were on track, Adrian spent the afternoon in deep concentration, finalizing the opening remarks for the inaugural video conference with all pilot sites. He carefully crafted his words, wanting to inspire and motivate the teams on the ground. His speech outlined the vision and the scientific foundation of their approach, emphasizing the transformative potential of their work.

Meanwhile, Elena worked in her office, meticulously plotting the data collection timelines. She coordinated with the IT department to ensure that the data management system was fully operational and that all pilot sites were proficient in using it. Real-time data collection was pivotal, and Elena was determined to prevent any technical glitches.

Late in the afternoon, they reconvened in Adrian's office to synchronize their final preparations. They reviewed the technical setup for the upcoming video conference, testing the connection and the presentation materials.

"Let's run through the presentation one last time," Adrian suggested. They went through each slide, ensuring the content was clear and that it flowed logically. Elena provided feedback, fine-tuning the language and adding notes on key points she knew would resonate with the international teams.

As the day wound down, the clinic began to quiet. The staff, aware of the significance of the upcoming launch, offered words of encouragement and support as they left for the evening.

Adrian and Elena stayed behind, their offices lit by the glow of their computer screens. The silence around them was a stark contrast to the flurry of activity that had characterized the day.

Finally satisfied with their preparations, they stood, stretching the stiffness from their limbs. They shared a quiet moment, acknowledging the magnitude of what they were about to undertake.

"Tomorrow starts a new chapter," Adrian said, a note of resolve in his voice. Elena nodded, her expression one of determined optimism.

They left the clinic together, the setting sun casting long shadows across the parking lot. The evening air was cool, a refreshing change after the day's intensity. As they parted ways, there was a mutual understanding that the coming days would not only test their work but also potentially change the landscape of therapeutic practices globally. They drove off into the evening, ready for the challenges and opportunities that awaited them.

Chapter 14
Aftermath and Doubts

The inaugural video conference for the international pilot program was set to begin in the main conference room of the clinic. Dr. Adrian Harrow and Elena Markham were there early, ensuring every technical setup was functioning seamlessly. As the clock neared the starting time, participants from various global locations appeared on the large screen, each framed by the unique backdrop of their local environments.

Adrian cleared his throat and started the meeting. "Welcome, everyone. Thank you for joining us today. This is a significant milestone for all of us as we embark on a journey that not only spans multiple countries but also bridges the gap between traditional therapeutic practices and innovative environmental psychology."

Elena added, "Our goal with this pilot program is not just to validate our research but to adapt and optimize our therapeutic environment model to suit diverse settings across the globe. We appreciate your commitment and enthusiasm as we move forward."

A participant from the UK, Dr. Fiona Reed, was the first to respond. "We're thrilled to be part of this initiative. Our team has been reviewing the training materials, and we're particularly interested in how the integration of specific environmental elements can be customized to our patient demographics."

"Thank you, Dr. Reed," Adrian replied. "Customization is key, and we expect to learn as much from you as you might from us. This collaborative approach will help ensure that our model is robust and versatile."

Dr. Carlos Mendoza from Brazil chimed in, "One question we have is about the data collection. Could you elaborate on how we should handle the real-time data streaming, especially considering some of the connectivity issues we occasionally face?"

Elena took this question. "Great question, Dr. Mendoza. We've set up a system that's relatively low bandwidth and can queue data to send when connectivity is stable. Also, we're available to help troubleshoot any issues that arise to minimize data loss."

The conversation flowed smoothly, with Adrian and Elena addressing various technical and procedural inquiries. They discussed everything from patient consent processes to detailed explanations of how the environmental sensors worked and how data would be secured and analyzed.

Dr. Sato from Japan raised a practical concern. "In terms of scaling, assuming the pilot is successful, what support can we expect in expanding the program within our region?"

"We plan to provide continued logistical and technical support to all our pilot sites," Adrian assured her. "If the data supports broad implementation, we will discuss further funding and resources to ensure that scaling up is feasible and effective."

Elena elaborated, "We're also developing a second phase of training materials based on the outcomes of this pilot. These will include best practices identified during the pilot and new strategies informed by real-world application."

The discussion then moved to a roundtable format, where each participant shared their initial thoughts and expectations for the pilot. This exchange not only fostered a sense of community among the diverse group but also highlighted the shared excitement and commitment to the project's goals.

As the conference neared its end, Adrian concluded, "This meeting has been incredibly fruitful. Your insights and feedback are invaluable as we fine-tune our approach. We're not just conducting research; we're setting the groundwork for what could be a new standard in therapeutic environments worldwide."

"Thank you all for your time today," Elena added. "We'll send a follow-up with the minutes of this meeting and the next steps by the end of the week. Please feel free to reach out to us with any further questions or comments in the meantime."

Participants nodded and expressed their thanks, their faces showing a mixture of satisfaction and anticipation. As the screen eventually went blank, Adrian and Elena sat back, a sense of accomplishment filling the room. They had successfully set the stage for what promised to be a transformative few months. As they left the conference room, their conversation was already turning to the next steps, ready to tackle the challenges and opportunities that awaited them.

Following the successful inaugural video conference, Dr. Adrian Harrow and Elena Markham shifted their focus to the ongoing monitoring of the international pilot programs. The clinic had been equipped with a dedicated operations center, replete with multiple screens displaying real-time data feeds from each of the pilot sites. This room became the heart of their daily activities, filled with charts and live updates, allowing them to oversee the global implementation closely.

Adrian spent most mornings in the operations center, reviewing the overnight data. He would meticulously note any anomalies or significant trends, comparing them against baseline measurements taken before the environmental enhancements were implemented. This routine had become a cornerstone of their research methodology, ensuring that any deviations were promptly addressed.

One morning, Adrian called Elena into the operations center to discuss a pattern he had noticed. "Elena, take a look at these stress level metrics from the Tokyo site. They've been consistently higher than average for the past week."

Elena, peering over Adrian's shoulder at the graphs, responded thoughtfully. "That is unusual. Do we have any environmental data anomalies that could explain this?"

"Nothing significant on the environmental front," Adrian replied, scrolling through various charts. "I suggest we schedule a call with Dr. Sato to discuss possible cultural or procedural differences that might be influencing these readings."

The rest of their day was spent preparing for that call, with Elena gathering additional data and Adrian drafting a list of specific questions and concerns. Their discussion with Dr. Sato later that afternoon was enlightening, highlighting subtle cultural nuances that were affecting how patients perceived and reacted to the therapy sessions.

Adjustments were made based on this conversation, proving the value of their hands-on, responsive approach to managing the pilot programs. Such interactions were crucial, enabling them to tailor the environment more precisely to each location's needs.

Beyond these immediate operational concerns, Adrian and Elena were also preparing for the first quarterly review of the project. This review would involve a comprehensive analysis of the collected data, intending to identify broader trends and insights that could inform future iterations of the project.

In preparation, Elena compiled data reports from each site, synthesizing the vast amounts of information into digestible summaries. She also coordinated with the local site managers to ensure that any qualitative feedback from staff and patients was included in the review.

As the date of the quarterly review approached, Adrian reviewed these summaries, developing hypotheses about the environmental factors most strongly correlated with positive therapy outcomes. This analysis would form the basis of their review presentation, aimed at demonstrating the preliminary success of the pilot and outlining areas for improvement.

The day before the review, Adrian and Elena met to finalize their presentation. They rehearsed their parts meticulously, discussing how to best convey their findings to the stakeholders. The meeting room was set up with displays for the data visualizations they had prepared, each one a testament to the project's depth and their commitment to rigor.

Their conversation was a mix of technical details and strategic planning, reflecting the dual nature of their roles as researchers and project managers. "We need to emphasize not just the successes but also how we've addressed challenges," Adrian reminded Elena as they wrapped up their preparation.

"Absolutely," Elena agreed, reviewing her notes. "It's important they see how adaptive and responsive our approach is."

With their presentation ready and the operations center quieting down for the evening, Adrian and Elena left the clinic. The setting sun cast long shadows across the parking lot, mirroring the lengthening reach of their project across the globe. They parted ways, each filled with a sense of accomplishment and anticipation for the critical review that awaited them, ready to share the impact of their work and to learn from the rich data they had gathered.

The day of the quarterly review dawned clear and crisp. Dr. Adrian Harrow and Elena Markham arrived early at the clinic, each carrying the weight of the day's importance. The conference room was set up meticulously with high-resolution screens displaying interactive graphs and charts ready to showcase the collected data from the international pilot programs.

As stakeholders and collaborators began to filter into the room, the air filled with a subtle buzz of anticipation. Adrian checked the setup one last time, ensuring that each click would lead to the correct visualization, each designed to convey complex data in an accessible manner.

The meeting began with Adrian opening the presentation, his voice steady and clear. "Thank you all for joining us today. We are here to review the first quarter of our international pilot programs, which have been an incredible journey of learning and adaptation."

Elena took over to delve into the specifics. "Our primary focus today is to evaluate the effectiveness of the environmental enhancements across diverse settings and to understand the variability in outcomes," she explained, transitioning smoothly to the first series of graphs that detailed patient stress levels.

The presentation was structured to first highlight key successes. Improved patient outcomes, as evidenced by decreased anxiety levels and increased satisfaction rates, were clearly linked to the environmental modifications in therapy rooms. Elena presented this data effectively, showcasing before-and-after scenarios that highlighted significant changes.

However, the core of the review was not just to celebrate successes but to critically analyze challenges and areas for improvement. Adrian discussed some of the operational challenges they had encountered, including issues with data transmission delays in certain regions and the need for more robust training programs to ensure consistency in the application of the environmental enhancements.

The dialogue portion of the meeting was brief but insightful. One stakeholder asked, "How are we addressing the challenges related to cultural differences in therapy practices?"

Adrian responded, "We are continuously working with local teams to tailor the interventions, ensuring they are culturally sensitive and appropriate. This is an ongoing process, and feedback from each site is invaluable."

As the review progressed, Elena presented a series of case studies from different sites, highlighting how specific challenges were addressed and what the outcomes were. These real-world examples provided a tangible connection to the data, illustrating the practical application of their findings and the flexibility of their approach.

In concluding the presentation, Adrian emphasized the forward-looking aspects of the project. "Based on what we've learned, we will be implementing revised protocols and enhanced training modules. Our goal is not only to expand but to enhance the quality and effectiveness of each site's implementation."

The meeting closed with a round of applause, the stakeholders expressing their appreciation for the thorough analysis and clear direction forward. Adrian and Elena fielded a few more questions before the room began to clear, the screens dimming as the last of the attendees left.

The clinic's hallways were quiet as Adrian and Elena returned to their office. They sat reviewing their notes from the meeting, discussing the next steps and scheduling follow-up tasks. The successful review had bolstered their confidence, reinforcing their commitment to the project's global potential.

As they left the clinic at the end of the day, the challenges ahead seemed less daunting, overshadowed by the clear path they had carved out. The impact of their work was already evident, and the road ahead, though long, was lined with opportunities for significant advancements in therapeutic environments worldwide.

After a successful quarterly review, Dr. Adrian Harrow and Elena Markham were back in their makeshift war room, surrounded by digital displays and stacks of documents. Today, they were joined via video conference by Dr. Lisa Mendez and several key team leaders from pilot sites across the globe to discuss the next phase of their expansion.

Adrian initiated the meeting with a focused agenda. "Thank you all for joining us. Today, we need to strategize on scaling our project based on the successful outcomes and valuable feedback from the quarterly review. We aim to double our reach while ensuring the fidelity of the model."

Elena took over, outlining the specifics. "Our first order of business is to address the training enhancements we discussed. We've seen that deeper cultural integration and understanding dramatically improve patient and staff reception. Lisa, could you share the new training modules you've developed?"

Lisa responded, her image crisp on the screen. "Certainly, Elena. Based on our discussions, I've tailored the training to include more comprehensive cultural competency components. This includes case studies specific to each region we're operating in, ensuring our teams can adapt the interventions effectively."

"That sounds excellent," Adrian said, nodding. "Now, regarding the expansion, we've identified ten new sites where we believe our model will be beneficial. These sites have been chosen based on demographic diversity and expressed need for innovative therapeutic environments."

Elena continued, "For each new site, we'll need to conduct initial environmental assessments similar to our first pilots. This means we'll need to allocate resources for our environmental psychology experts to travel and assess these sites personally."

One of the site leaders, Dr. Rajiv Nair from India, raised a concern. "While I understand the importance of these assessments, we also need to consider the ongoing pandemic restrictions. How flexible are we with the timeline for these assessments?"

Adrian replied thoughtfully, "That's a valid point, Dr. Nair. We'll schedule the assessments tentatively, keeping an eye on travel advisories. Our priority is the safety of our team and the communities we work in."

"Moving on," Lisa interjected, "I suggest we also enhance our data collection frameworks to include more qualitative data, which will give us richer insights into the user experience at these new sites."

Elena was quick to agree. "Absolutely, Lisa. Qualitative data will complement the quantitative metrics we're already collecting, giving us a fuller picture of the impact."

The conversation shifted to funding. Adrian outlined the approach. "We'll be approaching our existing sponsors with the results from our quarterly review and our plan for expansion. Additionally, we're drafting proposals for new funding sources who are interested in mental health innovations."

"Have we considered any partnerships with academic institutions? This could not only bolster our research but also provide us with additional funding channels," suggested Dr. Sophie Leung from the UK.

"That's an excellent suggestion, Dr. Leung," Adrian replied. "Elena, let's put together a list of potential academic partners and start reaching out next week."

As the meeting drew to a close, Elena summarized the action items. "I'll coordinate with each site leader to prepare for the environmental assessments and ensure that all logistical aspects are handled. Lisa will finalize the training modules, and Adrian will lead the funding initiatives."

"Thank you, everyone, for your dedication and hard work," Adrian concluded. "This is an ambitious phase of our project, but with our combined efforts, I'm confident in our success."

The video call ended with nods and words of encouragement, leaving Adrian and Elena to reflect on the road ahead. They gathered their notes and prepared for the next immediate tasks, motivated by the clear goals set during their productive discussion. The clinic was quiet as they left, stepping out into the evening with a sense of accomplishment and anticipation for the next steps in their pioneering work.

Chapter 15
Visions and Revelations

As the ambitious expansion of their therapeutic environment project unfolded, Dr. Adrian Harrow and Elena Markham were fully immersed in coordinating the complex logistics and operational details. The clinic, once a quiet place for contemplation and healing, had transformed into a bustling hub of international collaboration and strategic planning.

Adrian reviewed the latest updates from the environmental psychology experts who had begun their assessments at the new pilot sites. Each report was thorough, detailing the specific needs and adaptations required for each location, taking into account the diverse cultural and environmental factors that could influence the therapy outcomes. His office was strewn with maps, charts, and a plethora of digital devices that kept him connected with teams across different time zones.

Meanwhile, Elena was focused on the training rollout. She had organized a series of webinars and live sessions, all designed to ensure that the staff at each new site was not only familiar with the theoretical underpinnings of the environmental enhancements but also adept at implementing and maintaining these changes. Her days were a mix of training sessions, feedback assessments, and continuous improvements to the training modules based on real-time issues and challenges that were being reported.

One particular challenge was the integration of the new data collection protocols. The expanded framework meant that more data than ever was flowing into their systems, necessitating enhancements to their IT infrastructure. Elena worked closely with the IT team to oversee the installation of upgraded servers and more sophisticated data analysis software. This upgrade was critical to handle the influx of data and ensure its integrity, security, and usefulness for ongoing research.

Adrian and Elena met weekly to synchronize their efforts. During one such meeting, Adrian expressed concern about the varying rates of progress among the pilot sites. "We need to ensure that any site lagging behind receives more focused attention. It might be beneficial to send additional support staff to these sites to address any specific challenges they're facing."

Elena agreed, noting the importance of a tailored approach. "I'll arrange for our lead trainers to visit these sites personally. A hands-on approach will likely resolve many of the issues more quickly."

They also discussed the upcoming second round of funding applications. Adrian was preparing detailed progress reports and case studies from the initial months of the pilot programs, which would be crucial in securing the next wave of funding. "These reports need to clearly communicate not just our progress but also how we're innovating and adapting to challenges. It's these details that will convince our sponsors of the value of continuing their support."

Elena took on the task of compiling testimonials and case studies from the various sites, highlighting the positive impacts the project had already achieved. "I'll make sure these narratives are not only compelling but also backed by solid data. We want our sponsors to see and feel the impact of their support."

As they wrapped up their meeting, Adrian looked over the operations center, where live feeds displayed data from around the world. The scope of their project was immense, but so was its potential to revolutionize therapeutic environments globally.

In the weeks that followed, Adrian and Elena continued their diligent oversight of the project's expansion. They navigated time zone differences, language barriers, and the myriad details that needed their attention. Each decision they made, each problem they solved, brought them closer to realizing the full potential of their vision.

Their days were long and often merged into nights, but the satisfaction of seeing their project grow and succeed provided a profound sense of accomplishment and purpose. As they left the clinic late one evening, the quiet of the night was a stark contrast to the day's busyness, a moment of peace amidst the whirlwind of their groundbreaking work.

The complexities of rolling out an innovative therapeutic environment across diverse international landscapes were becoming increasingly apparent to Dr. Adrian Harrow and Elena Markham. As the project expanded, each day brought new challenges that required not just their attention but also their ability to adapt and innovate under pressure.

The clinic's operations center was abuzz with activity, with multiple screens showing real-time data from the pilot sites. Adrian often stood before these screens, analyzing patterns and trends, identifying any deviations that might indicate a problem or an opportunity for further improvement. His ability to decipher complex data into actionable insights had become crucial in steering the project forward.

Elena, on the other hand, was deeply involved in ensuring the logistical aspects of the training programs were executed flawlessly. She coordinated with local teams to schedule training sessions, which were crucial for the successful adoption of the new therapeutic environments. Her meticulous planning ensured that all materials and resources were available when needed, despite the logistical challenges posed by different geographical locations.

One afternoon, as a storm brewed outside, darkening the skies and reflecting the turbulent phase of their project, Adrian and Elena sat together in the clinic's main conference room, poring over feedback from the latest training sessions. They needed to assess the effectiveness of their educational materials and identify any gaps in understanding that could affect the project's success.

Adrian sifted through the feedback forms, noting areas of concern. "It seems like there's some confusion about the integration of environmental sensors. Some sites are struggling with the technical aspects more than others."

Elena nodded, tapping notes into her laptop. "I'll schedule some follow-up webinars focusing specifically on those technical issues. Perhaps we can also create a troubleshooting guide, something easily accessible that addresses common problems."

Their discussion briefly touched upon the upcoming review meeting with stakeholders. Adrian was aware that they needed to present not only the successes but also how they were addressing the challenges. "We should prepare a detailed report on how we're managing these obstacles. It will be important to show our proactive approach to problem-solving."

Elena agreed, her mind already running through the best formats for such a report. "I think case studies of specific sites could be effective. We can show before and after scenarios, detailing the issues we faced and how we resolved them."

As they continued their work, the storm outside intensified, mirroring the pressure they felt. Yet, inside the conference room, there was a sense of controlled urgency. Adrian and Elena were seasoned enough to manage the stress, understanding that the path to innovation is often lined with unexpected hurdles.

The day ended with them finalizing the agenda for the upcoming stakeholder meeting. They reviewed the financials, the data collected, and the qualitative feedback from all sites. Each piece of information was a tile in the larger mosaic of their project, essential for understanding the full picture.

They left the conference room late in the evening, the rain still pouring down outside. The clinic was quiet, most of the staff having left for the day. As they walked through the dimly lit hallways, there was a mutual understanding that the challenges they were facing were just as important as the successes. These challenges would refine their model, test their resilience, and ultimately contribute to the robustness of their innovative approach to therapy.

The drive home was a time for reflection. Adrian considered the day's discussions, while Elena thought about the logistics of implementing their solutions. Both knew that the next few months would be crucial. As they drove through the rainy streets, the glow of the streetlights flickered like beacons, guiding them through the darkness, much like their project's aim to illuminate and innovate within the world of therapeutic practices.

In the midst of their expansive project, Dr. Adrian Harrow and Elena Markham were preparing meticulously for an upcoming stakeholder meeting. It was crucial to address concerns about the recent complications and to maintain confidence in the ongoing international rollout of their therapeutic environment enhancements.

On the morning of the meeting, the clinic's largest conference room was set up with precision. Adrian reviewed the agenda, ensuring that it covered all necessary points, while Elena checked the technical setup for the presentation. Their preparation was thorough, as they understood the importance of clear communication in maintaining stakeholder support.

As the stakeholders began to arrive, Adrian greeted each one personally. "Thank you for coming," he often said, his tone both welcoming and confident. "We appreciate your continued support and involvement in this important initiative."

Once everyone was seated, Elena began the presentation. "We're here today to update you on the progress of the international pilot programs and to discuss some of the challenges we've encountered," she stated clearly, clicking to the first slide which outlined the agenda.

Adrian took over to delve into the specifics of the recent data. "Let's start with the successes. We've seen significant improvements in patient outcomes at several of our pilot sites, thanks to the environmental enhancements we've implemented. Here are some graphs that show the before and after metrics."

The screen displayed colorful charts that clearly depicted improvements in patient anxiety levels and overall satisfaction. The visual impact of these charts was strong, reinforcing the positive aspects of the project.

However, moving on to the challenges was equally important. "We've also faced some challenges, particularly with the integration of the new technology in certain regions," Adrian continued, his tone shifting to a more serious but still optimistic cadence. "These challenges have provided us with valuable lessons."

Elena picked up the thread of the conversation. "For instance, we encountered technical difficulties with the environmental sensors in two locations. This was largely due to local infrastructure issues. We responded by deploying a specialized tech team to provide on-site training and enhancements to the installation process."

A stakeholder, Mr. Jacobs, raised a question. "How are we ensuring that these kinds of issues won't continue to affect the project? What steps are being taken to prevent future complications?"

"That's an excellent question," Adrian replied. "We've established a rapid response team that's ready to address any technical issues within 48 hours. Additionally, we're improving our pre-deployment assessments to better predict and prepare for potential problems."

Elena added, "We're also increasing our focus on training for local staff, ensuring they are more self-sufficient in managing and troubleshooting the technology."

The discussion then turned to financials, with another stakeholder, Ms. Patel, inquiring about the budget implications of these adjustments. "Can you elaborate on how these changes impact our budget projections?"

Adrian answered, "We've allocated funds from the contingency budget to cover these unexpected expenses. We are committed to staying within our overall budget by optimizing other areas of the project, ensuring that these adjustments do not require additional funds from our stakeholders."

The meeting continued with more detailed discussions about the logistics, training, and data analysis. Adrian and Elena addressed each question with detailed responses, showcasing their deep engagement with every aspect of the project.

As the meeting drew to a close, the stakeholders expressed their appreciation for the transparency and detailed planning. Adrian and Elena reassured everyone of their commitment to the project's success and the measures in place to achieve it.

Walking out of the conference room, Adrian and Elena felt a sense of accomplishment. They had successfully navigated difficult discussions, providing clarity and reassurance. The clinic was quiet as they walked through the hallways, their conversation turning to the next steps and preparations for the coming months. They were ready to continue their work, strengthened by the support of their stakeholders and their own unwavering commitment to improving therapeutic environments worldwide.

The weeks following the stakeholder meeting were critical for Dr. Adrian Harrow and Elena Markham as they implemented the agreed-upon strategic adjustments to their international pilot program. Their focus was laser-sharp, driven by the dual goals of ensuring the project's continued success and addressing the concerns raised during the meeting.

Adrian was often found in the newly established rapid response operations center, which he and Elena had set up as a direct result of the feedback from stakeholders. This center was equipped with state-of-the-art communication tools and monitoring systems that allowed real-time oversight of all pilot sites. Here, Adrian coordinated with site leaders, troubleshooting issues as they arose and providing immediate support to ensure minimal disruption to the ongoing therapy sessions.

Elena, meanwhile, was deep into refining the training programs. She enhanced the curriculum with additional modules focused on technological proficiency, aiming to empower local staff with the skills needed to manage the environmental enhancements independently. She worked closely with training coordinators at each site, scheduling live sessions and webinars that were tailored to the specific challenges and needs of each locale.

One afternoon, Adrian and Elena met to discuss the progress of their new initiatives. "The rapid response team has already made a significant impact," Adrian noted, showing Elena the latest operational reports. "We've seen a decrease in downtime at several sites, and the feedback on their effectiveness has been overwhelmingly positive."

"That's great to hear," Elena replied, her tone reflecting relief. "On the training front, we've also seen improvements. The new modules have been well received, and the site staff feel more confident in handling the technology, which has reduced the number of calls to the response team."

Their conversation also touched on the upcoming second round of data collection. "With the new systems and training in place, I'm optimistic about this next phase," Adrian said. "It will be crucial to gather data that reflects the impact of these changes."

Elena agreed, "Absolutely. I'll coordinate with the data analysis team to ensure we're ready to process and review the incoming data efficiently. We need to be able to report back to our stakeholders with concrete results."

As they prepared for this next critical phase, Adrian and Elena also planned a series of site visits. They intended to personally assess the on-ground implementation of the project enhancements and to hold town-hall style meetings with the local teams and patients to gather direct feedback.

The site visits were eye-opening. Adrian and Elena traveled to several locations, engaging with teams and observing the environments. These visits not only allowed them to see the fruits of their labor but also to identify any subtle issues that might not be evident from data reports alone.

Back at the clinic, after completing the site visits, Adrian and Elena compiled their findings and prepared for an internal strategy session. They reviewed every aspect of the project, from technological integration to patient feedback, preparing to make further adjustments as necessary.

Their days were long, often extending into the evenings as they analyzed data, responded to emails, and planned for the next day's tasks. Despite the demanding schedule, there was a palpable sense of progress and optimism. Each step forward reinforced their commitment to the project's goals.

As they wrapped up another day, the clinic quiet around them, Adrian and Elena shared a moment of quiet reflection in the operations center. The screens around them displayed peaceful scenes from the various therapy rooms around the world, a reminder of the calm they were striving to create not just in their own clinic but globally.

With a sense of accomplishment and anticipation for the next phase, they left the clinic under the gentle glow of the streetlights, ready to continue their pioneering work in transforming therapeutic environments. The journey was far from over, but each step was a stride toward a better understanding and application of their innovative model.

Chapter 16
A New Ally

Dr. Adrian Harrow and Elena Markham were in the main conference room of the clinic, joined via video conference by Dr. Lisa Mendez and various site leaders from around the globe. The purpose of today's meeting was to review the progress of the international pilot programs and to outline the next steps based on the collected data and feedback.

Adrian opened the meeting with a brief overview. "Thank you, everyone, for joining today. We're here to assess our progress and discuss the strategic directions for the upcoming quarter. I'll start with a brief overview of the data we've collected so far."

Elena then took over to present the findings. "Our data shows significant improvements in patient outcomes at most sites. However, we've identified a few areas where the results are not as strong as we expected. We need to address these inconsistencies to ensure the success of our program."

Dr. Mendez added her insights. "The data from the Tokyo site shows less improvement compared to others. We suspect cultural differences in therapy practices might be influencing this. Adrian, Elena, have you looked into tailored interventions for such cases?"

Adrian replied, "Yes, Lisa, that's a good point. We are considering localized adjustments to better align with regional therapeutic traditions. This might involve more in-depth cultural training for our teams."

One of the site leaders, Dr. Rajiv Nair from India, shared his feedback. "In our location, we've seen great success with the environmental enhancements, particularly the use of natural elements in therapy rooms. However, technical issues with data collection have been a challenge."

Elena responded, "Dr. Nair, we're aware of the technical challenges and are working on upgrades to our data collection systems. We appreciate your patience and continued efforts to manually track data when necessary."

Another site leader, Dr. Fiona Reed from the UK, asked, "Could we possibly increase the frequency of training sessions? Some of our newer staff members require more support to fully grasp the nuances of the enhanced therapeutic environments."

"That's an excellent suggestion, Dr. Reed," Elena acknowledged. "We will schedule additional training sessions and make sure they are also available on-demand for any new team members."

Dr. Mendez then steered the conversation towards future planning. "Looking ahead, we should consider expanding the pilot to include more diverse environments. Are there plans to include rural settings or areas with different socioeconomic backgrounds?"

Adrian took this question. "Yes, Lisa, we are planning to expand our pilot to include such environments in the next phase. This will help us understand how our model performs across a broader spectrum of settings."

The discussion moved on to resource allocation, with several site leaders expressing the need for additional support in managing the environmental enhancements.

Elena reassured them, "We are allocating more resources to ensure that each site has what it needs to successfully implement and maintain the enhancements. This includes both physical resources and expert support."

As the meeting drew to a close, Adrian summarized the key points. "Today's discussion has been incredibly valuable. We'll take all your feedback and incorporate it into our strategy for the next quarter. Expect a detailed follow-up from us within the week with new guidelines and schedules."

"Thank you all for your hard work and dedication," Elena added. "Your contributions are what make this project successful. We look forward to continuing this journey with you."

The site leaders expressed their gratitude and anticipation for the next steps, logging off with renewed enthusiasm for the challenges ahead.

Adrian and Elena, left in the quiet conference room, reviewed their notes from the meeting, both satisfied with the productive exchange. They were ready to tackle the necessary adjustments, confident that their collaborative approach was the key to navigating the complexities of this global initiative. As they left the room, their conversation already turned to the tasks at hand, each step planned with the precision and care that had become their hallmark.

In a bustling conference room, Dr. Adrian Harrow and Elena Markham were engaged in a detailed virtual training session with new staff from various international pilot sites. The focus today was on cultivating local expertise to ensure each site could autonomously manage and adapt the therapeutic environments according to their specific regional needs.

"Welcome everyone," Adrian began, his voice clear and encouraging over the video link. "Today's session is crucial. We're not just transferring knowledge; we're empowering you to become experts in managing and adapting our therapeutic environments in ways that best serve your communities."

Elena chimed in, "Let's start with a review of the environmental control systems. These are central to maintaining the therapeutic atmosphere we've designed. Can anyone share how they've been managing these systems at their site?"

A site leader from Sweden, Dr. Henrik Larsson, responded first. "We've been closely monitoring the ambient settings according to the guidelines. However, we've noticed that during our long winter months, patients respond better when we slightly increase the warmth and lighting levels beyond the standard settings."

"That's a great observation, Dr. Larsson," Elena replied, making a note. "It's important to adapt the guidelines to fit local conditions and patient responses. This kind of feedback helps us refine our models."

Adrian then directed the conversation towards troubleshooting common technical issues. "Let's discuss some of the common challenges. For instance, sensor malfunctions can disrupt data collection. Does anyone have an example of how they handled such an issue?"

Dr. Maria Gomez from Mexico shared her experience. "We had a humidity sensor failure last week. Following the troubleshooting protocol, we first checked the connections and settings. When we couldn't resolve it, we used the hotline you set up, and the support team guided us through a replacement process. It was back online within a few hours."

"That's perfect, Dr. Gomez," Adrian responded with approval. "Using the hotline effectively and knowing when to escalate an issue are key components of managing these systems smoothly."

The training continued with a focus on cultural adaptations. Elena asked the group, "How have you tailored the therapeutic environments to better suit your cultural contexts?"

Dr. Amina Yusuf from Nigeria answered, "We incorporated local art and materials within the therapeutic rooms, which has made them more welcoming and relatable to our patients. It seems to enhance their comfort and overall therapy experience."

"That's an excellent adaptation, Dr. Yusuf," Elena praised. "Local relevance is crucial. It's about creating an environment where patients feel secure and understood."

As the session neared its end, Adrian addressed the group with a final point on continuous learning. "Remember, this is an ongoing process. We encourage you all to keep experimenting within the framework and share your findings with us. This collaborative approach is what will ultimately refine and perfect this model."

Elena concluded, "We'll have more of these sessions, and we'll also be setting up a forum where you can all share experiences and insights directly with each other. Think of it as a community of practice, where learning is constant and shared."

The session ended with a round of thanks and enthusiastic nods from the participants, each of them feeling more equipped and empowered. Adrian and Elena logged off, satisfied with the progress. They knew that supporting and educating the local teams was essential for the sustainability of the project.

As they left the conference room, the buzz of productive collaboration lingered in the air. They discussed their next steps, planning additional support materials based on today's insights. Their dedication to not just implementing but also nurturing the project's growth was evident in every decision they made.

Dr. Adrian Harrow and Elena Markham dedicated several weeks to synthesizing the data collected from the various international pilot sites. Their office, often quiet in the late hours, now buzzed well into the evening as they worked tirelessly, analyzing reports, and preparing for the strategic review that would determine the future direction of their expansive project.

Adrian focused on the quantitative aspects, delving deep into the analytics to draw out patterns and trends that could inform their understanding of which interventions were most effective and under what conditions. His desk was covered with graphs and charts, each representing different variables from patient satisfaction to therapy outcomes and environmental conditions.

Meanwhile, Elena concentrated on compiling qualitative feedback. She sifted through hundreds of responses from patients, therapists, and site managers, each providing insights into the personal and cultural impact of the therapeutic environments. Her work was crucial in painting a broader picture of the project's effect on individuals across diverse backgrounds.

One evening, as they reviewed their findings together, Adrian pointed to a series of graphs. "Look at this correlation between light intensity adjustments and patient anxiety reduction. It's particularly strong in sites located in northern latitudes."

Elena, looking over the data, nodded in agreement. "That's consistent with the qualitative feedback. Many patients in those regions reported feeling calmer and more at ease in the enhanced settings. It seems the seasonal affective disorder might be mitigated somewhat by these adjustments."

Their review also highlighted areas that needed more attention. Adrian and Elena identified several sites where the improvements were not as pronounced. These required a more nuanced approach to understand the local factors at play, which might include less optimal integration of cultural elements or technical challenges.

In preparation for the strategic review meeting with their stakeholders, they prepared a detailed presentation that included both their successes and the challenges. The goal was to provide a transparent overview of the project's progress and to outline their strategies for scaling up the successful interventions while addressing the less effective areas.

The night before the meeting, Adrian and Elena rehearsed their presentation, fine-tuning every detail and anticipating potential questions from their stakeholders. "We need to emphasize not just the successes but also how we plan to use what we've learned to improve," Adrian reminded Elena.

"Absolutely," Elena responded as she adjusted a slide on cultural adaptability. "It's about learning and evolving. Our flexibility in addressing these challenges is as important as the initial successes."

The day of the strategic review arrived, and the clinic's main conference room was set up meticulously. As stakeholders began to fill the room, the air was charged with anticipation. Adrian and Elena presented their findings confidently, supported by data and real-life anecdotes from the sites.

The stakeholders were particularly interested in the adaptations made for different cultural contexts. "How do you ensure these adaptations are both respectful and effective?" one stakeholder asked during the Q&A session.

"We work closely with local teams to integrate culturally significant elements into the therapeutic environments," Elena explained. "It's a collaborative process, and we continuously seek feedback to ensure these elements are having the intended positive impact."

As the meeting concluded, Adrian and Elena felt a sense of accomplishment. They had successfully navigated the complexities of a global project, learning and adapting as they went. The feedback from the stakeholders was overwhelmingly positive, with many expressing their support for the continued expansion of the project.

Leaving the conference room, Adrian and Elena discussed their next steps. They were determined to keep the momentum going, using the insights gained from this review to enhance the project further. As they walked through the quiet clinic, they were already planning their approach to the next phase, ready to tackle the challenges and opportunities that lay ahead.

In the aftermath of a successful strategic review, Dr. Adrian Harrow and Elena Markham convened in a small, well-lit meeting room within the clinic to finalize the enhancements and plan the next phase of their global expansion. Joined by Dr. Lisa Mendez via video call, they were poised to take decisive action based on the insights and feedback gathered.

Adrian started the meeting with a clear focus. "Based on our last review, it's clear that we need to fine-tune our approach before we can expand further. Lisa, could you share the modifications you've proposed based on the feedback from various sites?"

Lisa nodded, her image crisp on the screen. "Certainly, Adrian. First, we've noticed that sites in colder climates benefit significantly from an increase in ambient warmth and tailored lighting. I propose we standardize these adjustments across similar climates to enhance patient comfort and therapy effectiveness."

"That makes sense," Elena chimed in. "Have you considered the energy consumption implications of these adjustments?"

"We have," Lisa replied. "I'm working with the technical team to ensure these enhancements are energy-efficient. We're also exploring sustainable options that could be integrated into the existing systems without compromising their effectiveness."

Adrian noted this down, then shifted the conversation towards training. "Elena, how do you propose we handle the training for these new enhancements?"

Elena responded with a detailed plan. "I suggest we develop a modular training program that can be customized based on the specific needs of each site. This program would include virtual reality simulations that allow staff to experience and interact with the enhancements in a controlled environment before they go live."

"That's an innovative approach," Lisa commented, visibly impressed. "It could really help in reducing the learning curve and ensuring that the staff is fully prepared to implement these changes."

Adrian agreed, adding, "Let's ensure that these training modules are accessible in multiple languages to accommodate our diverse staff at the international sites."

The discussion then moved to expansion. Elena brought up the logistics, "We need to strategize our rollout to new sites more carefully. Given the complexities we've encountered, perhaps a phased approach would be more effective."

Lisa nodded in agreement. "A phased rollout will allow us to manage resources better and address any issues as they arise without overwhelming our support teams."

"What about the financial aspect? How do we ensure that the expansion is sustainable?" Adrian asked, always mindful of the budget.

Lisa had already considered this. "I recommend we seek additional funding based on the success of our pilot sites. We can present our data to potential investors and partners to secure the necessary funds."

"That's a good strategy," Elena said. "I'll start preparing a detailed report highlighting our successes and the potential benefits of investing in our project."

As they wrapped up the meeting, Adrian summarized their action items. "Lisa will finalize the technical enhancements and work with the technical team on sustainability. Elena will update the training modules and start working on the investment report."

"Sounds like a plan," Lisa responded, ready to get started on her tasks.

"Thank you both for your hard work and dedication," Adrian concluded, feeling optimistic about the next steps. "Let's reconvene next week to review our progress."

With that, the meeting ended, leaving Adrian and Elena in the quiet room, both filled with a renewed sense of purpose. They collected their notes and laptops, ready to tackle the tasks ahead. The clinic's hallways were quiet as they left, reflecting the late hour, but their minds were buzzing with activity, planning for the future of their innovative project.

Chapter 17
Dark Echoes

Dr. Adrian Harrow and Elena Markham convened in the operations center early one morning, surrounded by monitors displaying data feeds and digital maps pinpointing the locations of their expanded pilot sites. Today's agenda focused on initiating the phased rollout of their enhanced therapeutic environments to new international sites.

Adrian, reviewing the timeline on the main screen, turned to Elena. "We've set a solid strategy for this expansion, but as we initiate the rollout, let's ensure that we're fully synchronized with the site managers. I want to avoid any missteps that could delay our progress."

Elena nodded, pulling up a detailed checklist on her laptop. "I'll go through the final preparations with each site manager today. We need to confirm that they have received all necessary materials and training modules. It's crucial that they feel supported and ready."

"Good," Adrian replied, his tone reflecting the importance of these initial steps. "Let's also double-check the communication lines. Quick and clear communication will be essential, especially as we navigate the complexities of different time zones and languages."

Elena made a note, then looked up thoughtfully. "What about the support structures we discussed? Are the local rapid response teams fully operational?"

Adrian checked a report on his tablet. "They are mostly up and running. A few sites are still finalizing their setups, but we expect all teams to be operational by the end of the week. These teams will play a vital role in troubleshooting any immediate issues."

"That's reassuring," Elena said. "I'll schedule a simulation exercise for these teams next week. It will be a good test to ensure they're ready to handle anything that comes up."

As they continued their discussion, the room buzzed with the quiet intensity of a mission control center on the verge of a major operation. Each screen and dashboard was a window into the vast scope of their project, and the weight of responsibility was palpable.

Adrian looked over at another screen, showing feedback from a pilot site in Norway. "It looks like the modifications we made for colder climates are performing well. The feedback from patients and staff has been overwhelmingly positive."

"That's fantastic to hear," Elena responded, genuinely pleased. "It shows that our tailored approach is working. Adapting our model to meet the specific environmental and cultural needs of each location is definitely paying off."

"Yes, it is," Adrian agreed. "Let's ensure that these successes are well documented. We should prepare a case study for our next stakeholder meeting. It could help secure further support and funding."

Elena jotted this down, then shifted the conversation toward the logistical aspects of the rollout. "I've arranged for additional training sessions focusing on the technical aspects of the environmental controls, especially for the newer sites. We want to make sure that every team feels confident in managing the systems."

"That's important," Adrian said. "Confidence in handling the technology will translate into smoother operations and better overall outcomes."

As they finalized their plans for the day, their discussion was interspersed with check-ins from various team members, each reporting on different aspects of the rollout. Adrian and Elena addressed each update with focused attention, providing guidance and making decisions on the fly.

The meeting wrapped up with Adrian summarizing their immediate next steps. "Let's continue to monitor the initial rollouts closely. We need to be proactive in addressing any issues as they arise."

"Agreed," Elena said as she closed her laptop. "I'll keep a close eye on the feedback loops and make sure that any concerns are addressed immediately."

They left the operations center ready to tackle the day's challenges, each step marked by a shared commitment to their project's success. As they walked through the clinic, their conversation turned to the potential impacts of their work, not just in terms of patient care but also in how it might shape the future of therapeutic environments globally. Each discussion, each decision, brought them closer to realizing their vision.

In the operations center, which had become their mission control for the global project, Dr. Adrian Harrow and Elena Markham faced an array of monitors and communications equipment. Today, they were troubleshooting early-stage issues that had arisen during the initial rollout of their expanded pilot programs. Joining them via video conference were site leaders from various locations, each eager to resolve their specific challenges.

"Thank you all for joining at short notice," Adrian began, his tone serious but composed. "We're here to address the initial challenges reported across several sites. Let's tackle these one by one to ensure our rollout continues smoothly."

Elena took the lead on the first issue. "Let's start with the technical difficulties reported in Johannesburg. Dr. Nkosi, can you describe what's happening on the ground?"

Dr. Nkosi, appearing on the screen from South Africa, detailed the problems. "We've encountered persistent issues with the humidity sensors. They're crucial for maintaining the right environment here, given our local climate, but they've been failing intermittently."

Adrian responded quickly, "That's concerning. We've sent an update patch that should stabilize the sensor readings. Have you had a chance to install that update yet?"

"Yes, we applied the patch this morning. It's too soon to say if the issue is fully resolved, but we're monitoring it closely," Dr. Nkosi replied.

"Please keep us updated every few hours," Adrian instructed. "If the problem persists, we might consider replacing the entire sensor batch. I'll have our tech team on standby."

The discussion moved to a training issue in Tokyo. Elena addressed the site leader there, Dr. Sato. "Dr. Sato, you mentioned that the new staff are struggling with the environmental control systems. What specific aspects are they finding challenging?"

Dr. Sato explained, "The interface is quite complex, and while the training modules cover a lot, the practical application is proving difficult for newer team members who aren't as tech-savvy."

Elena nodded understandingly. "We anticipated some learning curves. Let's schedule additional hands-on training sessions. I'll also send over some simplified user guides that might help bridge this gap."

"That would be very helpful, thank you," Dr. Sato responded, her relief evident.

Moving to an issue in Brazil, Adrian engaged Dr. Lima. "Dr. Lima, you reported fluctuations in light levels affecting therapy sessions. What's been your observation?"

Dr. Lima's concern was clear. "The automated light adjustments aren't syncing well with our session timings, possibly due to software glitches. It's disrupting the therapeutic ambiance we're trying to maintain."

Adrian was quick to propose a solution. "Let's do a remote session where our tech team can log in and observe the system in real-time. We need to see the issue as it happens to diagnose it accurately."

"Let's organize that for tomorrow," Dr. Lima agreed.

As they addressed each issue, Adrian and Elena ensured that every solution was actionable and tailored to the specific needs of each site. The meeting continued with discussions around logistics, supply chain adjustments, and further technical support.

Concluding the session, Adrian reiterated their commitment. "Thank you all for your detailed reports and cooperation. Elena and I, along with our teams, are dedicated to supporting you through these teething problems. It's crucial for the success of our project that these issues are resolved swiftly."

Elena added, "We're here to assist you every step of the way. Don't hesitate to reach out if new challenges arise. Together, we'll ensure that these environments become a cornerstone of effective therapy worldwide."

The meeting ended with a round of thanks and a collective sense of determination. Adrian and Elena logged off, feeling reassured that despite the hurdles, their approach of direct engagement and rapid response was making a tangible difference. As they left the operations center, their conversation already shifted towards preventive measures for future rollouts, each step forward informed by the lessons learned today.

Dr. Adrian Harrow and Elena Markham were back in the clinic's main conference room, surrounded by the latest data visualizations projected on the walls. Today's session was focused on evaluating the impact of the newly implemented changes after addressing the initial rollout challenges. They were joined by Dr. Lisa Mendez via video conference, who had compiled comprehensive impact reports from each pilot site.

Adrian started the meeting with an overview. "Now that we've managed to stabilize the initial issues, it's crucial we understand the direct impact of these interventions on therapy outcomes. Lisa, could you start by summarizing the overall trends we're seeing?"

Lisa, her image clear and steady on the screen, nodded. "Certainly, Adrian. Since implementing the fixes, there's been a noticeable improvement in therapy outcomes across most sites. Patient satisfaction has increased by an average of 15%, and therapist feedback has been overwhelmingly positive regarding the environmental adjustments."

"That's excellent news," Elena responded, her tone reflecting relief and satisfaction. "Are there particular sites or regions where the impact has been more significant?"

Lisa scrolled through her data. "Yes, the sites in northern Europe have shown the most dramatic improvements, particularly in patient mood stability during sessions, which seems to correlate strongly with the enhanced lighting and temperature controls we prioritized for those regions."

Adrian made notes, then shifted the focus. "What about the sites that were lagging initially? Have the targeted interventions brought them up to par with others?"

"Some have improved significantly, while a few are still catching up," Lisa explained. "For instance, the Johannesburg site has seen a slower rate of improvement. We believe additional customizations might be necessary there, perhaps even more localized training for their staff."

Elena suggested, "Let's plan a focused review session with Johannesburg next week. We might uncover more underlying issues that our data isn't showing."

Adrian agreed, "Good idea, Elena. We need to ensure every site is benefiting equally from our project."

The discussion then turned to the feedback mechanisms they had put in place. "Are we getting consistent feedback across all sites, or do we need to adjust our methods?" Adrian asked, always concerned about maintaining robust data streams.

Lisa responded, "Feedback has been mostly consistent, thanks to the new digital tools we introduced. However, there's room for improvement in how quickly we process and react to this feedback at a few sites."

Elena, thinking ahead, added, "Maybe we should consider a bi-weekly virtual roundtable with site leaders. It could serve as a real-time feedback loop and help us address any issues more promptly."

"That would definitely tighten our feedback cycle," Lisa concurred, noting down the suggestion. "I'll organize the first of these roundtables and see how it enhances our communication."

As they wrapped up their meeting, Adrian summarized their next steps, "We'll focus on the specialized session for Johannesburg and start the bi-weekly roundtables as proposed by Elena. Lisa, please keep a close eye on the data trends and alert us to any anomalies immediately."

"Will do," Lisa confirmed, her tone professional and focused.

The meeting ended with a sense of accomplishment and a clear path forward. Adrian and Elena lingered for a moment to discuss their immediate tasks. They were pleased with the progress but aware that continuous monitoring and adaptation were key to the project's long-term success.

Stepping out of the conference room, they were already discussing the details for the upcoming session with Johannesburg, committed to ensuring that the project delivered on its promise of enhancing therapeutic environments across the globe. As they walked through the clinic, the late afternoon light streamed through the windows, casting long shadows and bathing their path in a warm glow—a subtle reminder of the positive changes they were fostering in so many lives.

In the clinic's dedicated strategy room, Dr. Adrian Harrow and Elena Markham were deep in discussion, surrounded by digital maps and live data feeds from their international sites. They were focused on integrating the enhancements more fully across all sites, ensuring that the project's impact was both broad and sustainable. Today, they were joined via video call by their global project coordinators from Europe, Asia, and South America, each ready to discuss the specifics of their regional challenges and progress.

Adrian opened the session with a clear agenda. "We need to ensure that our enhancements are not just implemented, but fully integrated into each site's daily operations. This is crucial for the sustainability of the project. Let's start with a status update from each region, focusing on the integration process and any obstacles you're encountering."

The European coordinator, Dr. Heinrich Weber, was the first to report. "In our region, the enhancements have been well received, particularly the ambient adjustments in therapy rooms. However, we are facing some resistance from older staff members who are less comfortable with the new technology."

Elena responded thoughtfully, "Dr. Weber, perhaps we can organize some additional hands-on training sessions specifically tailored for those who need more support. We could also pair them with tech-savvy colleagues who can mentor them through the transition."

"That sounds like a practical approach," Adrian agreed, making a note. "Let's implement that across all regions where similar challenges exist."

Next, the coordinator from Asia, Dr. Aisha Chen, shared her insights. "Our main challenge has been logistical, particularly with the timely delivery of sensor components due to customs delays. It's impacting our ability to maintain the scheduled enhancements."

Adrian considered this logistical hiccup. "Let's explore local sourcing options for some of these components. It might increase costs slightly, but it will give us greater control over supply chain delays. Elena, could you work with Dr. Chen to identify potential suppliers?"

"Absolutely," Elena confirmed, already listing potential contacts and suppliers she knew in the region.

The South American coordinator, Dr. Luis Rojas, then highlighted a different aspect. "Our challenge is primarily environmental. The high humidity in some areas is affecting sensor performance. We need a more robust solution to shield the sensors from these elements."

"That's a good point, Dr. Rojas," Adrian acknowledged. "Let's look into weather-resistant models that could better withstand such conditions. I'll coordinate with our tech team to fast-track this."

As the meeting progressed, it was clear that while the rollout of enhancements faced distinct challenges in each region, the solutions required thoughtful adaptation and sometimes creative problem-solving.

Elena suggested, "In addition to these specific actions, I propose we set up a quarterly review workshop where all regional coordinators can share their successes and challenges. It could foster a more collaborative approach to problem-solving and allow for the sharing of strategies that have been effective in various locales."

"That's an excellent idea," Adrian said. "Let's include it in our next global newsletter and start planning the first workshop. It will also help maintain the momentum of our global integration efforts."

As the meeting wrapped up, Adrian thanked everyone for their contributions. "Your insights are invaluable, and the solutions we've discussed today are testament to our collective commitment to this project's success. We'll reconvene next month with updates on the actions we've outlined today."

After the call, Adrian and Elena spent a few more minutes in the strategy room, reflecting on the discussions and planning their next steps. They were both aware of the complexities involved in managing such a diverse and wide-ranging project, but they were also confident in their team's ability to meet these challenges head-on.

Stepping out of the strategy room, they felt prepared and motivated, ready to tackle the ongoing tasks that lay ahead. The clinic was quiet as they walked through the dimly lit hallways, each step reinforcing their dedication to improving therapeutic environments across the globe.

Chapter 18
The Gathering Dark

As the global expansion of their therapeutic environment project continued, Dr. Adrian Harrow and Elena Markham found themselves increasingly occupied with the complexities of managing a worldwide initiative. Each pilot site offered unique insights and challenges, which they meticulously monitored from the operations center, now the nerve center of their global efforts.

The room was lined with large screens displaying real-time data from across the world. Adrian, sitting before one of the screens, analyzed the latest feedback from the European sites, noting trends and outliers in patient responses. He was particularly focused on the data visualization that depicted patient stress levels before and after the introduction of the environmental enhancements. The downward trends were promising, but some spikes of concern needed addressing.

Elena, meanwhile, was on a conference call with site managers from Asia, discussing the logistical challenges they faced. "We need to ensure that any delays in supply chains do not impact our project timelines," she stressed. "Can we increase our local stock of critical components to buffer against these delays?"

The site manager from Japan responded, "That would be helpful. We can use local storage facilities to keep an additional month's supply on hand. This should give us enough leeway to manage minor disruptions without affecting the ongoing sessions."

"Excellent," Elena replied, making a note of this. "I'll arrange for the finance team to adjust the budgets accordingly. Let's keep this strategy under review and see if it helps mitigate the issue."

Back in the operations center, Adrian met with Dr. Lisa Mendez, who had come in to discuss the integration of cultural elements into the therapy environments. "The feedback on the cultural adaptations has been overwhelmingly positive," Lisa reported. "Patients feel more at ease, and therapists find the sessions more engaging."

Adrian nodded in agreement. "That's great to hear. It validates our approach of customizing environments to reflect local cultures. Do we have quantitative data to back this up?"

"Yes, the initial analysis shows a significant correlation between these cultural adaptations and the improvement in therapy outcomes," Lisa confirmed, handing Adrian a graph showing the statistical relationship.

Adrian looked over the data with a critical eye. "We should consider a deeper study into this. If we can firmly establish the impact of cultural customization on therapeutic effectiveness, it could become a cornerstone of our global strategy."

Elena joined them, her part of the meeting concluded. "I've just off the call with our Asian sites. We're implementing a strategy to buffer stock locally to manage supply chain delays. It's a test approach, but if it works, we might roll it out to other regions facing similar issues."

"That sounds like a proactive approach," Lisa remarked. "Managing logistics effectively will be key as we continue to expand."

Adrian and Elena then discussed the upcoming week's schedule, which included visits to several new sites preparing to join the pilot. "We need to ensure these sites are fully integrated from the start," Adrian noted. "Let's make sure they benefit from the lessons we've learned from our existing sites."

Elena agreed, "I'll compile an integration package based on our most successful strategies. It'll include everything from environmental setup tips to cultural adaptation guidelines."

As they wrapped up their meeting, the operations center continued to buzz with activity. Adrian and Elena, along with their global team, were weaving together a complex tapestry of therapeutic environments that spanned continents.

They left the center late in the evening, satisfied with the progress but aware of the challenges ahead. The quiet corridors of the clinic provided a stark contrast to the global activity they were orchestrating. As they walked through the dimly lit hallway, their conversation turned to the upcoming site visits, each step echoing their commitment to transforming therapeutic practices worldwide.

Dr. Adrian Harrow and Elena Markham were embarking on a series of site visits designed to ensure that the newly integrated pilot locations were aligning with the project's high standards and unique approach. Their first stop was a newly incorporated site in Lisbon, where they were met by the local team leader, Dr. Sofia Mendes.

As they toured the facility, Adrian observed the ambient enhancements in the therapy rooms. "Dr. Mendes, the layout here aligns well with our specifications. How have the initial therapy sessions been received by the patients?"

Dr. Mendes responded enthusiastically, "The feedback has been very positive, Dr. Harrow. Patients have noted the calming effects of the environment, particularly the natural elements we've incorporated, such as plant installations and water features."

Elena, checking her notes on a digital tablet, followed up, "Have there been any challenges with the maintenance of these features, especially the water elements, which can be quite demanding?"

"We did encounter some minor issues initially," Dr. Mendes admitted. "However, after increasing our maintenance staff's training on these specific elements, we've managed to minimize any disruptions."

Adrian nodded, pleased with the proactive steps. "That's good to hear. Continuous staff training is key to sustaining the effectiveness of our environments. Are there any other areas where you think additional support from our team might be needed?"

"Actually, yes," Dr. Mendes said as they walked towards the patient relaxation area. "I believe further customization of the sensory elements, like adjusting light and sound to better suit the individual needs of our patients, could enhance the therapeutic experience. However, we're unsure how to implement these adjustments without compromising the standardized settings."

"That's a valid concern," Elena responded thoughtfully. "We could look into more advanced, user-friendly control systems that allow slight modifications without straying from the proven effective ranges. Let's schedule a technical session with our systems team to explore viable options."

"Thank you, that would be very helpful," Dr. Mendes replied, clearly relieved.

The next stop on their trip was a site in Madrid, where they met with Dr. Carlos Ruiz. During their meeting, Adrian began, "Dr. Ruiz, this site has been part of the pilot for a few months now. Based on the latest reports, your team has been doing exceptionally well with the integration. What do you attribute this success to?"

Dr. Ruiz smiled, "One of the major factors has been the extensive pre-launch training and the continuous online support we receive from your team. The real-time troubleshooting helpdesk has been particularly valuable."

Elena was quick to jot this down. "That's great to hear. Your feedback underscores the importance of our support structures. How do you feel about the scalability of these practices? Can they be enhanced further for wider application?"

"Definitely," Dr. Ruiz affirmed. "Especially the helpdesk component. If it could be expanded to offer multilingual support, it would greatly benefit sites like ours where English is not the first language."

"That's an excellent suggestion," Adrian noted. "We'll look into enhancing the linguistic capabilities of our support services."

As their visit concluded, Adrian and Elena thanked Dr. Ruiz and his team for their hospitality and insights. On their way back, they discussed the key takeaways from both visits.

Elena summarized, "Both sites highlighted the importance of local adaptations and strong support systems. It's clear that our ongoing success depends on how well we tailor and support each site's specific needs."

"Absolutely," Adrian agreed as they prepared to board their flight back. "Let's use these insights to refine our approach further. Each site gives us a clearer picture of what works and what can be improved."

Their conversation continued as they flew home, each discussion point helping to refine their strategies and approaches, ensuring that their global initiative would continue to grow and succeed, guided by the real-world experiences of their international teams.

After returning from their site visits, Dr. Adrian Harrow and Elena Markham were deeply engrossed in integrating the feedback and insights gathered into the broader framework of their global project. The operations center, with its array of glowing screens and continuous data feeds, served as their base of operations where they spent long hours analyzing data, strategizing, and planning.

The focus of this phase was to implement a series of enhancements based on the specific needs and feedback from each site. Adrian dedicated himself to overseeing the development of new technological tools designed to allow sites to make minor adjustments to the environmental settings without deviating from the proven effective ranges. This task involved collaborating with tech specialists who were integrating advanced, user-friendly interfaces into the existing systems.

Meanwhile, Elena was busy enhancing the training modules with additional sections that included best practices derived from the most successful sites. She was determined to ensure that all sites could benefit from the proven strategies that Dr. Mendes in Lisbon and Dr. Ruiz in Madrid had highlighted during their visits. This required her to work closely with educational designers and clinical psychologists to ensure the information was both accessible and clinically valuable.

One afternoon, they convened in a small meeting room to discuss the progress of these enhancements. Adrian shared updates from the tech team, "The new interfaces are in development. We're focusing on intuitive design to ensure ease of use. We're planning a pilot test next month at a few select sites."

Elena nodded, looking over her notes. "On the training front, I've incorporated interactive elements into the modules, such as virtual reality scenarios that replicate real-life challenges. This should help in better preparing the staff for on-the-ground issues."

Their conversation briefly turned to the upcoming community engagement initiative they were planning. "We need to ensure that our project continues to align with community needs and expectations," Adrian mentioned. "This means more than just making technological and training adjustments; it involves ongoing dialogue with the communities we serve."

Elena agreed, "I've been coordinating with community leaders to set up a series of forums where patients and local residents can share their experiences and suggestions directly with us. It's crucial that their voices help shape our project."

As the day wound down, Adrian and Elena reviewed the extensive list of tasks still ahead of them. They were both aware of the challenges, but also confident in the robustness of their approach. They had a clear vision and a comprehensive plan that was continuously refined by the real-world data and feedback they were gathering.

Leaving the operations center that evening, the clinic was quiet, with most of the staff gone home. The silence allowed them a moment to reflect on the importance of their work and the impact it was already having on so many lives. They discussed their next steps as they walked through the dimly lit corridors, each step a progression towards a more responsive and effective global health initiative.

Their commitment to enhancing therapeutic environments worldwide was more than just a professional endeavor; it was a mission driven by data, enhanced by technology, and guided by the voices of those it aimed to help. As they left the building, the cool night air was a crisp reminder of the world outside their project, a world that was ever-changing and that they were striving to improve, one therapy session at a time.

Dr. Adrian Harrow and Elena Markham embarked on a new phase of their project: the implementation of community engagement forums designed to foster open dialogue between the project team and the communities served by their global initiative. These forums were intended to gather firsthand feedback on the therapeutic environments, gauging their effectiveness and gathering suggestions for further improvements.

The first of these forums was scheduled in a community center close to one of their most successful pilot sites. Adrian and Elena prepared diligently, ensuring that the event was well-publicized and accessible to a broad segment of the community, including patients, local healthcare providers, and interested residents.

As they set up for the event, Adrian checked the audiovisual equipment while Elena reviewed the printed feedback forms and discussion guides. "It's crucial that everyone feels they can speak openly. We need honest feedback to truly understand how our environments are impacting their therapy experiences," Elena remarked, arranging the chairs into a welcoming circle.

Adrian nodded, testing the microphone. "Absolutely, and we need to listen more than we speak today. Let's encourage them to share their thoughts and experiences without steering the conversation too much."

As the community members began to arrive, Adrian welcomed them warmly. "Thank you for joining us this evening. Your input is invaluable in helping us improve and adapt the environments we're developing. We're here to listen and learn from all of you."

Once everyone was seated, Elena facilitated the first part of the forum, focusing on participants' general impressions of the therapeutic environments. "Can anyone share how the new settings have affected your therapy sessions? Any specific elements that stand out, either positively or negatively?"

A local therapist took the opportunity to speak. "The natural elements you've incorporated, like the indoor plants and water features, have been particularly well-received. They seem to soothe the patients and make the space feel more open and less clinical."

However, a patient raised a concern. "While the aesthetic changes are nice, I find some of the automated features, like the lighting adjustments, a bit disruptive. They don't always align with what I find comfortable."

Elena made a note of this. "That's very useful feedback, thank you. Adjusting our systems to accommodate individual preferences is something we're looking into."

The discussion then shifted towards suggestions for improvements. Adrian encouraged the participants to think creatively. "If there were no constraints, what changes or additions would you suggest to make these environments even more supportive of your needs?"

Responses varied, with some suggesting more personalized control over environmental settings, while others expressed a desire for spaces designed for group therapy that encouraged interaction among patients.

As the forum concluded, Adrian and Elena thanked everyone for their candidness and insights. "This has been incredibly enlightening," Adrian said. "We take your suggestions seriously and will be looking to integrate as many of your ideas as possible into our project."

Post-forum, Adrian and Elena stayed back to discuss the feedback with some of the attendees who lingered, deepening their understanding of the community's needs and expectations.

Driving back to the clinic, they discussed how to systematically analyze the feedback they had collected. "We should categorize the feedback into immediate actions and long-term developmental ideas," Elena suggested.

"Agreed," Adrian replied. "And let's schedule these forums more regularly. This direct interaction is invaluable."

They arrived back at the clinic after nightfall, energized by the day's interactions. The clinic was quiet, providing a stark contrast to the lively discussions of the evening. As they locked up for the night, they felt reassured that the path they were on was not just informed by their data and research, but was continually shaped by the very people it aimed to help. This connection to the community not only grounded their work in reality but also propelled it forward with a renewed sense of purpose and direction.

Chapter 19
Threads of Fate

After the success of the initial community engagement forums, Dr. Adrian Harrow and Elena Markham dedicated their efforts to refining their global project strategies based on the valuable feedback received. The operations center, usually a hub of technical monitoring, today transformed into a strategic planning room where they, along with Dr. Lisa Mendez, discussed the integration of community suggestions into their project.

"Let's start by categorizing the feedback into themes," Adrian suggested, projecting a list of comments and suggestions onto the screen. "We have significant comments on environmental controls, personalization of therapy settings, and requests for more natural elements in the therapy rooms."

Elena nodded, reviewing the notes she had taken during the forums. "One recurring theme was the request for personal control over the environment settings. Patients expressed a desire to adjust lighting and sound according to their comfort levels."

Lisa, joining via video call, added her perspective. "It's a valid request. We could explore smart technology solutions that allow patients to adjust settings via a control panel or even a mobile app, within the ranges that we know are therapeutic."

"That's a great idea, Lisa," Adrian responded, making a note. "We need to ensure that any such technology is user-friendly and doesn't become a distraction itself. Perhaps we can pilot this in one of our more tech-savvy sites and see how it goes."

Elena considered the logistical aspects. "We'll also need to assess the cost implications of installing such technology across all sites. But first, a pilot could help us understand the benefits versus the costs."

The discussion then shifted towards the natural elements that were highly favored by forum participants. "There's overwhelming evidence that the natural elements are beneficial," Elena said. "We should consider standardizing larger, more interactive natural installations across all sites."

"Perhaps we can collaborate with local artists and landscapers to create these installations," suggested Lisa. "It would add a local flavor and also support the community."

"That's an excellent point," Adrian agreed. "Engaging local talents would indeed resonate well with the community-focused model we are striving for. Let's draft a proposal for incorporating local arts into our sites."

As they continued their discussion, they also tackled the feedback on group therapy spaces. "There's a clear demand for better-designed group therapy areas that encourage interaction but also allow for individual comfort," Adrian noted.

"We could redesign these spaces to be more modular," Elena proposed. "Adjustable partitions, for instance, could offer flexibility—providing privacy when needed or open spaces for group activities."

Lisa liked the idea. "Modularity is key. It offers the versatility required for different types of therapy sessions and client needs. Let's include that in our next design update phase."

As the meeting drew to a close, Adrian summarized their action items. "Okay, we will move forward with piloting the smart environmental controls, initiate collaborations for natural installations, and plan for modular group therapy spaces. Each of these aligns directly with our mission to make therapy environments more effective and personalized."

"Sounds like we have a solid plan," Elena concluded. "I'll start reaching out to potential tech partners for the smart controls and set up a task force for the redesign of the therapy spaces."

With their strategies refined and clear tasks ahead, Adrian, Elena, and Lisa felt confident about the next steps. They ended the meeting with a sense of accomplishment and a renewed commitment to enhancing their project based on the direct input from those it aimed to help.

As they left the operations center, their conversation continued, focusing on the immediate steps to implement the discussed changes. Each was

aware of the challenges ahead but also energized by the potential to
significantly enhance the therapeutic experiences of patients around the
world.

In a brightly lit meeting room, Dr. Adrian Harrow and Elena Markham
sat across from their tech team, along with Dr. Lisa Mendez joining via
video conference, ready to discuss the pilot testing of the smart
environmental controls they had decided to integrate based on
community feedback. This meeting was crucial to determine the feasibility
and design of these controls before wider implementation.

Adrian opened the meeting with a clear focus. "Let's ensure that we are
all on the same page about what we need from these smart controls. They
need to be intuitive for the users, but also secure and reliable. What
progress do we have so far?"

The head of the tech team, Simon, displayed a prototype interface on the
screen. "We've developed a preliminary design that allows users to adjust
light, sound, and temperature within therapeutic ranges. The interface is
simple—users can control settings using a touchscreen panel installed in
each therapy room."

Lisa, observing from her screen, interjected, "It looks user-friendly, but
how are we ensuring that these adjustments truly stay within therapeutic
ranges?"

Simon responded, "We've programmed hard limits into the system. Users
can only adjust settings within these limits, ensuring that all changes are
safe and beneficial."

Elena, always concerned with practical application, questioned, "What
about feedback mechanisms? Can the system track user preferences and
adjust automatically over time to suit individual patient needs?"

"We've included an AI component that learns from adjustments and can
suggest settings based on previous preferences," Simon explained.
"However, this feature will be closely monitored during the pilot to ensure
it's functioning as intended without compromising patient care."

Adrian nodded, satisfied with the technical explanations. "Let's talk about the pilot. Where are we planning to implement this first?"

Elena answered, "We've selected our site in Amsterdam for the initial pilot. The staff there are tech-savvy, and the patient demographic is diverse enough to give us good data on a wide range of preferences and needs."

Lisa added, "I recommend that we conduct thorough staff training on how to use and troubleshoot the system before we go live. It's important that the team feels confident in managing the technology."

"Absolutely," Adrian agreed. "Simon, can your team prepare training materials and conduct a training session next week?"

"Will do," Simon confirmed. "We'll also set up a direct line for the Amsterdam site to our tech support team to address any issues in real-time during the pilot."

Elena, thinking ahead to the evaluation of the pilot, suggested, "We should design a detailed feedback form for both therapists and patients to fill out after each session. We need to know not just if the system works, but how it affects the therapeutic process."

"That's a good point, Elena," Adrian supported. "We need qualitative data as well as quantitative. Lisa, could you help design these feedback mechanisms?"

"I'd be happy to," Lisa responded. "I'll draft something that lets us capture both subjective impressions and objective data."

As the meeting concluded, the team felt prepared and motivated. Adrian summarized, "We have a solid plan moving forward. Let's execute it carefully and learn as much as we can from this pilot. It has the potential to significantly enhance patient experience across all our sites."

The team dispersed, each member clear on their responsibilities. Adrian and Elena stayed behind to discuss further the strategic impacts of integrating such technology across all sites, contemplating the broader implications for patient care and operational efficiency.

Their conversation was a blend of optimism and caution, typical of their approach to innovation—a careful balance between embracing new technologies and maintaining the highest standards of patient care. As they left the meeting room, the corridors of the clinic seemed to echo with the potential of their discussions, each step forward marked by careful planning and hopeful anticipation.

Two months after initiating the pilot test for the smart environmental controls at the Amsterdam site, Dr. Adrian Harrow, Elena Markham, and Dr. Lisa Mendez convened via a video conference to review the collected data and feedback to decide on the next steps for potential expansion.

"Let's start with the overall performance of the smart controls," Adrian began, looking at the comprehensive reports displayed on the screen. "Simon, can you walk us through the data?"

Simon, the head of the tech team, was prepared with a detailed analysis. "The pilot results have been largely positive. The system's reliability was 98%, and user feedback indicates a high level of satisfaction with the interface. Most users found it intuitive and appreciated the ability to customize their environment."

Elena, always focused on the human aspect, asked, "What about the therapeutic outcomes? Any noticeable trends in the feedback from therapists and patients regarding the impact on therapy sessions?"

Lisa took this question. "The qualitative data is encouraging. Therapists reported that patients seemed more relaxed and engaged during sessions. Many patients commented that the ability to adjust the settings made them feel more in control of their therapy experience, which aligns well with our therapeutic goals."

Adrian nodded thoughtfully, then said, "That's excellent to hear. It supports our hypothesis that environmental control can enhance therapeutic efficacy. What were the challenges, if any?"

Simon shifted slightly, ready to address this part. "There were a few technical glitches initially, mainly with the AI learning component, which caused slight discomfort for a couple of patients due to inappropriate temperature settings. However, we've since made adjustments, and the issue hasn't reoccurred."

"Good," Adrian responded. "Moving forward, how scalable do you believe this system is across other sites?"

Simon was optimistic. "The architecture of the system is designed for scalability. With the modifications we've made following the pilot, I believe we can roll this out to additional sites with minimal disruption."

Elena, thinking about implementation, added, "We need to consider the training for each site. The success in Amsterdam was partly due to the high level of technical proficiency of the staff there. Other sites might require more intensive training."

"That's a valid point," Lisa agreed. "I suggest we create a tiered training program. Sites with less technical experience could receive a more hands-on approach, while others might only need basic orientation."

Adrian liked the tiered approach. "That's a smart way to handle it. Let's draft a rollout plan based on that training model. We also need to keep an eye on the budget impacts of a wider implementation."

Elena noted, "I'll work with the finance team to ensure our projections for the next fiscal year include the costs for this expansion. We should also consider applying for additional funding or grants, given the positive outcomes of the pilot."

Lisa concluded, "I'll start refining the training materials based on our learnings from the pilot. Additionally, I'll collaborate with Simon to ensure that any further technical enhancements are included in the training sessions."

Adrian summarized, "Excellent. Let's proceed with caution but confidence. The potential benefits to patient care and therapy outcomes could be significant."

As the meeting ended, each member of the team was clear on their next steps. Adrian and Elena spent a few more minutes discussing the potential long-term impacts of this initiative on their overall project goals.

Their conversation was a blend of strategic planning and a shared commitment to improving patient care through innovation. As they left the conference room, they felt a renewed sense of purpose, energized by the progress and potential of their work.

After concluding their strategic meeting with positive decisions regarding the expansion of smart environmental controls, Dr. Adrian Harrow and Elena Markham dedicated themselves to the meticulous planning required for the global rollout. Their goal was to implement these controls across all pilot sites, enhancing therapeutic environments worldwide.

The duo began by coordinating with regional managers to assess each site's readiness for the new technology. This involved evaluating the existing infrastructure and the technical proficiency of the site staff. Adrian took the lead in developing an implementation timeline that accounted for these variables, ensuring a smooth transition.

"Each site will receive customized support based on their current setup and capabilities," Adrian explained as he drafted the timeline. "We'll stagger the rollout to manage our resources effectively and ensure each site gets the attention it needs."

Elena, meanwhile, focused on updating the training programs. "I'm incorporating interactive elements and simulations into the training modules," she shared with Adrian during one of their strategy sessions. "This will allow staff to get hands-on experience with the controls before they go live."

Adrian nodded in approval. "That's crucial. We need to ensure everyone feels confident using the new systems. Have we set up the support lines?"

"Yes, the tech support lines are being expanded to handle queries from all time zones. We're also including a feedback mechanism to gather real-time user experiences which will help us make any necessary adjustments quickly," Elena responded, detailing the support structure.

In preparation for the rollout, Adrian and Elena hosted a series of webinars with site leaders to discuss the deployment phases and address any concerns. "Your feedback is essential to us," Adrian emphasized during one webinar. "Please be proactive in reporting any issues, no matter how small they seem."

Elena added, "And remember, this technology is designed to enhance therapeutic outcomes. It's a tool to help you provide better care, not a replacement for your expertise."

As the first phase of the rollout began, Adrian and Elena monitored the progress from their operations center. They had set up a dashboard that allowed them to see real-time data from each site, which included system status reports and user feedback.

The initial reports were encouraging. Sites that had gone live with the new controls reported a smooth transition, and the feedback from therapists and patients was positive. "Look at this data coming in from Berlin," Adrian pointed out one morning, showing Elena the user statistics. "The adoption rate is higher than we expected, and the preliminary feedback is very positive."

Elena, pleased with this news, replied, "That's fantastic. It shows that the training and preparation were effective. Let's make sure we maintain this momentum."

However, not all sites experienced a seamless transition. A few reported technical glitches and user errors, which were promptly addressed by the support teams. "These are teething problems," Adrian reassured the concerned site manager during a follow-up call. "We're on top of it, and we appreciate your quick reporting."

As the global rollout continued, Adrian and Elena kept a close eye on every aspect of the implementation. They were determined to ensure that the project not only met but exceeded its goals.

Their days were long, often extending into late evening discussions and planning sessions. Despite the workload, there was a palpable sense of achievement in seeing their project impact therapy practices globally.

Each step forward was documented and analyzed, ensuring that lessons were learned and successes were replicated. As they left the operations center one evening, with most of the sites successfully transitioned to the new system, they discussed the next steps in their journey to revolutionize therapeutic environments. Their conversation, always forward-looking, was filled with ideas for further enhancements and innovations.

Chapter 20
Reflections of Despair

In the conference room adorned with screens showcasing global data, Dr. Adrian Harrow and Elena Markham convened a crucial meeting to review the comprehensive feedback received following the global rollout of smart environmental controls. They were joined by Dr. Lisa Mendez and regional representatives via a video conference, each ready to share insights from their respective territories.

Adrian initiated the session with a clear directive. "Let's begin by reviewing the feedback from each region to gauge the impact of our environmental controls. We need to understand both the successes and the areas where adjustments may be necessary."

Lisa started with an overview. "From a global perspective, the feedback has been largely positive. There's been a noticeable improvement in patient engagement and overall satisfaction. However, there are variations in feedback that are worth discussing."

Elena took over to delve deeper. "Let's start with North America. Tom, can you summarize the feedback from the sites there?"

Tom, the North American regional manager, responded confidently. "Certainly, Elena. Our feedback has been very positive, especially regarding the user interface of the controls. Patients and therapists find it intuitive. However, there is a request for more customizable options, particularly in sound settings, which some users find too limited."

Adrian nodded thoughtfully. "That's good to know. Simon, from our tech team, could we enhance the sound settings without compromising the therapeutic integrity of the environments?"

Simon, who was also on the call, replied, "Yes, we can definitely expand the options. I'll need a couple of weeks to work with the team on this, but it's certainly feasible."

Elena then directed the conversation towards Europe. "Maria, what has been the response in your region?"

Maria, the European regional manager, shared her insights. "The feedback here is a bit mixed. The control systems are well-received in urban centers, but there are connectivity issues in rural areas which affect system reliability. We need to address this to ensure uniform effectiveness."

"That's an important point," Adrian acknowledged. "Lisa, could we explore additional training or support for rural sites to help them manage these issues more effectively?"

Lisa agreed, "Absolutely, Adrian. I'll coordinate with Maria to identify specific needs and develop targeted support plans."

The discussion moved to Asia, where Ken, the regional manager, highlighted a different challenge. "In Asia, we're seeing cultural variations in how the environments are used. Some settings that work well in Western contexts aren't as effective here. We may need to consider regional customizations."

"That's a vital observation," Elena responded. "Let's set up a task force to work on regional adaptations. Ken, could you lead this and report back with proposed modifications?"

"Happy to," Ken confirmed, noting down his new responsibility.

Adrian, summing up the discussions, stated, "This feedback is invaluable. It shows we're on the right track, but also that there's room for refinement. Let's proceed with the proposed enhancements and address the connectivity issues in rural areas as a priority."

Lisa concluded, "I'll oversee the follow-up on these action items and ensure we maintain momentum. It's crucial that we continue to adapt and respond to feedback promptly."

As the meeting ended, Adrian and Elena stayed back to discuss the broader implications of the feedback. "This kind of detailed review is essential for continuous improvement," Adrian reflected.

Elena agreed, "It keeps us aligned with our goal of providing the best possible therapeutic environments. Let's keep pushing for innovation and responsiveness."

Their dialogue continued as they left the room, each step echoing their commitment to a project that was reshaping therapeutic practices globally. Their conversation was not just about immediate tasks but also about future strategies, underlining their dedication to sustained impact and improvement.

In the weeks following their comprehensive review meeting, Dr. Adrian Harrow and Elena Markham worked diligently on implementing the strategic adaptations and technical enhancements discussed. Their focus was not only on refining the smart environmental controls but also on ensuring that these enhancements met the specific needs of diverse global populations.

Adrian dedicated much of his time to overseeing the development of the enhanced sound settings for the North American sites. Working closely with Simon and the tech team, they developed a more sophisticated sound module that allowed for a broader range of adjustments, providing users with the ability to customize their auditory environment to a greater degree. This technical refinement was aimed at enhancing patient comfort and ensuring that the therapeutic sessions were as effective as possible.

Meanwhile, Elena focused on the connectivity issues that had been a significant concern in rural European areas. She collaborated with local service providers to improve internet services at these locations, which was crucial for the reliable operation of the smart control systems. Additionally, Elena initiated a series of workshops for the staff at these sites, designed to equip them with the skills needed to troubleshoot minor technical issues independently, reducing downtime and improving overall system reliability.

The task force led by Ken, aimed at customizing the environmental controls for Asian sites, was making substantial progress. They conducted extensive research into regional preferences and cultural nuances that influenced therapy outcomes. The task force's findings were insightful, revealing specific environmental factors that resonated more positively within different cultural contexts. Based on these insights, Ken's team developed a set of region-specific guidelines for environmental settings, which were then integrated into the control systems to ensure they were more aligned with local user expectations.

Throughout this period, Adrian and Elena maintained regular communication with all regional managers, providing guidance and receiving updates on the implementation process. Their approach was hands-on, yet they allowed enough flexibility for site managers to make decisions that best suited their local conditions.

One afternoon, as they reviewed the latest reports from the pilot sites, Adrian and Elena were pleased to see positive trends emerging from the adjustments made. Feedback from the North American sites indicated a marked improvement in patient satisfaction with the new sound settings. Similarly, the rural European sites reported fewer disruptions due to improved connectivity and local staff training.

"This shows that our targeted approach is working," Adrian remarked as he analyzed the data. "By addressing specific issues with tailored solutions, we're seeing a significant improvement in system performance and user satisfaction."

Elena, looking over the cultural adaptation guidelines from Ken's task force, added, "These guidelines will be invaluable as we continue to expand. They not only enhance the effectiveness of our environments but also ensure that our interventions are respectful and sensitive to cultural differences."

As they planned the next steps, Adrian and Elena were aware that the project was entering a new phase of global integration. Each decision they made was underpinned by data-driven insights and a deep commitment to user-centered design. They were not just solving technical problems but were also weaving a complex tapestry of technology, culture, and therapy into a cohesive global strategy.

Their workday extended into the evening as they prepared a presentation for the upcoming international conference, where they planned to share their findings and learn from other leaders in the field. The quiet of the operations center late at night was a stark contrast to the bustling day, but for Adrian and Elena, it was a productive solitude that allowed them to concentrate fully on their mission.

Leaving the clinic that night, their conversation continued, with discussions about potential innovations and strategies for further enhancements. Each step they took was driven by a vision of a world where therapeutic environments were not only universally accessible but also uniquely responsive to the needs of those they served.

In the spacious conference room bathed in the soft glow of the afternoon sun, Dr. Adrian Harrow and Elena Markham met with their core strategy team, including Dr. Lisa Mendez, who was present via video call. They were there to discuss the integration of feedback received from the global sites and to refine their strategic approaches based on this input.

Elena opened the meeting, her tone focused and pragmatic. "The feedback from our last set of enhancements has been very instructive. Let's use today to discuss specific issues and plan our next steps accordingly."

Adrian nodded in agreement, then turned his attention to the screen where Lisa appeared. "Lisa, can you start by giving us an overview of the feedback trends you've compiled?"

Lisa adjusted her papers before speaking. "Certainly. The most consistent feedback has been about the smart environmental controls. Users appreciate the ability to adjust settings, but there have been requests for even greater customization options. Additionally, some sites have reported intermittent issues with the AI learning component, which seems to be adjusting settings based on incorrect data patterns."

Adrian, concerned, leaned forward. "That's troubling. Simon, what can be done to enhance the AI's accuracy?"

Simon, the lead tech officer, responded quickly. "We're currently developing a software update to refine the AI's data analysis algorithms. This should address the inaccuracies by allowing the system to better differentiate between typical and atypical user patterns."

"That sounds promising," Elena remarked. "How soon can we implement this update across all sites?"

"We're targeting to roll out the update in the next two weeks," Simon answered. "We'll need to run some preliminary tests, but if all goes well, it should be ready."

Turning the discussion towards customization, Adrian asked, "What specific customization features are being requested, and how feasible is it to implement them without compromising the therapeutic integrity of our environments?"

Lisa took a moment before replying, "The requests vary, but the most common are for more granular control over lighting and acoustic settings. We could design a few preset configurations that users can choose from, each scientifically vetted to ensure they're within therapeutic limits."

Elena considered this suggestion. "Presets sound like a balanced approach. It gives users the feeling of control without risking the therapeutic outcomes. Let's develop a range of presets and see how they are received."

The conversation shifted to the feedback from cultural adaptation initiatives. Adrian was keen on understanding how these were being perceived across different regions. "Ken, how are the culturally adapted environments performing? Is the feedback as positive as we hoped?"

Ken, responsible for overseeing these adaptations, was optimistic. "Overall, very positive. The culturally relevant modifications have been well received, particularly in Asia and South America. However, there is a desire for even deeper cultural elements to be incorporated, especially in communal spaces."

"That's an insightful observation," Adrian mused. "We should consider more extensive collaborations with local cultural consultants to enrich these spaces. It could significantly enhance patient engagement."

As the meeting drew to a close, Elena summarized the action items. "We'll proceed with the AI software update and develop a range of customizable presets for environmental controls. Additionally, we'll expand our cultural consultations to make our spaces more resonant with local traditions."

Lisa, satisfied with the productivity of the meeting, added, "I'll coordinate with all site managers to ensure these changes are implemented smoothly and continue to gather feedback on these new initiatives."

The team agreed on the strategies moving forward, and as the meeting ended, Adrian and Elena stayed back to discuss some of the finer details of implementation. Their conversation reflected a deep commitment to continuous improvement and responsiveness to the needs of their diverse global clientele.

Stepping out of the conference room, they felt reassured by the robustness of their project's framework and the collaborative spirit of their team, confident that each step taken was a stride toward enhancing therapeutic environments worldwide.

In the final week leading up to an important international conference where Dr. Adrian Harrow and Elena Markham were scheduled to present their findings and insights from the global rollout of smart environmental controls, the pair found themselves in a series of intensive preparation sessions. They aimed to showcase the project's success and the innovative strategies they had employed, focusing on how their work could be a model for similar initiatives worldwide.

In a small, quiet room filled with their presentation materials and notes, Adrian reviewed the outline of their presentation. "Elena, I think we should start with a strong introduction about the project's scope and the initial challenges we faced. Then we can transition into discussing the global implementation and the feedback we've integrated."

Elena, who was fine-tuning the slideshow, agreed. "That sounds good. I've prepared some slides with graphs showing the before and after effects of our enhancements on patient outcomes. We should also highlight the AI improvements and the customizations that we've implemented based on user feedback."

Adrian suggested further, "Let's not forget to include case studies from specific sites. The Amsterdam site, with its high user engagement and positive feedback, would be a great example. And we should also mention how we addressed the technical challenges in rural European sites."

"That's a great point," Elena responded as she added notes to the slide deck. "I'll make sure those case studies are detailed but concise. We want to keep the audience engaged and show them tangible results."

As they continued to refine their presentation, they also rehearsed their speaking parts, ensuring a smooth delivery. "When we discuss the AI enhancements, I'll take the lead since that's been a significant part of the tech team's focus," Adrian planned out loud.

Elena nodded, "And I'll handle the section on cultural adaptations and community feedback since I've been directly involved with that. It will give a personal touch to the presentation."

They also prepared for potential questions from the audience. "We should anticipate questions about scalability and potential applications in other settings," Adrian pointed out. "Let's prepare some talking points on how our project can be adapted for other health interventions."

Elena added, "And let's be ready to discuss the budget implications and funding strategies. That's always a key concern at these conferences."

The day before the conference, they held a final review session with Lisa Mendez and Simon from the tech team via video call. "Lisa, can you give us a quick rundown of the latest feedback from the sites? We want to be up-to-date if we're asked about current user satisfaction," Adrian requested.

Lisa provided the latest statistics and user comments, "Overall satisfaction has continued to improve, especially with the latest AI tweaks. I'll send you the summary so you can refer to it during the Q&A session."

Simon added, "I've also included a technical appendix to our presentation material. It has details about the AI algorithms and the backend processes, in case there are any technical questions from the audience."

With their presentation refined and their materials packed, Adrian and Elena felt prepared and confident. As they left the clinic that evening, their conversation was a mix of anticipation and excitement about the opportunity to share their hard work and success.

The clinic was quiet as they walked through the hallways, reflecting on the journey they had undertaken. They were not just going to a conference to present; they were going to demonstrate how thoughtful innovation and user-centered design could make a tangible difference in the field of therapeutic environments. Their steps echoed in the empty corridor, a rhythmic reminder of the progress they had made and the impact they hoped to continue.

Chapter 21
Beneath the Surface

After their successful presentation at the international conference, Dr. Adrian Harrow and Elena Markham returned to their clinic, energized by the positive reception and insightful questions they had received. The clinic, usually a hub of clinical activity, served today as a quiet space for reflection and strategic planning.

In the late afternoon, with the sunlight casting long shadows across the floor of Adrian's office, the two sat down to discuss the implications of their findings and the feedback they received, and to chart the future course of their project.

Adrian, leaning back in his chair, broke the silence. "The response at the conference was incredibly affirming. It's clear that our approach not only works but also sets a benchmark in therapeutic environment design. We now need to think about how we can scale and sustain this impact."

Elena, flipping through her notes from the conference, added, "Absolutely. One thing that stood out was the interest in how we manage real-time data to continually improve the user experience. There's potential there for developing a more advanced data analytics service that could benefit other health sectors."

Adrian nodded thoughtfully. "That's a good point. Our data-driven approach is one of our strongest assets. Expanding that capability could indeed offer new avenues for growth and impact."

Their discussion then shifted towards the feedback regarding cultural adaptability, a topic that had generated much interest among the conference attendees. "We need to delve deeper into cultural nuances," Elena proposed. "Perhaps we could establish a dedicated research team to work specifically on cultural adaptation. This team could work closely with local communities to tailor environments that are not just physically, but also culturally supportive."

"That's an excellent idea," Adrian agreed. "It ties back to our commitment to patient-centered care. Let's draft a proposal for setting up this team. We'll need to outline potential research goals, methodologies, and the expected outcomes."

As they continued to plan, their conversation also touched on expanding their technology offerings. "The feedback on the smart environmental controls was overwhelmingly positive," Adrian pointed out. "There might be an opportunity to commercialize this technology. We could offer it to other healthcare providers as a packaged solution."

Elena was cautious but optimistic. "That's a significant step. We need to ensure that any commercial venture we undertake doesn't distract from our core mission. Perhaps a separate commercial arm could be established to handle these opportunities?"

"That might work," Adrian mused. "Let's explore that further. We could consult with business development experts to understand the implications and best practices."

Their strategic session extended into the evening as they mapped out specific tasks and timelines for the next few months. They discussed strengthening their current sites with the latest enhancements and technologies, and also explored new sites where they could replicate their successful model.

The day's end found them still in Adrian's office, surrounded by charts and digital models of therapeutic spaces. The clinic was quiet, most staff having left for the day, giving them the space to think and plan without interruption.

As they finally stood to leave, their conversation shifted to the personal impact of their work. "It's been quite a journey," Elena said, a reflective tone in her voice. "Seeing how much we've accomplished, and the lives we've touched, it's profoundly gratifying."

Adrian nodded in agreement, locking his office door. "It is. And the potential for future impact keeps growing. Let's keep pushing the boundaries."

They walked down the corridor, their steps echoing softly, each echoing their commitment to a future where therapeutic environments would not just heal but would do so in a way that respected and embraced the diversity of human experience.

In a well-lit conference room, Dr. Adrian Harrow and Elena Markham were gathered with key members of their team, including Simon from the tech team and Lisa from research and development. They were there to discuss the expansion of the research team and to explore the possibilities of commercializing their smart environmental control technology.

Adrian started the meeting with a clear focus. "Today, we need to outline our plan for expanding the research team, particularly with a focus on cultural adaptability. We also need to discuss the feasibility of setting up a commercial arm for our technology."

Lisa was the first to speak. "On the research expansion, I've already drafted a proposal. The plan is to bring on board cultural researchers and social scientists who can help us understand and integrate cultural nuances more deeply into our environments."

Elena, looking pleased, responded, "That sounds promising, Lisa. Can you elaborate on how you envision this team working with our existing sites?"

"Absolutely," Lisa continued. "This team will initially work closely with our pilot sites, conducting in-depth studies and community engagement sessions. Their findings will directly influence how we adapt and refine our environments. The idea is to make each site a reflection of its community's values and needs."

Adrian nodded thoughtfully, then shifted the topic. "Turning to the potential commercialization of our technology—Simon, you've been looking into this. What are your thoughts?"

Simon adjusted his glasses before answering. "The commercial potential for our smart environmental controls is significant. However, to successfully commercialize, we would need to establish a separate entity or a subsidiary that focuses purely on business development, marketing, and customer support."

Elena raised a concern. "It's crucial that any commercial venture does not detract from our core mission. How can we structure this subsidiary to ensure it aligns with our ethical guidelines and mission?"

"That's a valid point," Simon agreed. "We could set up the subsidiary so that it operates independently but still adheres to the core values and principles that define our main operations. Additionally, profits from the subsidiary could be funneled back into supporting our non-commercial research and development efforts."

Lisa added her perspective, "This could actually broaden the impact of our work by making our technology accessible to a wider range of healthcare providers. Plus, the feedback and data from a commercial venture could further inform our research."

Adrian considered this, then said, "That's a compelling argument. Let's start putting together a business plan. We'll need detailed market analysis, a clear business model, and a strategic plan for the initial launch."

Elena, always focused on implementation, suggested, "I think it would be wise to consult with a business development expert to ensure we're considering all angles. We should also think about potential partners or investors who align with our mission."

"Good idea," Adrian agreed. "Simon, can you take the lead on drafting the initial business plan? And Lisa, continue to refine your proposal for the research team expansion."

Both nodded, acknowledging their tasks. "Will do," they said in unison.

As the meeting drew to a close, Adrian summarized, "We have our work cut out for us, but these are exciting developments. Expanding our research capabilities and exploring commercialization could really take our impact to the next level."

The team members left the room energized by the discussions and the road ahead. Adrian and Elena lingered for a moment, reflecting on the steps they were about to take. As they walked out of the conference room, their conversation turned to the broader implications of their decisions, not just for their project but for the communities they served. Each step they took was filled with purpose, driven by their commitment to improving therapeutic environments globally.

In the weeks following their decision to explore the commercialization of their smart environmental control technology, Dr. Adrian Harrow and Elena Markham found themselves deeply involved in the structural and strategic planning of the new commercial subsidiary. This phase was crucial, as it involved laying down the foundational principles that would ensure the subsidiary not only thrived as a business but also upheld the ethical standards and mission of their original project.

The clinic's quiet library, usually a place for medical research and patient consultation preparation, served as their planning headquarters. Here, Adrian and Elena worked with a hired business development expert, Mr. Jacob Reynolds, who specialized in ethical business practices in healthcare innovations. Their goal was to create a business model that would facilitate the commercialization process while reinforcing their commitment to improving patient care through innovative environmental design.

"Jacob, based on your experience, how can we structure this subsidiary to ensure it operates independently but remains aligned with our core values?" Adrian asked, marking out a key concern in their strategy.

Jacob, a seasoned professional with deep knowledge of ethical business strategies, suggested, "One effective approach could be to establish a governance board that includes members from both the main organization and the subsidiary. This board could oversee operations to ensure they meet ethical standards and support your mission."

Elena, considering the logistical implications, added, "That sounds practical. We'll need a clear set of guidelines on how the board interacts with both entities to prevent any conflicts of interest."

Adrian nodded in agreement, jotting down notes. "Absolutely, we must maintain transparency and accountability at all levels. Let's draft a charter for this governance board outlining their roles and responsibilities."

As part of the structural planning, they also discussed the financial aspects of establishing the subsidiary. It was essential to determine how profits would be utilized to support ongoing research and development efforts without compromising the subsidiary's growth and sustainability.

"We should consider reinvesting a significant portion of the profits back into research and development," Elena proposed. "Not only does this support our ongoing mission, but it also helps in innovating and improving the products we offer."

Jacob agreed, "Reinvestment is a wise strategy, especially in the tech-driven markets you're entering. It keeps the company at the forefront of innovation and ensures continued relevance and competitiveness."

In addition to these discussions, Adrian and Elena spent time developing a detailed rollout plan for the subsidiary. This plan included timelines for market entry, product development milestones, and strategies for marketing and customer engagement. They aimed to launch with a robust product that reflected the high standards of their research initiatives while appealing to a broad healthcare audience.

The final task for the day was setting up a meeting schedule to regularly review the progress of the subsidiary's development and to adjust strategies as needed based on real-time market feedback and operational experiences.

As they wrapped up their session in the library, Adrian looked over the plans they had outlined. "This subsidiary has the potential to significantly impact how therapeutic environments are designed and implemented worldwide. It's crucial we get this right."

Elena, closing her laptop, responded, "We're on the right track. With careful planning and adherence to our values, we can make this a success."

They left the library with a clear sense of direction and a commitment to overseeing this new venture with the same diligence and ethical rigor that had characterized their original project. The quiet of the clinic in the evening mirrored the thoughtful mood they carried with them; a reflection of the responsibility they felt towards their work and the people it served. Each step forward was measured and intentional, aimed at broadening the reach and impact of their innovations in therapeutic environmental design.

In the light-filled conference room, Dr. Adrian Harrow and Elena Markham convened a critical meeting with Jacob Reynolds, the business development expert, and Simon, the head of their technology team. The agenda was focused on finalizing the commercial strategy and preparing for the official launch of the subsidiary.

Adrian began the discussion with a clear sense of purpose. "We need to lock down our commercial strategy today. It's crucial that we have a solid plan in place that reflects our ethical standards and supports our growth. Jacob, can you start us off with the latest version of the business plan?"

Jacob nodded, opening his laptop to bring up the document. "Certainly, Adrian. The business plan has been refined to emphasize our dual goals: market penetration and support for ongoing research. We're proposing a phased launch, starting in regions where our pilot studies were most successful, as these areas already recognize the value of our technology."

Elena leaned in, interested in the specifics. "How are we addressing the marketing aspect? We need to ensure that our communication highlights not just the functionality of our products but also their contribution to patient well-being."

Jacob responded, "We've developed a marketing strategy that leverages case studies and testimonials from our pilot sites. These real-world examples will illustrate the tangible benefits of our technology. Additionally, we're planning a series of workshops and seminars to educate potential clients about the applications and advantages of our systems."

Simon chimed in, "From a technical standpoint, we've ensured that our products are scalable and adaptable. This will be a key selling point, as it allows clients to customize solutions based on their specific needs."

Adrian, satisfied with the progress, moved the conversation forward. "What about the support infrastructure? Once we launch, we must be able to support our clients effectively."

Simon was prepared for this question. "We're setting up a dedicated support team that will handle both pre-sales questions and post-sales service. This team will be trained extensively on every aspect of our products to ensure they can provide the best possible support."

Elena considered the human resources aspect. "Let's make sure that our support team not only understands the technology but also the therapeutic contexts in which it will be used. This understanding will be crucial for providing relevant and sensitive support."

Jacob added, "On the financial side, we've structured the pricing to be competitive yet reflective of the high value our products provide. We've also included options for leasing, which could make the technology accessible to a broader range of clients."

Adrian directed the final part of the meeting towards the launch timeline. "We need to set a realistic but ambitious timeline for our launch. We want to capitalize on the momentum we've built but also ensure that everything is in place for a smooth rollout."

Elena suggested, "How about aiming for a launch in Q3? That gives us enough time to finalize our preparations and conduct a comprehensive pre-launch marketing campaign."

"That works," Adrian agreed. "It gives us a clear target to work towards. Let's all focus on what needs to be finalized to meet this timeline."

As the meeting concluded, the team felt a collective sense of achievement and anticipation. They had a clear strategy and were ready to take the next steps to bring their innovative technology to the market.

Adrian and Elena stayed behind to discuss some finer points of the strategy. Their conversation reflected their excitement and the weight of their responsibilities. As they left the conference room, the setting sun cast long shadows through the windows, mirroring the lengthening impact of their work on the world outside.

Chapter 22
Resurfacing Truths

With the launch of their commercial subsidiary only weeks away, Dr. Adrian Harrow and Elena Markham convened an urgent meeting with their core team to address last-minute preparations and any emerging hurdles. The atmosphere in the clinic's largest conference room was tense yet charged with anticipation as they gathered around the large oak table, each member equipped with laptops, reports, and a sense of purpose.

Adrian opened the meeting with a direct approach. "We're close to our goal, but as with any project of this scale, we're facing some last-minute challenges that we need to address. Let's go through these systematically to ensure our launch is as smooth as possible."

Elena, always focused on coordination and details, took the lead. "First on our list is the issue with the supply chain for our sensor components. Simon, can you update us on this?"

Simon quickly responded, "Yes, we've encountered some delays with our main supplier due to unexpected demand on their end. However, I've already initiated talks with an alternative supplier who can meet our specifications and timeline. We should have a confirmation by the end of today."

"That sounds promising," Adrian replied. "Keep us updated, Simon. It's crucial that we have those components on time."

The conversation then shifted to the marketing front. Elena addressed the team's marketing director, Lisa. "Lisa, how are we progressing with the pre-launch marketing campaign? Are we on track with the planned activities?"

Lisa, flipping through her digital planner, confirmed, "We're mostly on track. The digital ads are rolling out as scheduled, and the response has been encouraging. However, we're a bit behind on the educational seminars for potential clients. We need a bit more time to finalize the content and confirm the speakers."

Elena nodded thoughtfully. "It's vital that those seminars provide substantial value to attendees. Let's prioritize finalizing them. Maybe we can shift some resources from less critical tasks to get these ready."

The discussion then moved to training for the support team, a critical component of the post-launch plan. Adrian asked, "How is the training going for our support team? They need to be fully prepared by launch."

The head of customer support, Michael, reassured the group. "Training is going well. The team is responsive and enthusiastic. We're conducting final role-plays next week to ensure they can handle all types of customer inquiries and issues."

"Excellent," Adrian responded. "Elena, perhaps you and I should sit in on some of those sessions. It would give us a good sense of how prepared the team really is."

Elena agreed, "That's a good idea. We need to be confident in their ability to represent our brand and support our users effectively."

Lastly, Adrian addressed the overall readiness for the launch. "We need to ensure that every team is aligned and ready for the launch. Let's have a final review session next week. I want every team lead to report on their readiness and any potential issues that might impact the launch."

Each team lead nodded in agreement, understanding the importance of this final push. As the meeting drew to a close, Adrian reiterated the significance of the upcoming weeks. "This launch is not just about bringing a product to market. It's about setting a new standard in therapeutic environments. Let's make sure we live up to our own expectations."

As they left the conference room, the team felt a renewed sense of urgency and commitment. Adrian and Elena lingered for a moment, discussing the day's outcomes. Their conversation was pragmatic but optimistic, reflecting their readiness to tackle the challenges head-on and their anticipation of the positive impact their work was about to make.

As the launch date of their commercial subsidiary approached, Dr. Adrian Harrow and Elena Markham found themselves deep in the throes of final preparations. The clinic, usually a sanctuary of calm and order, had transformed into a bustling command center, with team members moving quickly and conversations about logistics and last-minute details filling the air.

Adrian was in his office, poring over the latest deployment schedule when Elena knocked and entered, her expression a mix of anticipation and concern. "We're nearly there," she announced, sitting down across from him. "I've just reviewed the final checklist with the team. There are a few minor issues still to be resolved, but nothing that should delay our launch."

"That's reassuring to hear," Adrian replied, leaning back in his chair. "What's the status of the marketing materials? Are they ready to go live?"

Elena nodded. "Yes, all materials have been finalized and are scheduled for release. The media buy is in place, and our online campaigns are queued up for launch day. Lisa has done a tremendous job ensuring everything aligns with our branding and message."

Adrian's attention then shifted to the technical side of things. "And the support team? Are they ready to handle customer inquiries from day one?"

"They've undergone extensive training and completed several simulation exercises. Michael confirmed they're well-prepared," Elena responded, her tone confident.

Satisfied with the updates, Adrian stood and suggested they walk through the operations center to get a feel for the atmosphere and address any last-minute concerns the team might have. As they walked, the palpable buzz of activity around them was a testament to the hard work and dedication of their team.

Passing through the bustling hallways, they paused to speak with Simon, who was coordinating the final tests on the environmental control systems. "Simon, how are the systems holding up? Any issues with scalability now that we're going live?"

Simon looked up from his monitor, a slight frown on his face that quickly turned into a smile. "We had a couple of hiccups during the stress tests, but I'm happy to report that all issues have been resolved. The systems are stable and ready for the rollout."

"That's excellent," Adrian said, clapping Simon on the shoulder. "Great work."

Their next stop was the customer support hub, where Michael was overseeing the final training session. Observing the team in action, Adrian and Elena listened as the support staff confidently handled mock inquiries, demonstrating their expertise and readiness.

Feeling reassured, Adrian whispered to Elena, "They seem ready to me. What do you think?"

Elena, observing the operations, nodded in agreement. "They're more than ready. Michael has done a fantastic job here."

As they continued their tour, the last stop was the marketing department, where Lisa was overseeing the launch of the digital campaign. "Everything's set to go, Elena," Lisa reported, her eyes never leaving her screens. "We're synchronized across all platforms. Once we give the green light, everything will go live according to plan."

"Thank you, Lisa. Keep us posted on the initial responses once we launch," Elena instructed, satisfied with the progress.

Returning to Adrian's office, they reviewed the events of the day. Each department had confirmed readiness, and all that remained was for the launch to commence. They discussed the significance of the next few days, knowing that their efforts could potentially reshape how therapeutic environments were perceived and utilized globally.

As they concluded their day, the clinic began to quiet down, the evening shift leaving for the night. Adrian and Elena shared a quiet moment of reflection, looking over the clinic grounds from the office window. The peace of the evening was a stark contrast to the day's busyness, a reminder of the impact of their work extending far beyond the walls of the clinic.

On the morning of the launch, the atmosphere in the clinic was electric. Dr. Adrian Harrow and Elena Markham were in the central hub where all major operations were being coordinated. Teams from marketing, tech support, and product management were in their final positions, ready to manage the rollout.

Adrian, checking his watch, turned to Elena. "It's almost time. How are you feeling about everything?"

Elena, with a cautious smile, responded, "Optimistic, but you know me—I won't relax until we see how the market responds. How about you?"

"I'm the same," Adrian admitted. "Let's do a final check-in with the teams. I want to make sure everyone is confident and ready."

They started with the marketing team, where Lisa was monitoring the digital dashboards. "Lisa, are we all set here?"

Lisa nodded, her focus unwavering from the screens. "All systems are go, Adrian. We're ready to launch the campaign the moment you give the word. The team is prepared for all scenarios."

"Excellent," Adrian replied. "Let's move on to the tech support team."

At the tech support hub, Michael was double-checking communication lines and system readiness. "Michael, are your teams ready for the incoming queries?"

Michael looked up, his expression one of focused readiness. "We are prepared, Elena. The team is well-drilled, and we have all the troubleshooting protocols in place. We can handle the initial queries and any issues that come up."

"Great to hear," Elena said, visibly relieved. "And Simon, how are the systems holding up?"

Simon, nearby, overseeing the technical monitoring team, gave a thumbs-up. "All systems are operational. We've done all the checks and rechecks. The infrastructure is holding steady, and we'll keep an eye on everything as we go live."

Adrian, feeling reassured, suggested, "Let's gather the team for a quick pep talk. This is a big moment for all of us."

Gathering everyone in the central hub, Adrian addressed the team. "This is a milestone day for us. Each of you has played a crucial role in getting us to this point. Whatever happens today, know that I'm proud of the work we've done and the integrity with which we've done it."

Elena added, "Your hard work and dedication reflect not just in this project but in the impact we're about to make in healthcare environments globally. Let's keep our focus and execute as we've planned. We're doing something great here."

The team, energized by their leaders' confidence, clapped and cheered, ready to launch.

Adrian, looking at Elena, said, "It's time. Let's do this."

Elena nodded, and together they gave the final nod to Lisa to initiate the launch.

As the digital campaigns went live and the product officially hit the market, Adrian and Elena watched the real-time reactions and data pouring in. The early responses were positive, a testament to the meticulous planning and effort of their team.

Throughout the day, they stayed in the hub, addressing minor hiccups and making slight adjustments based on real-time feedback. The day was long, and the work was intense, but as the sun began to set, the initial data confirmed the successful uptake of their technology.

As the team began to wind down, Adrian and Elena took a moment to step outside. They stood in the quiet of the early evening, watching the sunset over the clinic.

"Today was a good day," Adrian finally said, a small smile playing on his lips.

"It was," Elena agreed, "And it's just the beginning."

Together, they walked back inside to join their team in celebrating the day's success and to plan for the next phase of their journey. The clinic's corridors, now quiet, seemed to echo with the day's achievements and the promise of what was yet to come.

As the excitement of the launch day settled, Dr. Adrian Harrow and Elena Markham shifted their focus towards analyzing the outcomes and planning the next steps for their newly launched subsidiary. The clinic was quiet in the aftermath, providing a stark contrast to the previous day's buzz, allowing them both a moment to reflect and strategize without interruption.

Adrian spent the early morning hours in his office, surrounded by various reports and analytics on his desk. He meticulously went through the data, noting trends and outliers in the customer uptake and the feedback collected through the support lines. The numbers were promising, but he knew that the real work of sustaining the growth and managing the roll-out effectively was just beginning.

Elena, meanwhile, was in her office, coordinating with the marketing and customer support teams to synthesize the feedback received from the first batch of clients. She organized the information into actionable categories, prioritizing issues that needed immediate attention and those that could enhance the product offering in the future. Her focus was on maintaining the momentum generated by the successful launch and leveraging it to improve service delivery.

Late in the morning, Adrian and Elena convened in a small meeting room to consolidate their findings and discuss their strategy moving forward. They laid out all the data they had gathered, along with feedback reports and market analysis documents.

Adrian began the discussion. "The initial sales figures have exceeded our projections, which is excellent. However, there are a few areas where the feedback suggests we could improve, particularly in simplifying the user interface for less tech-savvy clients."

Elena added, "I've noticed that too. The support team has flagged several calls regarding difficulties with some of the advanced settings. We might need to consider a quick update or perhaps a supplemental user guide."

They both agreed that educating their users would be crucial. Adrian suggested, "Let's schedule some webinars and interactive Q&A sessions for our users. It could help alleviate some of the basic issues and improve user satisfaction."

Elena, noting this down, proposed, "We should also look into enhancing our customer service response time. While the feedback has been positive about the quality of support, faster response times could significantly boost our client satisfaction ratings."

The discussion then moved to future expansions. With the successful launch in their primary markets, Adrian and Elena considered the possibility of introducing their product to additional regions. "We need to start preparing for the next phase of expansion," Adrian noted. "Let's begin by conducting market research in other regions where our pilot studies suggest high potential."

Elena, always methodical in her approach, outlined the next steps. "I'll coordinate with the research team to start this analysis. We'll need to understand not just the market potential but also any regulatory hurdles we might face."

As they wrapped up their meeting, they planned a series of departmental briefings for the following week to communicate the current status and next steps to their teams. They knew the importance of keeping everyone aligned and motivated.

Leaving the meeting room, Adrian and Elena felt a mix of relief and anticipation. The launch was only the beginning of what they hoped would be a significant contribution to the field of therapeutic environments. Walking back to their offices, they discussed the upcoming briefings and the importance of maintaining clear and open communication with their teams.

The clinic was bathed in the soft light of the late afternoon sun as they parted ways at the corridor junction, each headed to continue their preparations. The quiet hallways echoed their steps, a reminder of the journey they had embarked on and the long path still ahead.

Chapter 23
Preparing the Seal

Following the successful launch and immediate aftermath of their commercial subsidiary, Dr. Adrian Harrow and Elena Markham were now focused on the next phase: strategic expansion into new markets. This phase was crucial, requiring careful navigation of regulatory environments and strategic decision-making to ensure the global reach of their innovative therapeutic environments.

In Adrian's office, stacked with market research reports and regulatory guidelines, he and Elena were deep in discussion over the expansion strategy. They needed to ensure that every new market they entered was approached with a thorough understanding of local regulations and cultural nuances.

Elena was examining a detailed report on regulatory hurdles in various countries. "Based on this report, our next big challenge is to navigate the diverse regulatory frameworks in Asia and Europe. Each region has its own set of rules that we need to comply with, which could affect our timelines and costs."

Adrian, looking over the market analysis charts, nodded in agreement. "Yes, and it's crucial that we understand these fully before we make any moves. We need to consider hiring local experts or perhaps even partnering with local firms who understand these markets intimately."

The room was quiet, save for the rustling of papers and the occasional click of a computer mouse, as they absorbed the information in front of them. Their strategy had to be meticulous, balancing ambition with careful planning to avoid potential pitfalls.

Elena then suggested, "What about setting up advisory boards in each region? They could provide us with ongoing advice not just on regulatory matters but also on cultural aspects that might affect product reception."

"That's an excellent idea," Adrian replied. "Local insights could make a significant difference in how we position ourselves in each market. Let's put together a list of potential candidates for these advisory boards."

As they discussed potential candidates, they also contemplated the expansion's impact on their operations. They needed to ensure that their infrastructure could support the increased demand. Adrian was particularly concerned about the supply chain. "We need to ensure our supply chain can handle the expansion without hiccups. Perhaps it's time to look into additional manufacturing partners."

Elena agreed, marking down action items. "I'll arrange meetings with our current suppliers to discuss scaling up operations. Additionally, I'll start scouting for new suppliers who can meet our quality standards and delivery timelines."

Their conversation also touched on the importance of maintaining the quality and efficacy of their products as they scaled. "It's imperative that our expansion doesn't dilute the quality of our offerings," Adrian stressed. "We must keep our R&D team in the loop and ensure they are part of the expansion discussions."

"Agreed," Elena said. "Let's schedule a meeting with the R&D team next week to discuss how they can support the expansion effectively."

As they wrapped up their strategic session, Adrian and Elena felt prepared but cautious. They had a clear roadmap but were aware of the challenges that lay ahead. They left the office to brief their senior management team, ready to communicate the strategies and gather additional insights.

Walking through the clinic's corridors, their conversation turned to the team they would need to build to manage these new challenges. Each decision they made, each step they took, was with the aim of transforming therapeutic environments on a global scale. The clinic, quiet in the late afternoon, echoed with their determined steps, a testament to the journey they were navigating together.

In a spacious, brightly lit conference room, Dr. Adrian Harrow and Elena Markham sat across from each other, surrounded by their core team. The focus of today's meeting was to discuss and finalize the formation of global partnerships and ensure compliance with international regulatory standards, crucial steps for their strategic expansion.

Adrian began the meeting with a clear directive, "We need to solidify our global partnerships and make sure we're fully compliant with all international regulations before we proceed further. This is key to our successful expansion."

Elena added, "I've contacted several potential partners in Asia and Europe. We need partners who not only understand the local market but can also navigate the regulatory landscape effectively."

Simon, their tech lead, chimed in, "From a technical standpoint, it's crucial that any partner we choose has the capability to integrate our systems seamlessly with the local healthcare infrastructures. Compatibility is essential for the smooth deployment of our technology."

Adrian nodded in agreement, "Absolutely, Simon. Let's ensure that our due diligence covers technical compatibility extensively. Elena, could you update us on the regulatory hurdles?"

Elena had prepared a detailed report. "Each region has its unique challenges. For instance, in Europe, GDPR compliance is a significant concern, particularly how we handle patient data. In Asia, the regulatory environment varies widely from country to country, which complicates our compliance efforts."

Adrian considered this, "That's complex but manageable. We might need to tailor our approach to each country, which could affect our timelines and costs."

Lisa, the head of regulatory affairs, suggested, "I recommend we set up a specialized regulatory team for each region. This team can work closely with our partners to ensure compliance and handle any legal challenges that might arise."

"That's a good approach, Lisa," Adrian responded. "Let's draft a proposal for these teams by the end of the week. We need to move quickly but carefully."

Elena, thinking ahead about the operational aspects, said, "Once we establish these teams, we should start with a pilot project in one of the less complex markets. This would give us valuable insights and help us refine our approach before tackling more challenging regions."

Adrian liked the idea, "A pilot project sounds like a prudent first step. Let's choose a market where we have strong potential partners and a relatively straightforward regulatory environment. Simon, could you work with Elena to identify such a market?"

Simon nodded, "I'll start on that immediately. We'll consider both technical and regulatory perspectives to select the right market."

As the meeting drew to a close, Adrian summarized, "We have a solid plan in place. Elena will finalize potential partnerships and start forming the specialized regulatory teams. Simon will identify the best market for our pilot project. I want us to reconvene next week with updates on all fronts."

The team felt a renewed sense of purpose as they left the conference room. Their discussions were not just theoretical; they were planning and acting on strategies that would expand their reach and impact globally.

Adrian and Elena stayed back to discuss some of the finer points of their strategy. As they walked out of the conference room, their conversation continued, focused on how best to align their resources to meet the upcoming challenges. The clinic's corridors, now quiet, seemed to absorb their strategic deliberations, a backdrop to the unfolding narrative of their ambitious global expansion.

In a well-equipped meeting room filled with digital displays and global maps, Dr. Adrian Harrow and Elena Markham were gathered with their international expansion team. Today's session was dedicated to initiating the pilot project in their selected market—Singapore. The team was poised to dissect every aspect of the operation, from logistical setups to compliance checks.

Adrian started the discussion with a direct focus, "We've chosen Singapore as our pilot market due to its robust healthcare system and straightforward regulatory environment. The goal here is to establish a successful model that can be replicated in other regions. Simon, what's the status on the technical preparation?"

Simon looked up from his laptop, where he displayed a detailed timeline. "All systems are go for Singapore. The tech infrastructure there aligns well with our requirements, and preliminary tests show our systems are fully compatible. We've also set up data handling and security protocols that comply with local regulations."

Elena jumped in, her tone reflective of the task's magnitude, "That's great, Simon. On the partnership front, we've secured a strong local partner who is well-versed in the healthcare landscape. They'll assist not just in deployment, but also in navigating ongoing regulatory and market dynamics."

Adrian nodded, pleased with the progress. "Excellent work, Elena. Now, let's talk about the operational rollout. Michael, how is the support team gearing up for this?"

Michael, responsible for customer support, was ready with his update. "We have trained a dedicated team specifically for the Singapore market. They're not only tech-savvy but also trained in local customer service etiquette to ensure they meet cultural expectations. Additionally, we're setting up a localized call center to handle any on-the-ground issues promptly."

"Good foresight, Michael. It's crucial that our support system is as robust as our technology," Adrian replied, marking notes on his digital pad. "Lisa, can you update us on the regulatory compliance side of things?"

Lisa, who had been coordinating closely with legal advisors, responded confidently, "We're fully compliant with all local healthcare regulations. We've conducted several reviews with our legal team and our local partner to ensure that every aspect of our operation meets or exceeds statutory requirements. We'll continue monitoring any changes in the regulatory landscape to stay compliant."

Adrian, looking around the room, felt a sense of collective achievement. "This pilot is not just about testing our product in a new market—it's about setting a standard for all our future operations. Everyone's clarity on their role and the thoroughness of your preparations will make this a success."

Elena, always focused on strategic implications, added, "Once we launch in Singapore, we'll need to gather data and feedback rigorously. This information will be invaluable as we refine our model before expanding further. We need to capture not just operational data, but also user satisfaction and any market-specific challenges that arise."

"Absolutely," Adrian agreed. "Let's make sure our feedback mechanisms are as effective as our deployment strategies. We need real-time data to make real-time decisions."

As the meeting concluded, the team felt well-prepared and motivated. They had a clear plan and defined roles, and the pilot project was more than just a test—it was the blueprint for their future global strategy.

Walking out of the meeting room, Adrian and Elena discussed the day's outcomes. Their conversation was detailed and strategic, reflecting not only the complexities of their undertaking but also their commitment to transforming therapeutic environments on a global scale.

Their steps echoed through the empty hallways of the clinic, each echo a reminder of the progress they were making toward a broader, more impactful future.

The early stages of the Singapore pilot project had been set in motion, and it was time for Dr. Adrian Harrow and Elena Markham to review the initial results and feedback. They convened a meeting in the clinic's main strategy room, where the walls were lined with digital screens displaying real-time data and analytics from the pilot.

Adrian initiated the meeting with a focused question, "Let's start with the initial feedback. Simon, can you provide us with an overview of how the systems are performing?"

Simon, who had been closely monitoring the technical aspects, replied, "The systems are performing well within the expected parameters. We've had a few minor technical queries, but nothing outside the ordinary. The real-time data integration with local healthcare providers has been particularly smooth, which is a great sign."

Elena, keen on understanding the user interaction, turned to Michael. "Michael, what's the word from the ground? How are the users responding to our systems?"

Michael had the latest user feedback reports ready. "The response has been overwhelmingly positive. Users appreciate the customization features we've incorporated, especially the ability to adjust environmental settings to their preferences. However, there is feedback about wanting more intuitive controls for older demographics, who find the current interface a bit challenging."

"That's important feedback," Adrian noted. "We should consider simplifying the interface in our next update. Simon, can you work with your team on that?"

"Absolutely," Simon confirmed. "We can look at user-friendly designs that have worked well in other markets and see how we can adapt those for our systems."

Elena then raised another critical point, "It's not just about user interface. We need to ensure that the overall experience is aligned with our brand promise. Lisa, how are we doing on compliance and overall service quality?"

Lisa, having coordinated the compliance efforts, responded, "Compliance is on track, and service quality is high. Our local partners have been instrumental in maintaining our standards, and continuous training has kept our service team sharp. However, we need to keep an eye on response times, which have edged up slightly as demand increases."

Adrian, always looking at the bigger picture, suggested, "We should consider scaling our support team if demand continues to grow. Maintaining high service quality is crucial."

"Agreed," Elena said. "I'll look into logistics and budgeting for scaling the support team. It's better to plan for growth now rather than be caught unprepared."

The discussion then turned to future steps. "Based on the success we're seeing, how soon can we start replicating this model in other markets?" Adrian asked, addressing the group.

Simon was optimistic but cautious. "Given the positive data, I think we could start preparations for other markets soon. However, I recommend a phased approach, where we gradually introduce the system based on regional readiness and compliance."

"That sounds prudent," Adrian agreed. "Let's start identifying potential markets and prepare a phased rollout plan. Elena, could you lead that effort?"

"Of course," Elena replied. "I'll start with a market analysis to identify where our systems could have the most impact and outline potential challenges."

As the meeting concluded, the team felt confident about the progress of the Singapore pilot and the prospects of expanding their reach. They had a clear set of actions and were prepared to adjust their strategies based on real-world data and feedback.

Walking out of the strategy room, Adrian and Elena continued their discussion about the next phases, committed to adapting and evolving their approach to meet global needs. The clinic, quiet in the evening, echoed with their purposeful conversation, a testament to their dedication to making a global impact on therapeutic environments.

Chapter 24
The Final Confrontation

Dr. Adrian Harrow and Elena Markham were seated in a high-tech conference room surrounded by their strategic planning team, focusing on the expansion of their innovative therapeutic environments into new global markets. Today's meeting was particularly crucial as they aimed to finalize decisions based on the comprehensive market analysis Elena had overseen.

Elena opened the discussion, presenting the core findings of her analysis. "The market research has given us a clear indication of where our next opportunities lie. Based on healthcare infrastructure readiness and regulatory environments, our top candidates for expansion are Japan, Germany, and Canada."

Adrian, looking over the documents in front of him, nodded in approval. "These markets have robust healthcare systems and a high receptivity to technological innovations in healthcare. What are the specific challenges we face in each?"

Elena flipped through her digital report, highlighting key points. "In Japan, the challenge will be navigating the language barrier and local business practices, which are quite unique. For Germany, the regulatory requirements are stringent, but it's nothing we haven't handled before. Canada, on the other hand, will be the easiest in terms of regulatory and cultural adaptation but has intense competition in the healthcare technology sector."

Simon, the tech team lead, chimed in, "For Japan and Germany, we'll need to invest significantly in localization of our software and training materials. This means not just translation, but also cultural adaptation to ensure our product is user-friendly and meets local expectations."

"That's a good point, Simon," Adrian responded thoughtfully. "Localization can be resource-intensive. How prepared are we to handle this?"

Simon assured him, "We've started vetting agencies that specialize in medical technology localization and have a good track record. Once we decide to move forward, we can engage one of them to ensure our materials and systems are appropriately adapted."

Elena then directed the conversation towards potential partners in these markets. "I've identified several potential partners in each region. These are firms that not only have the distribution channels we need but also align with our ethical values and commitment to quality."

Adrian considered this. "Partnerships will be crucial. We need to ensure any partners we choose can truly represent our brand and manage the nuances of their local markets effectively. Elena, could you initiate preliminary talks to gauge their interest and compatibility with our goals?"

"I'm on it," Elena confirmed. "I'll start with setting up exploratory meetings with each to discuss potential collaboration."

The discussion then shifted towards the investment required for these expansions. "We need to be mindful of our budget allocations," Adrian pointed out. "While all three markets are attractive, we may need to prioritize based on the potential return on investment and strategic value."

"That's true," Elena agreed. "Perhaps we should consider launching in one market first, possibly Canada, as it presents the least regulatory hurdles and allows us to refine our approach before tackling more complex markets like Japan and Germany."

"That sounds like a strategic approach," Adrian approved. "Let's prepare a detailed proposal for entering the Canadian market first. We can use it as a pilot for broader European and Asian expansions."

As the meeting drew to a close, the team felt well-prepared and aligned on the next steps. They had a clear direction and a strategy that balanced ambition with careful planning.

Adrian and Elena stayed behind to summarize the day's decisions and prepare for their upcoming presentations to the board. Their discussion was detailed, reflecting both the opportunities and the challenges ahead.

Walking out of the conference room, they continued their conversation, their voices echoing slightly in the now-quiet corridor, discussing the transformative potential of their next moves. Their commitment to enhancing healthcare through innovative therapeutic environments was evident, driving them to navigate new territories with precision and care.

As the decision to prioritize the Canadian market was set into motion, Dr. Adrian Harrow and Elena Markham shifted their efforts towards detailed planning and preparation for this new venture. The clinic, usually a bustling hub of innovation and patient care, took on the added buzz of strategic market entry discussions.

In the days following the strategic meeting, Adrian and Elena worked meticulously to compile all necessary documentation and plans for a successful market entry. They reviewed reports on Canadian healthcare technology trends, competitor analyses, and potential partner profiles, ensuring that each step they took was informed and strategic.

Elena took the lead on refining the partnership strategy. She reached out to potential Canadian partners, arranging meetings to explore synergies and collaborative possibilities. Her approach was methodical, focusing on partners with strong local networks and a reputation for quality and innovation.

Meanwhile, Adrian focused on operational logistics. He coordinated with Simon and the tech team to ensure that their technology would be fully compatible with Canadian healthcare standards and practices. He also oversaw the adaptation of their systems to include French language options, recognizing the importance of bilingual support in Canada.

Throughout this process, regular meetings were held to ensure all team members were aligned and aware of their responsibilities. In one such meeting, Adrian addressed the group, emphasizing the importance of thoroughness. "It's crucial that we enter the Canadian market with a strong, well-prepared presence. We need to demonstrate not only the superiority of our technology but also our commitment to adapting to local needs."

Elena added, "Our partnerships here will set the tone for future expansions. We must choose partners who share our vision and can help us navigate the local landscape effectively."

The team's preparation also included developing a robust marketing plan tailored to the Canadian audience. They planned targeted campaigns highlighting the benefits of their technology in improving patient outcomes, with a particular focus on the Canadian healthcare system's specific challenges and needs.

As the launch date approached, Adrian and Elena reviewed the final checklist, ensuring nothing was overlooked. They double-checked everything from marketing materials and legal compliances to logistical arrangements for the deployment of their systems.

Their thorough preparation was evident in the calm yet focused way they approached the final days before the launch. The clinic, while still a center for patient care, had seamlessly incorporated these expansive operational tasks.

In the quiet moments of the evening, after the staff had left and the preparations for the day were complete, Adrian and Elena often found themselves reflecting on the magnitude of their undertaking. They discussed the potential impacts of their entry into the Canadian market and how it could pave the way for further international expansions.

These moments of reflection were crucial, not just for strategic planning but also for reaffirming their commitment to their mission. As they left the clinic under the soft glow of the streetlights, their conversation continued, a blend of strategic foresight and mindful planning, echoing softly in the empty streets.

Their steps were measured, mirroring the deliberate pace of their project's expansion, each step forward a testament to their careful planning and hopeful anticipation of the impact they were about to make in a new market.

With the strategy set and all preparations checked and rechecked, Dr. Adrian Harrow and Elena Markham approached the launch of their therapeutic environments in Canada with a mixture of excitement and the natural apprehension that accompanies stepping into new terrain. The clinic had become the operational heart from which all planning and execution for the expansion pulsed.

On launch day, the early morning light filtered through the blinds of Adrian's office where he and Elena were seated, going over the day's schedule. Each item on their agenda was pivotal, designed to ensure that the rollout proceeded smoothly and any unforeseen issues could be managed swiftly.

The morning was spent in briefings with the tech and support teams. Adrian had arranged for a virtual meeting with the Canadian partners to synchronize their efforts, ensuring that everyone was on the same page. The partners were enthusiastic, having fully bought into the vision and potential of the new therapeutic environments. They discussed final details, emphasizing the importance of maintaining a clear line of communication throughout the day.

Elena, meanwhile, coordinated with the marketing team, ensuring that the promotional materials were launched according to the planned schedule. The marketing campaign was tailored to highlight the innovative features of the technology, emphasizing how it could revolutionize patient care in Canada. Social media channels buzzed with activity, and the initial responses were encouraging, showing a keen interest from both healthcare providers and potential users.

Throughout the day, Adrian and Elena kept close tabs on the deployment, monitoring the installation of their systems in several key Canadian healthcare facilities. They had chosen these initial locations carefully, aiming to demonstrate their technology's effectiveness across a variety of healthcare settings.

As reports came in from the field, it was clear that the installations were proceeding without significant issues. Minor technical queries were quickly resolved by the support team, who were well-prepared and responsive. Feedback from the healthcare staff was positive, with many expressing excitement about the potential benefits for their patients.

In the afternoon, Adrian and Elena reviewed the real-time data being collected from the new installations. This data was crucial not only for ensuring the smooth operation of their systems but also for gathering early insights into their effectiveness in a real-world setting. The data showed promising usage patterns and user engagement, aligning with their expectations and projections.

As the sun began to set, casting long shadows across the clinic, Adrian and Elena finally had a moment to breathe. The initial phase of the launch had been a success, but they knew that the real work—ensuring sustained success and acceptance of their product—was just beginning.

They spent the early evening strategizing the next steps, discussing how to leverage the day's success to further penetrate the Canadian market. They planned follow-up visits and additional training sessions for the healthcare providers, wanting to ensure that the technology was used to its fullest potential.

As they left the clinic, the weight of the day's efforts felt lighter on their shoulders, tempered by the satisfaction of having navigated this complex undertaking effectively. The quiet of the evening was a stark contrast to the day's dynamism, offering a moment of reflection.

Their conversation as they walked to their cars was less about the immediate tasks and more about the broader implications of their work. Every successful installation and every positive report was a step towards changing the therapeutic landscape, not just in Canada but globally. As they parted ways, the fading light seemed to underscore the significance of their efforts—a reminder of the impact they were beginning to make on a global scale.

After a successful launch day, Dr. Adrian Harrow and Elena Markham were now focused on monitoring the long-term success of their initiative in Canada and planning for further expansion. The clinic served as their base, from which they orchestrated an extensive follow-up on the installation of their systems across various healthcare facilities.

In the weeks following the launch, Adrian and Elena set up a comprehensive monitoring system that allowed them to track the usage, effectiveness, and user satisfaction of their products in real time. This data was crucial not only for ensuring operational success but also for gathering insights that could inform their approach in other markets.

One morning, as they reviewed the latest data, Adrian commented on the positive trends. "It looks like our systems are not only being adopted as intended but are also enhancing patient care significantly. The feedback on user interface and functionality has been overwhelmingly positive."

Elena, who was examining user satisfaction reports, added, "Yes, and it seems our focus on training and support has paid off. The staff at these facilities are not just using the technology; they're really maximizing its potential. This is exactly the kind of outcome we were hoping for."

Their discussion then shifted towards expansion. Adrian pulled up a map on the screen showing potential new markets. "Based on our success in Canada, I think we're ready to start planning our next phase of expansion. The question now is, where do we focus our efforts next?"

Elena leaned in, pointing to a few key areas on the map. "Given our analysis, I believe Germany and Japan are our next best bets. Both markets have robust healthcare systems, are receptive to new technologies, and we've already started the groundwork on regulatory compliance."

"That makes sense," Adrian agreed. "Let's initiate detailed market entry plans for these countries. We'll need to adapt our approach slightly for each to account for cultural and regulatory differences, but I think we can replicate our success in Canada."

Elena nodded, making a note. "I'll start by deepening our partnerships in these regions. We need strong local allies not just for distribution and sales, but also to help navigate the local business landscape."

Adrian considered the broader implications. "As we expand, we'll also need to scale up our operations and possibly look into additional manufacturing partnerships. We have to ensure that we can meet increased demand without compromising on quality."

"Absolutely," Elena responded. "I'll also coordinate with Simon and the tech team to ensure our systems can be easily adapted for these new markets. The last thing we want is technical issues slowing us down."

As they concluded their meeting, they decided to schedule regular updates on the progress of these plans. They knew that managing this expansion would require careful coordination and a deep understanding of each new market.

Walking out of the meeting room, they discussed the need to maintain a balance between rapid growth and the meticulous attention to detail that had made their Canadian launch a success. Each step they planned was with an eye towards sustainable growth and the long-term vision of their company.

As they parted ways, the quiet of the clinic in the early morning hours gave way to a day full of potential. Adrian and Elena were not just running a clinic or a tech company; they were at the helm of a venture that was setting new standards in healthcare environments globally. Their conversations might have quieted with distance, but their shared commitment to their vision continued to echo in their respective paths.

Chapter 25
Shattering Shadows

In a conference room filled with morning light, Dr. Adrian Harrow and Elena Markham were seated across from each other, their laptops open, and numerous documents spread out in front of them. Today's focus was on refining their expansion strategies for Germany and Japan, countries identified as key targets in their global growth plan. Joining them via video call were their regional managers for Germany and Japan, providing local insights crucial for adapting their strategy effectively.

Adrian initiated the meeting with a strategic prompt. "Let's start by discussing our entry strategy for Germany. Klaus, can you update us on the regulatory progress and any potential barriers we might face?"

Klaus, the German regional manager, was prepared. "Yes, Dr. Harrow. We've made good progress with the regulatory bodies here. However, the certification process is rigorous, and we'll need to ensure our systems meet all local standards, which are quite strict, especially regarding data security."

Elena, noting this, asked, "How long do you anticipate this will delay our launch timeline?"

Klaus responded, "If we prioritize our efforts on compliance, I believe we can manage to stay on schedule. We might need additional support from our tech team to adapt our systems to these standards."

Adrian turned his attention to the Japanese market. "Now, moving to Japan, Akemi, what's the status there, particularly regarding partnership development?"

Akemi, the Japanese regional manager, answered, "We've identified several potential partners who are enthusiastic about our technology. However, building trust and finalizing partnerships here involves a lengthy process, given the business culture in Japan. We need to be seen as committed to long-term relationships, not just entering the market for short-term gains."

"That's an important point, Akemi," Adrian acknowledged. "Elena, perhaps we should consider a series of engagements in Japan to demonstrate our long-term commitment to the market and our potential partners."

Elena agreed, "Absolutely, I suggest we arrange a series of workshops and possibly even a local conference to showcase our technology and its benefits directly to potential partners and healthcare providers."

Turning the conversation towards marketing strategies, Adrian asked, "Klaus and Akemi, what are your thoughts on how we should approach marketing in your respective markets?"

Klaus shared his perspective first. "In Germany, our marketing should focus on the precision and reliability of our technology. German consumers respond well to products that are technically robust and offer clear, practical benefits."

Akemi then provided insights for Japan. "In Japan, it's essential that our marketing highlights how our technology can improve patient care, emphasizing personalization and comfort. Additionally, we should use testimonials and case studies, as personal stories are very persuasive here."

Adrian considered these insights thoughtfully. "Thank you both. Let's integrate these specific marketing strategies into our overall plan. Elena, could you oversee the adaptation of our marketing materials to align with these strategies?"

"Yes, I'll coordinate with our marketing team and ensure that we localize our materials effectively for each market," Elena confirmed.

As the meeting concluded, Adrian summarized their action items. "Klaus will focus on navigating the regulatory landscape in Germany with support from our tech team. Akemi will continue to deepen relationships with potential partners in Japan. Elena will manage the localization of our marketing efforts. Let's reconvene next week with updates."

Everyone nodded in agreement, understanding their roles and the importance of the tasks at hand. Adrian and Elena stayed behind to discuss some additional details about resource allocation for these markets.

As they left the conference room, their conversation shifted to the broader impact of their global strategy, reflecting on how each market's success could influence their operations worldwide. Their steps through the hallway echoed with a sense of purpose, each stride taking them closer to realizing their vision on a global scale.

As the sun began its descent, casting a golden hue across the bustling clinic, Dr. Adrian Harrow and Elena Markham were deeply entrenched in their efforts to tailor their innovative therapeutic environments for the German and Japanese markets. The success of their Canadian expansion provided a blueprint, yet each new market demanded a unique approach, especially in the realms of technology adaptation and relationship building.

In Germany, Adrian focused on ensuring the technological adaptations met the stringent local standards. He worked closely with Simon and the tech team, who were tasked with integrating advanced data security measures into their systems—a critical requirement in the German market. They tested and retested the systems, simulating various security scenarios to identify any potential vulnerabilities. This meticulous process was vital, not just for meeting regulatory approvals but for maintaining the trust of their future German clients.

Meanwhile, Elena spearheaded the initiative to deepen their market engagement in Japan. Understanding the importance of relationships in Japanese business culture, she arranged for a series of in-person visits to Tokyo. During these visits, she and the local team met with potential partners and healthcare providers, presenting detailed demonstrations of their technology and discussing potential collaboration opportunities. These meetings were more than just business transactions; they were opportunities to build trust and mutual understanding.

The dialogue during these meetings was carefully crafted to resonate with their Japanese counterparts. Elena ensured that every word spoken underscored their commitment to the Japanese market and their respect for its culture and business practices. This approach helped to slowly but surely cement the relationships that would be crucial for their long-term success in Japan.

Back at the clinic, the preparation for these market-specific strategies was exhaustive. Adrian and Elena reviewed countless reports and feedback sessions, ensuring no detail was overlooked. They understood that the success of their global expansion depended not only on the superiority of their technology but also on their ability to adapt and respond to each market's unique needs.

As the plans for Germany and Japan progressed, the team also kept a close eye on the operational aspects of these expansions. They coordinated logistics for shipping, installation, and training in both countries, ensuring that their teams were prepared to execute the rollouts flawlessly.

Throughout this period, regular updates were communicated to all stakeholders. Adrian and Elena held frequent briefing sessions with their team, discussing progress, addressing challenges, and iterating on strategies. These sessions were crucial for maintaining alignment and momentum.

As one particularly long day drew to a close, Adrian and Elena took a moment to reflect on the progress made and the journey ahead. They stood by the large windows in Adrian's office, looking out over the city as it lit up for the night. The quiet of the office provided a stark contrast to the complexity of their tasks.

Their conversation touched on the upcoming steps and the anticipation of seeing their plans come to fruition. They discussed the potential impacts of their technology on healthcare in Germany and Japan, and how successful integration in these markets could set the stage for further global expansion.

As they left the office, the weight of their responsibilities was palpable, yet there was a clear sense of direction and purpose in their steps. Each decision they made, each strategy they implemented, was a building block in their mission to transform therapeutic environments across the globe.

In a brightly lit conference room, with a large table covered in maps, digital tablets, and stacks of documents, Dr. Adrian Harrow and Elena Markham were deep in discussion with their respective teams for Germany and Japan. The agenda was focused on finalizing the preparations for the upcoming launches in both countries, ensuring that every detail was meticulously planned.

Adrian addressed the team, his tone marked by a mix of determination and anticipation. "We're on the brink of launching in two of the most challenging yet rewarding markets. Let's go through the final checklist and address any last-minute concerns."

Elena took the lead on the discussion, starting with the German market. "Klaus, can you confirm that all regulatory requirements have been met and that we're ready to go from a compliance standpoint?"

Klaus, joining via video link from Berlin, responded confidently, "Yes, Elena. We've passed all regulatory checks. The final documentation was approved this morning. We're fully compliant and ready for launch."

"That's excellent news," Adrian commented, then turned his attention to Akemi in Japan. "Akemi, how are things on your end? Are the partnerships solidified and the systems ready for deployment?"

Akemi's face appeared on another screen, her expression calm yet enthusiastic. "Yes, Dr. Harrow. Our partners are fully on board, and their support teams have been trained on our systems. We've also completed a series of successful pilot tests last week. Everything is set for a smooth rollout."

Elena, looking over a digital document, added, "I see we have a series of promotional events lined up in both countries. Can you give us a brief on how we plan to manage these events to maximize our impact post-launch?"

Klaus detailed his strategy for Germany. "We are coordinating with major healthcare facilities to host demonstrations of our systems. These events are paired with educational seminars on the benefits of our technology, specifically targeting leading healthcare professionals to create advocates for our systems."

Akemi outlined a similar yet culturally tailored approach for Japan. "In addition to demonstrations, we are utilizing respected figures in the healthcare community to endorse our technology. Given the importance of relationships and trust in Japan, having these endorsements will greatly enhance our credibility and acceptance."

"That sounds well thought out," Adrian acknowledged. Then, turning to Elena, he asked, "What about the media coverage? Are we prepared to handle inquiries and potentially high exposure?"

Elena nodded, "We've prepared press kits and have briefed our public relations teams in both countries. They're ready to handle media inquiries effectively. We're also monitoring social media closely to gauge public reaction and respond promptly."

Adrian, satisfied with the responses, concluded, "It sounds like we are well-prepared. I want to emphasize the importance of responsiveness during the first few weeks post-launch. We need to be agile and ready to address any issues that arise immediately."

Elena agreed, "Absolutely, staying on top of feedback and being ready to make quick adjustments will be key to our success. Let's keep our lines of communication open and ensure we support our teams on the ground."

As the meeting wrapped up, Adrian and Elena stayed behind to discuss some final thoughts. "These launches are just the beginning," Adrian remarked. "How we handle these will set the tone for future expansions."

Elena responded, "I'm confident in our preparation and our teams. It's going to be a learning experience, but I believe we're ready for whatever comes our way."

They left the conference room, their conversation continuing as they walked down the corridor, each step bringing them closer to seeing their global vision come to life. The quiet hum of the clinic in the background served as a reminder of the journey that had brought them here and the new paths they were about to forge.

The launch days in Germany and Japan had arrived, marking significant milestones in the global expansion of Dr. Adrian Harrow and Elena Markham's therapeutic environments. Early in the morning, they gathered their core team in the strategy room, filled with an air of cautious optimism and focused energy.

Adrian addressed the group, his voice steady and purposeful, "Today is a pivotal day for us. We're not just launching products; we're introducing new standards of care. Let's start with a status update from Germany. Klaus, how are things proceeding on the ground?"

Klaus, appearing on the screen from Berlin, reported enthusiastically, "The launch in Germany has started strongly. The first installations at major clinics in Berlin and Munich went smoothly, and the feedback from the medical staff has been very positive. We've encountered minor queries about system functionalities, but nothing our support team couldn't handle efficiently."

Adrian nodded, pleased with the progress. "Great work, Klaus. Keep us updated throughout the day. Now, let's hear from Akemi in Japan. How are things going there?"

Akemi's face lit up with a confident smile as she responded from Tokyo, "We've had a fantastic start, Dr. Harrow. The launch event in Tokyo was well-attended by key industry players and the media. Our demonstration sessions were particularly well-received, and we've already had inquiries about extended collaborations."

Elena chimed in, her tone mixed with relief and anticipation, "That sounds promising, Akemi. How are we handling the inquiries and potential collaborations?"

Akemi detailed her approach, "We're scheduling follow-up meetings with interested parties for next week. I've also arranged for our tech team to provide additional demonstrations to potential large-scale clients who are interested in custom solutions."

Elena, taking notes, suggested, "Make sure to keep those interactions as interactive and informative as possible. We want to build on the momentum and establish strong, long-lasting partnerships."

Adrian, shifting focus, asked, "What about the public and media response? Are we managing that effectively?"

Klaus responded first, "In Germany, the media coverage has been overwhelmingly positive. Our PR team is actively engaging with journalists to provide them with all the information they need. We're also monitoring social media to respond to any queries or concerns promptly."

Akemi added, "Similarly, in Japan, our social media engagement has spiked significantly. We're using this opportunity to boost our visibility and communicate directly with both potential clients and the general public."

Adrian, satisfied, concluded, "Excellent. It's crucial that we maintain this level of engagement and responsiveness. These launches are just the beginning of our journey in these markets."

Elena, looking ahead, proposed, "Let's also start planning the post-launch reviews. I want us to analyze what worked well and where we can improve. This will be crucial for our further expansions."

Adrian agreed, "Absolutely, Elena. Let's schedule a detailed review session two weeks from today. We'll gather all the data and feedback to make informed decisions moving forward."

As the meeting wrapped up, Adrian and Elena stayed behind to discuss the broader implications of the day's events. They spoke about the future, planning how to leverage the success of these launches to accelerate their expansion into other markets.

Walking out of the strategy room, their conversation continued, reflecting on the significant strides they had made. Each step they took through the quiet hallways of the clinic was a reminder of the impact their work was having on a global scale. The day was not just another milestone; it was a testament to their vision and dedication to improving healthcare environments worldwide.

Chapter 26
Aftermath and Understanding

As the early morning sun illuminated the quiet halls of the clinic, Dr. Adrian Harrow and Elena Markham were already immersed in the task of analyzing the global impact of their recent launches in Germany and Japan. With data streaming in continuously, their offices had become command centers for overseeing international operations and strategizing further expansions.

Adrian was reviewing a comprehensive set of performance metrics that outlined user engagement, system efficacy, and customer satisfaction across the new markets. The data was encouraging but highlighted a few areas needing refinement. He made detailed notes, planning to discuss these with Elena and the respective regional managers to ensure continuous improvement.

Elena, meanwhile, was engaged in compiling feedback from the various stakeholders involved in the deployment and daily operation of their systems. This included direct feedback from healthcare professionals, patient satisfaction surveys, and partner communications. She was particularly focused on understanding the nuances of how their technology was being integrated into different healthcare settings and any cultural adaptations that were proving either effective or challenging.

Mid-morning, they convened in a small, glass-walled meeting room to synthesize their findings and discuss their next strategic moves. Adrian shared the performance data, highlighting the high user satisfaction rates and the robust functionality of their systems. However, he pointed out, "While the overall performance is strong, there are indications that we need to enhance our training modules. The feedback suggests that more comprehensive training could help users utilize our systems more effectively, particularly in complex cases."

Elena responded, noting the importance of such refinements, "That's a critical insight. I've noticed from the stakeholder feedback that different regions have slightly different needs based on their existing protocols and patient demographics. Tailoring our training to address these specificities could significantly boost our system's efficacy and user satisfaction."

Adrian agreed, and they decided to develop a plan for advanced, region-specific training programs. This would not only involve updating their existing materials but also conducting additional onsite training sessions with their tech teams.

They also reviewed the marketing strategies that had been employed during the launches. The initial buzz had created significant interest, but sustaining that interest was now the challenge. Adrian mused, "We need to keep the momentum going. Perhaps introducing case studies and long-term data on system performance could help. Showing tangible benefits over time can strengthen our position in these markets."

Elena proposed an ongoing marketing initiative that would include regular updates on system impacts, user testimonials, and independent reviews. "Making this information readily available and easy to digest will help reinforce the value of our systems and keep our stakeholders engaged," she suggested.

Their conversation also touched on potential new markets. With the success in Germany and Japan under their belt, they were better positioned to tackle other regions. However, they agreed that consolidating their presence in the current markets was crucial before undertaking further expansions.

As they wrapped up their meeting, Adrian and Elena felt cautiously optimistic. They had a clear understanding of their current standing and a solid plan to enhance their operations. The next steps involved detailed work on training enhancements and marketing strategies, which they scheduled to discuss in upcoming meetings with their teams.

Walking back to their respective offices, their conversation shifted towards personal reflections on the journey thus far. They discussed how their roles had evolved and how the project that had started as a small initiative was now making significant global impacts.

The clinic, now coming to life as more staff arrived and the day's activities began, was a testament to the growth and success of their venture. Adrian and Elena continued their day, each step and decision guided by the data-driven insights they had gathered, all aimed at improving healthcare environments worldwide.

In the bustling heart of the clinic's innovation lab, Dr. Adrian Harrow and Elena Markham were deep in strategic planning. Their focus was sharp: to refine the user interface of their therapeutic environments, ensuring that every enhancement directly addressed the varied needs of their global user base. The room was lined with whiteboards filled with flowcharts and user feedback, underscoring the task at hand.

Adrian was examining the latest user interface mock-ups, his eyes tracing over the sleek, intuitive designs that promised easier navigation and accessibility. "These new interfaces look promising," he commented, adjusting his glasses. "They seem to simplify the processes significantly. How are the initial user tests going?"

Elena, who had been coordinating the feedback sessions, responded with a note of optimism. "The response has been overwhelmingly positive. We've seen a marked improvement in user engagement, especially among older demographics who found our previous interface challenging. The addition of visual aids and step-by-step prompts has made a significant difference."

"That's excellent to hear," Adrian said, his voice carrying a mix of relief and satisfaction. "What about the multi-lingual support features? Are they integrating well with the existing systems?"

"We've successfully implemented multi-lingual support in three pilot facilities so far, and the feedback has been encouraging," Elena explained. "The ability to switch languages has been particularly appreciated in diverse settings, helping staff and patients interact with the system more fluently."

Adrian nodded, his mind already turning to the next issue. "Let's ensure that these enhancements are scalable. It's vital that as we expand, these features can be adapted to new markets without extensive overhauls. Simon mentioned something about modular design during our last tech review. Could you elaborate on how that's being implemented?"

Elena leaned forward, her hands clasped on the table. "Yes, Simon and his team have developed a modular approach for our software updates. This allows us to plug in new features as independent modules without disrupting the core system. It's not only cost-effective but also reduces the implementation time significantly."

"Good," Adrian responded, his tone approving. "That modular design will be crucial as we prepare for further international expansion. Speaking of which, how are we handling the training for these new updates?"

Elena switched tabs on her laptop, bringing up a detailed training schedule. "We're updating our online training modules to include interactive simulations of the new features. Additionally, we're planning a series of webinars to walk through the changes with current users. For new installations, our on-site teams are equipped to provide hands-on training tailored to the specific needs of each facility."

Adrian considered this, his gaze thoughtful. "I want to ensure that our support teams are also well-versed in these updates. Perhaps we should consider a separate session for them, focusing on troubleshooting common issues that might arise with the new system features."

"That's a prudent idea," Elena agreed, making a note. "I'll arrange for a series of in-depth training sessions for our support staff. It's important they're as confident in using the new systems as they are with the old."

As the meeting drew to a close, Adrian and Elena reviewed the action items they had discussed. They were satisfied with the progress but aware of the challenges that lay ahead. Ensuring the new system enhancements were embraced by users and seamlessly integrated into existing workflows would require careful management and ongoing support.

Leaving the innovation lab, their conversation continued, focused on the strategic decisions that would guide the next phases of their project. Each step they took through the clinic was a reminder of the impact of their work and the continuous improvement it demanded. The echo of their footsteps in the quiet corridor was a soft underscore to their dedicated pursuit of excellence in healthcare technology.

In a spacious, sunlight-filled conference room, Dr. Adrian Harrow and Elena Markham were seated with key members of their innovation and development teams. The focus of today's meeting was to finalize their continuous improvement strategy—a critical component in ensuring their technology remained at the forefront of therapeutic environments.

Adrian opened the meeting with a strategic question, setting the tone. "As we push forward with our expansions, it's crucial that our technology not only meets current standards but also anticipates future healthcare needs. Simon, can you start us off by outlining the main pillars of our proposed continuous improvement strategy?"

Simon, always ready with a detailed plan, responded, "Certainly, Dr. Harrow. Our strategy is built around three main pillars: technological advancement, user feedback integration, and predictive market analysis. For technological advancement, we are setting up a dedicated R&D team whose sole focus will be on emerging technologies and innovations that can be integrated into our existing systems."

Elena, interested in the practical applications, followed up, "That sounds robust, Simon. How will we integrate user feedback more dynamically into this process?"

Simon explained, "We plan to utilize real-time data collection tools that will gather user feedback continuously. This data will be analyzed by our AI algorithms to identify patterns and potential areas for enhancement. The idea is to make our improvement loop as responsive as possible to user needs."

Adrian nodded in approval, then turned to Elena, "And what about the predictive market analysis? How are we planning to stay ahead of market needs?"

Elena was prepared with an answer, "We are enhancing our market research capabilities by partnering with analytics firms that specialize in healthcare trends. This will allow us to not only react to current trends but also to forecast future developments in healthcare that could impact our product roadmap."

Adrian, satisfied with the responses, shifted the discussion towards implementation. "These pillars are well thought out. Let's talk about the timelines and resources needed to implement this strategy effectively."

Simon took the lead, "To kickstart the R&D focus, we'll need to recruit additional specialists in AI and machine learning. I propose we launch a recruitment drive next quarter to find the right talent. As for the feedback integration tools, we can start development immediately with our current team and aim for a rollout in six months."

Elena added details about market analysis, "For the predictive market analysis, I'll coordinate with the procurement team to identify and contract with suitable analytics firms. We should have a firm onboard within three months, giving us actionable insights by the end of the year."

Adrian, thinking about the broader implications, remarked, "This strategy will require significant investment in both talent and technology. We need to ensure our financial planning is aligned with these initiatives. Elena, could you work with the finance team to ensure we have the budget to support this?"

"Absolutely," Elena confirmed. "I'll make sure that our financial projections include these strategic investments. It's crucial that we maintain a balance between innovation and fiscal responsibility."

As the meeting concluded, the team felt a renewed sense of purpose. They had a clear strategy and the beginnings of a detailed implementation plan. Adrian and Elena stayed behind to discuss some of the finer points of the strategy, ensuring that every aspect was aligned with their long-term vision.

Walking out of the conference room, their conversation continued, focused on the future and the impact of their continuous improvement strategy. Each step through the clinic was a step towards a future where their technology would continually set the standard in therapeutic environments, driven by innovation and a deep understanding of user needs and market dynamics.

Dr. Adrian Harrow and Elena Markham were settled into the clinic's main conference room, the late afternoon sun casting long shadows across the table strewn with laptops and documents. They were joined by Simon and a few department heads, all pivotal to the launch of their new Continuous Improvement Team.

Elena began the meeting with a sense of urgency. "Today, we officially set our Continuous Improvement Team in motion. This team is essential for keeping our technology at the forefront of therapeutic environments. Simon, could you update us on the staffing for this team?"

Simon, looking up from his notes, responded confidently, "We've successfully recruited three specialists in AI and machine learning, each with impressive credentials in healthcare technology. They will be joining us next week. Additionally, we are in the final stages of securing two senior data analysts who will drive our predictive market analysis efforts."

Adrian, pleased with the progress, turned to discuss the operational aspects. "That's great news, Simon. Now, let's talk about integration. How will this team interact with our existing structures?"

Simon detailed his plan, "The Continuous Improvement Team will operate semi-autonomously but will closely collaborate with all tech and product development teams. We've established protocols for sharing data and insights across teams to ensure that all enhancements are aligned with user feedback and market demands."

Elena, focusing on the financial implications, added, "I've worked with the finance team to ensure that the budget for this initiative is in place. We've allocated funds not only for staffing but also for the necessary tech upgrades and research tools they'll need to be effective."

Adrian nodded, then raised a crucial point about accountability. "With the autonomy this team will have, we need robust oversight mechanisms. How will we track and evaluate their impact?"

Simon was ready with an answer. "We'll implement a quarterly review process to assess the team's contributions to our product lines. This will include metrics on system enhancements, user satisfaction improvements, and alignment with market trends. The first review is scheduled three months from now, giving the team some time to make an impact."

Elena considered this, then suggested an addition. "I think it would also be beneficial to have an annual strategy session where the Continuous Improvement Team can present their roadmap for the next year. This will help us ensure that their plans are in sync with our broader company objectives and market evolution."

Adrian agreed, "An excellent idea, Elena. Let's formalize that in our operational calendar."

As the meeting drew to a close, the team discussed the initial projects for the Continuous Improvement Team. They decided to prioritize enhancements to the user interface based on recent feedback from Germany and Japan, as well as integrating new data analytics capabilities to better predict maintenance and upgrade needs.

The group disbanded, each member clear on their role in supporting this new initiative. Adrian and Elena lingered in the room, discussing the broader impacts of fostering a culture of continuous improvement.

"It's not just about keeping our technology competitive," Adrian reflected as they prepared to leave the room. "It's about continuously enhancing the way we impact patient care, making it more effective and intuitive."

Elena nodded in agreement, "Exactly. By being proactive, we're not just responding to the market — we're anticipating its needs, staying ahead of the curve."

Their conversation continued as they walked down the corridor, their discussion deepening into how this new approach would be communicated across the company to ensure everyone understood its value and objectives. The clinic was quieting down for the evening, but for Adrian and Elena, the work was ongoing, each step forward driven by a commitment to innovation and excellence.

Chapter 27
Healing Wounds

In the clinic's expansive conference room, Dr. Adrian Harrow and Elena Markham were gathered with their top management team, including Simon and the leaders of the newly formed Continuous Improvement Team. The large screen at the end of the room displayed a series of graphs and metrics, reflecting the recent performance data from their initiatives in Germany and Japan, along with the early impacts of the Continuous Improvement Team.

Adrian initiated the session with an analytical focus. "Let's start by reviewing the quarterly performance metrics from our operations in Germany and Japan. I want us to identify any trends that need immediate attention and areas where we can capitalize on our current momentum."

Simon, leading the presentation, highlighted key data points. "Overall, user satisfaction has remained high, and system performance is stable. However, there have been some concerns regarding the integration of the latest updates in Germany. It appears there's a learning curve associated with the new features that we underestimated."

Elena responded thoughtfully, "That's a critical insight. We need to enhance our training modules for these updates. Perhaps more interactive, on-site training could help. What's the feedback from the Continuous Improvement Team on this?"

The head of the Continuous Improvement Team, Julia, joined the conversation. "We've analyzed the feedback and agree with Simon's assessment. Our team is proposing a new set of training webinars that include virtual reality simulations, making the learning process more intuitive and engaging."

Adrian, pleased with the proactive approach, asked, "Julia, could you elaborate on how soon we can implement these new training webinars?"

"We can roll out the first set of enhanced training sessions within the next month," Julia replied. "We've already developed a prototype that's shown promising results in our pilot tests."

Elena, considering broader implications, shifted the discussion toward market responses. "Turning to market expansion, how are our efforts in adapting marketing strategies to local preferences impacting our reach and user acquisition?"

Simon took the lead again, "Our localized marketing campaigns, especially in Japan, have significantly improved engagement. We've seen a 20% increase in inquiries and system demos requests after we launched our targeted ad series last quarter."

Adrian, looking satisfied, nodded and then posed another strategic question, "And how are we doing in terms of scalability? Are the systems and support structures we've put in place capable of handling this growth without compromising quality?"

Julia was quick to reassure, "Our scalability tests are positive. The modular design of our systems allows for relatively easy expansions and updates. Plus, our support teams are scaling well, thanks to the predictive staffing models we've implemented."

Elena then asked about the financial health of the operations, "With all these enhancements and expansions, how are we standing financially? Are we within the budget, and how are our investments performing against our forecasts?"

Simon displayed another chart, showing the financial metrics. "We're on track with our budget. The initial costs of the Continuous Improvement Team and the training enhancements were significant, but they're balanced by the efficiency improvements and the reduction in system downtime, which cuts long-term costs."

Adrian wrapped up the meeting with a forward-looking statement, "This feedback is invaluable. Let's continue to adapt and innovate, ensuring that our technology not only meets current needs but sets new standards in healthcare technology. Elena, Simon, Julia, please proceed with the proposed strategies and keep this momentum going."

As the team dispersed, Adrian and Elena stayed back to discuss some of the finer details of the feedback and the strategies. They walked out of the conference room, their conversation a blend of strategic deliberation and innovative ideas, each step echoing through the quiet of the clinic, signaling their unwavering commitment to improving healthcare across the globe.

In the calm ambiance of the clinic's main strategy room, Dr. Adrian Harrow and Elena Markham convened an emergency meeting with their international operations team. Recent challenges in supply chain logistics had surfaced, threatening to disrupt their service continuity in several key markets. Today's meeting was critical to devise immediate solutions and ensure the resilience of their operations.

As everyone settled, Adrian opened the discussion with a sense of urgency. "The recent supply chain issues have brought some risks to the forefront that we need to address immediately. Simon, can you give us a detailed rundown of the current situation?"

Simon, looking prepared and focused, began, "The main issue is with our component suppliers in Asia. Due to unexpected political unrest in the region, our usual shipments are being delayed, which has started to affect our installation schedules in Europe and North America."

Elena, always keen on finding proactive solutions, responded, "We need a contingency plan that doesn't just patch these issues temporarily but strengthens our supply chain for the future. What are our options for alternative suppliers?"

Simon replied, "I've identified two potential suppliers in Europe and one in Canada. They meet our quality standards and have the capacity to handle our orders. However, transitioning will take at least a month, and there might be initial cost implications due to the change."

Adrian considered this, then turned to Elena. "We should evaluate the long-term benefits versus the short-term costs. Elena, could you analyze the financial impact of this transition?"

Elena nodded, "I'll run the numbers and see how it aligns with our current budget. We might need to adjust our forecasts, but ensuring supply chain stability is crucial."

Turning to broader operational concerns, Adrian asked, "Beyond the supply chain, how robust are our systems against similar disruptions? Are there other vulnerabilities we need to be aware of?"

Julia, the head of the Continuous Improvement Team, joined the conversation. "We've been reviewing all our operational protocols. While our systems are generally resilient, we've noticed that our data centers are overly reliant on single-source energy providers. This could be a potential risk factor."

Adrian, recognizing the importance of redundancy, suggested, "Let's explore alternative energy solutions, perhaps even renewable options that could provide us with more security and sustainability. Julia, could you take the lead on this?"

"Absolutely," Julia affirmed. "I'll investigate sustainable and reliable energy options and prepare a proposal on how we can integrate these into our data centers."

Elena, looking at the broader picture, added, "It's also essential that we communicate effectively with our clients about these changes and what they mean for their service. Transparency is key to maintaining trust."

Adrian agreed, "Good point, Elena. Let's prepare a communication strategy that outlines these challenges and our steps to address them. We need to reassure our clients that these measures are in place to enhance service reliability."

As the meeting concluded, the team had a clear action plan and assigned responsibilities. Everyone was aligned on the urgency of the tasks and committed to implementing the solutions swiftly.

Adrian and Elena lingered after the meeting to discuss the strategic implications of the day's decisions. Their walk back to their offices was thoughtful, with discussions on ensuring the company not only overcame the current challenges but emerged stronger and more resilient.

Their conversation continued, a mix of strategic decision-making and operational adjustments, echoing softly in the quiet hallways of the clinic. Each step they took reinforced their commitment to navigating the complexities of global operations with foresight and precision.

In the days following their strategic meeting, Dr. Adrian Harrow and Elena Markham dedicated themselves to overseeing the implementation of the new supply chain solutions and the integration of sustainable energy sources into their data centers. The clinic, usually a place of calm and controlled activity, had become a buzzing hub of strategic innovation as these crucial changes were put into place.

Adrian spent the morning reviewing contracts from alternative energy suppliers, ensuring that the options being considered aligned with both their operational needs and their commitment to sustainability. The chosen solution needed to not only offer reliability and reduce potential disruptions but also adhere to their corporate responsibility towards environmental impact.

Meanwhile, Elena was deep in discussions with the operations team, mapping out the logistics of shifting to the new component suppliers. This transition was complex, involving negotiations on timelines, costs, and quality assurance processes. Ensuring that these new relationships were solidified without affecting the production schedules was her top priority.

Throughout the process, both Adrian and Elena were in constant communication with their teams, receiving updates, addressing issues, and making decisions on the fly to keep the transition as smooth as possible. They were particularly focused on minimizing any disruption to their clients, who relied on their technology in critical healthcare environments.

The shift to new suppliers was accompanied by a series of audits and quality checks, ensuring that all components met their strict standards. Simultaneously, the implementation of a new energy solution for their data centers was underway. This initiative was led by Julia, who coordinated with energy experts to design a system that not only powered their data centers more efficiently but also contributed to their sustainability goals.

As these projects progressed, Adrian and Elena monitored the impacts closely. They reviewed performance reports, checked in on operational metrics, and adjusted their strategies as needed. The challenge was not just in implementing these changes but in integrating them into their existing operations without losing momentum.

By the end of the week, the first phase of the transition was complete. The new component suppliers had begun delivering, and the initial setup for the renewable energy implementation was in place. Adrian and Elena convened a brief meeting with their team to review the progress.

"This has been a monumental effort," Adrian acknowledged in the meeting, "but we've managed to not only address the immediate challenges but also set ourselves up for more sustainable operations moving forward."

Elena added, "It's crucial that we continue to monitor these changes closely. Let's ensure that our teams are on top of any issues that may arise and that we're learning from this process. Continuous improvement is key."

With the immediate crises addressed, the clinic began to return to its usual rhythm. Adrian and Elena continued their day, moving from one meeting to another, always keeping an eye on the broader strategic goals of their organization.

As they walked through the quieter corridors of the clinic late in the afternoon, their conversation turned to future projects and innovations. Each discussion reflected their ongoing commitment to enhancing healthcare through technology, driven by a philosophy of resilience, sustainability, and continuous improvement.

The day wound down with the clinic bathed in the soft glow of the setting sun, symbolizing the close of a challenging yet productive phase and the beginning of the next stage in their journey. Each decision they had made over the past few days was a step towards a more robust and responsive operation, ready to meet the future with confidence and innovation.

As dusk settled over the clinic, casting a serene glow through the expansive windows of the conference room, Dr. Adrian Harrow and Elena Markham gathered with their senior management team to review the progress of the newly implemented strategies and to plan for the future. The room buzzed with the low hum of conversation as team members prepared their notes and presentations.

Adrian initiated the session with a focused query, "Let's begin by evaluating the effectiveness of the changes we've implemented in our supply chain and energy sources. Simon, can you provide us with an update on how the new suppliers are integrating with our operations?"

Simon, ever prepared, began confidently, "The transition to our new suppliers has gone smoother than anticipated. We've seen a 15% improvement in delivery times and a 20% reduction in logistical issues. The quality of components has been consistent with our high standards, and I'm happy to report that we've managed to maintain our production schedules without any disruptions."

Elena, keen on details, followed up, "That's excellent news, Simon. How about the renewable energy sources for our data centers? Julia, can you give us an overview of the initial impacts?"

Julia, the head of the Continuous Improvement Team, responded, "The integration of renewable energy sources has started to show positive outcomes. We've reduced our energy costs by 10% and significantly lowered our carbon footprint. However, it's important to note that we're still in the early phases, and I expect these numbers to improve as we optimize the system."

Adrian, satisfied, nodded and turned the discussion towards client feedback, "With these internal improvements, have we seen any changes in client satisfaction or feedback in the markets we're focused on?"

Elena answered this, "Our client feedback has been very positive, particularly regarding our faster response times and the increased reliability of our systems. Our recent client satisfaction surveys show an improvement of 8% in overall satisfaction."

The conversation then shifted towards future strategies. Adrian directed his next question to the entire room, "Given these positive developments, what are the next steps we should take to ensure continued growth and innovation?"

Simon was quick to suggest, "I believe we should look into further diversifying our supplier base to include more regions. This could not only safeguard us against regional disruptions but also potentially reduce costs and improve our market responsiveness."

Julia added, "On the sustainability front, we should consider expanding our use of renewable energy beyond our data centers. If we could apply this to our manufacturing processes as well, we could see even greater efficiency improvements and cost savings."

Elena, thinking strategically, proposed, "It might also be time to revisit our market expansion plans. With our operations now more robust and scalable, we could accelerate our plans for entering new markets, particularly in South America and Asia where we've identified significant demand."

Adrian considered these suggestions thoughtfully. "These are all excellent points. Let's prioritize these initiatives based on our strategic objectives and resource availability. Simon, Julia, Elena, please prepare detailed proposals on each of these suggestions for our next meeting."

As the meeting drew to a close, Adrian concluded, "This has been a productive discussion. It's clear that the changes we've implemented are having a positive impact, and there are substantial opportunities ahead of us. Let's continue to push forward with innovation and operational excellence."

The team members nodded in agreement, energized by the roadmap laid out before them. They filed out of the conference room, leaving Adrian and Elena to linger for a moment, reflecting on the progress made and the exciting challenges ahead.

Their conversation continued as they walked toward their offices, their steps echoing softly in the now-quiet clinic, a testament to the day's successful planning and strategic advancements.

Chapter 28
New Beginnings

As the early morning sun began to fill the spacious conference room with a gentle light, Dr. Adrian Harrow and Elena Markham were already deep in discussion about their strategic expansion into South America. The room was set up with maps and charts detailing demographic and economic data from various South American regions, illustrating potential markets for their therapeutic environments.

Adrian opened the discussion, his tone serious yet optimistic. "South America presents a significant opportunity for us, given the rising demand for advanced healthcare solutions. Elena, can you start by giving us an overview of the market research findings?"

Elena, prepared with her notes and interactive data displays, responded, "Certainly, Adrian. Our research indicates that Brazil and Argentina are the most promising entry points for our expansion. Both countries have shown substantial growth in healthcare infrastructure and a keen interest in integrating new technologies."

"That's promising," Adrian remarked. "What are the regulatory hurdles we might face in these markets?"

Elena continued, "Regulatory frameworks in these countries are quite robust, but they are actively seeking to attract foreign healthcare technologies, which works in our favor. However, we will need to navigate local certification processes, which can be time-consuming."

Simon, who had been working closely with the operations team, added his perspective. "To address potential delays in certification, we could consider partnering with local firms that already have a presence and understand the regulatory landscape. This could expedite our entry and help us establish a local footprint more efficiently."

Adrian considered this suggestion thoughtfully. "That's a solid strategy, Simon. Can you initiate contact with potential partners and start preliminary discussions?"

"Absolutely," Simon affirmed. "I'll begin reaching out this week and set up exploratory meetings."

Elena, shifting the conversation to logistics, said, "We also need to consider our supply chain strategy for South America. Establishing a regional distribution center could significantly improve our logistics and reduce delivery times."

Adrian agreed, "Yes, let's explore locations for a regional hub. It needs to be accessible and well-connected to both Brazil and Argentina. Perhaps we can look into areas with established transport links and favorable business conditions."

The discussion then moved to marketing strategies. "Given the cultural diversity in South America, our marketing approach must be highly localized," Elena pointed out. "We should develop campaigns that resonate with local healthcare professionals and patients, emphasizing how our technology can be adapted to meet regional needs."

"That's a crucial point," Adrian noted. "Let's ensure our marketing team collaborates closely with our new partners to tailor our messages appropriately. We need to make sure our brand is perceived as both innovative and sensitive to local needs."

As the meeting drew to a close, the team outlined a clear plan of action for entering the South American market, including steps to address regulatory, logistic, and marketing challenges.

Adrian concluded, "This is an exciting step forward for us. Let's proceed with caution but also with confidence. We have a strong plan and a great team to execute it."

The team members nodded in agreement, energized by the clear direction and the new opportunities ahead. As they left the conference room, Adrian and Elena stayed behind to discuss some final strategic details, their conversation a blend of anticipation and meticulous planning.

Their dialogue continued as they walked back to their offices, each step echoing through the corridor, signaling the start of yet another ambitious phase in their global expansion. The morning light that filled the room seemed to symbolize the new horizons they were set to explore, casting long shadows that hinted at the depth and reach of their upcoming endeavors.

In a well-lit meeting room lined with documents and digital screens showcasing regulatory frameworks and timelines, Dr. Adrian Harrow, Elena Markham, and Simon were joined via video conference by Lucia, a consultant specializing in South American healthcare regulations. Today's discussion was focused on understanding and navigating the regulatory pathways in Brazil and Argentina to ensure a smooth and compliant market entry.

Adrian initiated the discussion with an overarching question. "Lucia, can you provide us with an overview of the regulatory environment in Brazil and Argentina, and highlight any significant challenges we might face?"

Lucia, displaying a detailed chart of the regulatory processes for each country, began explaining, "In Brazil, the regulatory body ANVISA requires a comprehensive review of all medical technologies before they can enter the market. The process involves several stages, including clinical trials, which must be conducted locally. Argentina has a similar process managed by ANMAT, though slightly less rigorous than Brazil's."

Elena, considering the implications, followed up, "Given these requirements, what would you suggest as our best approach to minimize delays and ensure compliance?"

Lucia advised, "I recommend that we start the clinical trial process in Brazil as soon as possible. For Argentina, leveraging the data from Brazil might streamline the approval process, as ANMAT often recognizes findings from reputable international trials, including those conducted in Brazil."

Simon, concerned about the operational aspects, added, "Regarding the clinical trials, how can we ensure they are conducted efficiently? Do we have partners or facilities in mind that could facilitate this?"

Lucia responded, "I have contacts with several clinical research organizations (CROs) in São Paulo and Buenos Aires that specialize in medical device trials. They are well-equipped and have a track record of managing efficient and compliant trials."

Adrian, thinking strategically, asked, "Could you facilitate introductions to these CROs? Also, could you help us understand the potential costs involved in these trials?"

"Absolutely," Lucia confirmed. "I can arrange meetings with the top CROs in both cities. As for the costs, I'll provide you with a detailed breakdown based on the typical expenses of similar trials we've overseen in the past."

Elena, always keen to address multiple angles, inquired, "Beyond the regulatory approvals, what other local compliance issues should we be prepared for? Are there any specific legal or ethical considerations unique to these markets that we need to address?"

Lucia elaborated, "Both countries have strict data protection laws, especially concerning patient information. We'll need to ensure that our systems are fully compliant with these regulations. Additionally, there are specific import regulations for medical devices that we need to comply with, which include labeling in Portuguese and Spanish."

Adrian concluded, "Thank you, Lucia, for the insights. Let's proceed with setting up those introductions and start the groundwork for the clinical trials. Meanwhile, Simon, please work with Lucia to ensure all our systems meet local compliance standards."

As the meeting drew to a close, the team felt better prepared to navigate the complexities of the South American market. Adrian and Elena stayed back to discuss the integration of these regulatory strategies with their overall market entry plan.

Their conversation continued, focused on timelines and resource allocation, as they walked back to their offices. Each discussion, each decision, was a step toward expanding their reach, driven by careful planning and expert guidance. The quiet of the evening settled around them, echoing the depth of their commitment to bringing their technology to new markets.

In a spacious conference room adorned with panoramic views of the city skyline, Dr. Adrian Harrow and Elena Markham met with Simon and representatives from potential local partners in Brazil and Argentina. The focus of today's strategic session was to solidify partnerships and outline a comprehensive market entry plan for South America, incorporating all the regulatory, logistical, and marketing strategies they had developed.

Elena opened the meeting with a warm welcome. "Thank you all for joining us today. We are excited about the opportunities in both Brazil and Argentina and look forward to building strong partnerships that align with our vision and values."

Adrian continued, "Our goal is to not only introduce our technology into these markets but to ensure it is integrated in a way that maximizes its effectiveness and accessibility. Simon, could you start by giving us an update on our discussions with the clinical research organizations?"

Simon, flipping through his notes, responded, "We have initiated promising discussions with several CROs in São Paulo and Buenos Aires. They are ready to start the clinical trials as soon as we finalize our agreements. These trials are crucial for our regulatory submissions and will also provide valuable data to inform our product adaptations."

One of the local representatives, Carlos, from a leading healthcare distribution company in Brazil, then spoke up. "We are prepared to assist with navigating the local business landscape and expediting the regulatory process. Our network within the healthcare community can also facilitate quicker adoption and integration of your technology."

Elena, noting Carlos's points, asked, "Carlos, can you elaborate on how we can leverage your networks to enhance our training and support systems once we launch?"

Carlos explained, "Certainly, Elena. We can organize workshops and training sessions through our healthcare contacts. This will not only help in educating practitioners about your technology but also in gathering early feedback to fine-tune the system according to local needs."

Turning the discussion towards marketing, Adrian inquired, "What specific marketing strategies do we think will be most effective in these markets?"

Marina, representing the Argentine partner, suggested, "In Argentina, there is high value placed on health technology that demonstrates clear patient outcomes. We should focus on case studies and testimonials from the clinical trials to build trust and credibility. Additionally, engaging local health influencers can greatly enhance our visibility."

Elena, pleased with the suggestion, responded, "That's a great approach, Marina. We'll integrate these elements into our marketing campaigns. Also, aligning our launch with local health observances could amplify our impact."

Adrian wrapped up the session by outlining the next steps. "Based on today's discussion, we'll proceed with finalizing our partnerships and begin the setup for clinical trials. Simon, please coordinate with Carlos and Marina to ensure all logistical aspects are addressed."

As the meeting concluded, the participants exchanged handshakes and shared looks of mutual respect and anticipation. Adrian and Elena stayed behind to debrief.

Adrian reflected, "I believe we have strong partners who not only understand our technology but also the nuances of their local markets."

Elena agreed, adding, "It's about building relationships as much as it is about deploying technology. Our approach needs to remain flexible to adapt to new insights as we move forward."

Their discussion continued as they walked back to their offices, planning for a future where their innovative technology could make a significant impact in South America. Each step was taken with a clear sense of direction, guided by detailed planning and the partnerships they hoped would turn their vision into a reality.

The atmosphere was charged with a mix of excitement and focused tension in the conference room where Dr. Adrian Harrow, Elena Markham, and their team were gathered for one of the final meetings before launching their product in South America. The walls of the room were lined with digital displays showing timelines, marketing materials, and logistical plans, each detail meticulously organized to ensure a smooth rollout in both Brazil and Argentina.

Adrian started the meeting with a direct approach. "We're on the cusp of entering two very dynamic markets. This meeting is crucial to address any last-minute concerns and to ensure that every team is aligned and ready. Let's start with the status of our clinical trials. Simon, where do we stand?"

Simon, checking his notes, responded promptly. "The clinical trials in São Paulo are concluding next week. Preliminary results are promising and indicate strong performance metrics. Buenos Aires trials are a week behind but progressing well. We expect full reports on both by month's end."

Elena then took the floor, her focus on operational readiness. "Our local teams are trained and ready to go. Distribution channels have been established, and inventory levels will support the initial launch phase. Carlos, can you confirm the logistics are all in place for next week's launch?"

Carlos, joining via video link from Brazil, confirmed, "Yes, Elena. All logistics from our side are set. The products have cleared customs, and our distribution centers are fully stocked. We've also coordinated with local healthcare facilities to schedule installations and training sessions starting from day one."

Elena, nodding in satisfaction, continued, "Excellent. Marina, what's the status on the marketing front? Are we ready to go live with our campaigns?"

Marina, also on video from Argentina, was enthusiastic. "Our marketing teams are poised to launch. The campaign leveraging health influencers is scheduled to begin simultaneously with the product launch. We have also synchronized our digital ads to go live across various platforms to maximize reach from the outset."

Adrian, ensuring every base was covered, then asked, "What about post-launch support? It's crucial that we maintain high customer satisfaction, especially during the initial rollout phase."

Simon reassured him, "Our support teams in both countries have been briefed and trained extensively. They're ready to handle inquiries and provide technical support. We've also set up a hotline specifically for healthcare professionals to reach out directly with any operational queries."

Elena added, "I'd also like to confirm that our feedback mechanisms are in place. We need to be agile and responsive to any user concerns that arise post-launch."

Carlos responded, "We have implemented a real-time feedback system that will allow users to report issues directly via the app. This data will be monitored 24/7, allowing us to respond quickly to any critical issues that might arise."

Adrian concluded the meeting with a strategic outlook. "Thank you, everyone, for your hard work and dedication. This launch is not just about expanding our footprint; it's about establishing a strong presence and demonstrating the value of our technology in improving patient care. Let's keep our communication lines open and ensure a seamless launch."

As the team members logged off and the room began to clear, Adrian and Elena lingered to discuss the broader implications of their expansion efforts. They walked towards their offices, their conversation filled with plans for monitoring the launch and adjusting strategies as needed.

Their dialogue, a blend of strategic foresight and detailed planning, echoed softly in the now quiet corridor, a testament to their commitment to revolutionizing healthcare landscapes across continents.

Chapter 29
Reflections on the Past

In the wake of their ambitious South American launch, Dr. Adrian Harrow and Elena Markham convened an early morning meeting in the clinic's main conference room to assess the initial impact and gather feedback from their teams in Brazil and Argentina. The room was quiet, save for the soft hum of the projector displaying real-time data and customer feedback on the screen.

Elena initiated the discussion with a focus on customer reactions. "Let's start with the initial feedback from our new users in South America. Carlos, can you share how our products are being received in the Brazilian market?"

Carlos, appearing on the screen from São Paulo, responded with a note of optimism. "The response has been very positive, Elena. We've successfully installed systems in over thirty healthcare facilities, and the reports highlight significant improvements in patient management and satisfaction. However, there are some concerns regarding the adaptability of the software to smaller clinics with less tech-savvy staff."

Adrian, concerned but proactive, inquired, "What steps can we take to address these concerns quickly?"

Carlos suggested, "We're planning additional training sessions specifically tailored for these smaller clinics. Our local team is also developing simplified guides and video tutorials that should help bridge the technology gap."

Elena, pleased with the proactive measures, turned her attention to Argentina. "Marina, what's the situation on your end?"

Marina, connecting from Buenos Aires, shared her insights. "Similar to Brazil, the feedback has been largely positive. The healthcare community here is excited about the potential of our systems. However, we've encountered some logistical issues with distribution in more remote areas, which has delayed a few installations."

Adrian addressed the issue, "That's something we need to fix immediately. Simon, could you work with Marina to streamline our distribution process to ensure timely installations?"

Simon, ready with a plan, replied, "Absolutely, Adrian. I'll collaborate with Marina to assess our current distribution channels and explore the possibility of partnering with local logistics companies to enhance our reach and efficiency."

Elena, knowing the importance of continuous feedback, asked, "How are we tracking user satisfaction and system performance in real-time?"

Carlos answered, "We've implemented a dashboard that collects data from all installed systems. This allows us to monitor performance and user satisfaction metrics continuously. We are also encouraging users to submit their feedback directly through the app, which has been incredibly valuable."

Adrian, satisfied with the progress, shifted the discussion towards future improvements. "These insights are crucial for our continuous improvement strategy. Julia, how can we integrate this feedback into our development cycle quickly and effectively?"

Julia, who had been listening intently, responded, "We're already analyzing the data collected to identify common issues and areas for enhancement. Our development team is agile and can prioritize updates based on this feedback. I propose setting up a bi-weekly review with all regional teams to ensure we stay on top of these improvements and implement them efficiently."

Elena concluded the meeting with a directive, "That sounds like a solid plan. Let's ensure that these meetings are productive and focused on actionable outcomes. We need to maintain the momentum and ensure that our technology not only meets but exceeds expectations."

As the meeting adjourned, Adrian and Elena remained behind to discuss the broader strategic implications of the feedback. Their walk back to their offices was contemplative, filled with discussions about leveraging their initial successes to further solidify their presence in the South American market. Each step was taken with a renewed commitment to making a significant impact on global healthcare.

The morning was brisk as Dr. Adrian Harrow and Elena Markham settled into their strategy session in the clinic's glass-walled conference room, overlooking a serene garden. Today's agenda was to discuss strategic adjustments based on the initial feedback from the South American markets and to outline plans for further expansion.

Elena began by summarizing the key points from their previous meeting. "We have seen encouraging responses in both Brazil and Argentina. However, the challenges with technology adoption in smaller clinics and the logistical issues in remote areas need our immediate attention."

Adrian nodded thoughtfully. "It's crucial that we address these effectively. Let's consider partnerships with local tech training organizations to enhance our support for less tech-savvy users. Simon, have you made any progress in identifying potential partners?"

Simon, joining the meeting via video call, responded, "Yes, I've been in contact with several organizations that specialize in tech education and support in rural areas. We are close to finalizing a partnership with TechAid Brazil, which has a wide network and a robust training platform."

"That sounds promising," Adrian replied. "Ensuring that our systems are user-friendly across all user bases is essential. Let's move forward with that partnership as soon as possible."

Elena then shifted the discussion towards logistics, "Regarding the distribution challenges in Argentina, I suggest we establish a local distribution center. This could streamline our operations and improve delivery times."

Adrian considered this carefully. "A local center could indeed solve many of our logistical issues. Have we looked into the cost implications and potential locations for this?"

"Yes, we have preliminary reports on several locations that are strategically positioned to serve both urban and rural areas effectively. The initial investment is significant, but the long-term savings and improvement in service quality could justify the expense," Elena explained.

Adrian agreed, "Let's prepare a detailed proposal for this and review the financials thoroughly. We need to ensure that this move aligns with our overall budget and expansion goals."

The conversation then turned to the potential for further market expansion. Adrian outlined his vision, "With our operations stabilizing in Brazil and Argentina, we should start looking at other countries in the region. Peru and Chile could be our next targets. Both have shown growth in healthcare investments and could benefit significantly from our technology."

Elena was quick to support the idea. "I agree. I'll start a preliminary market analysis for both countries, focusing on regulatory environments and healthcare infrastructure. We'll need to understand the challenges and opportunities in these markets to tailor our entry strategy effectively."

Adrian concluded, "Excellent. Let's keep our focus on adapting and improving our offerings while we prepare for further expansion. Continuous improvement based on user feedback should remain a priority."

As the meeting came to a close, Adrian and Elena continued their discussion while walking back to their offices. Their conversation was a mix of strategic planning and operational adjustments, reflecting their commitment to not only expand their reach but also deepen their impact in existing markets.

Each step they took was a move towards optimizing their operations and extending their innovative healthcare solutions further into South America, guided by a clear strategy and a deep understanding of the challenges and needs of the regions they served.

The morning at the clinic was particularly vibrant as Dr. Adrian Harrow and Elena Markham prepared for a critical operational review with their South American teams. The meeting, held in a conference room filled with the latest digital interfaces for real-time data analysis, was focused on enhancing operational efficiency and deepening market penetration in both Brazil and Argentina.

Adrian initiated the meeting with an immediate focus on operational metrics. "Let's dive into the current operational data. We've implemented several strategic changes over the past quarter. Simon, can you start by giving us an update on the impact of these adjustments?"

Simon, displaying a series of charts and graphs, responded, "Certainly, Dr. Harrow. Since establishing the local distribution center in Argentina, we've seen a 30% improvement in delivery times and a 25% reduction in logistical costs. This has significantly improved our service levels in remote areas."

Elena, pleased with the progress, shifted the discussion towards training initiatives. "That's great news, Simon. On another note, Carlos, how have the new training partnerships impacted our technology adoption rates in smaller clinics?"

Carlos, joining from São Paulo, shared an enthusiastic update. "The impact has been very positive, Elena. Our partnership with TechAid Brazil has allowed us to offer tailored training sessions, which have increased user confidence and system utilization by 40%. Feedback suggests that clinics now feel more supported and are utilizing more features of the system."

Adrian, thinking strategically, proposed further enhancements. "That's a significant improvement. I believe we can build on this by introducing a mentorship program where tech-savvy users can assist new adopters in their region. What are your thoughts on this, Carlos?"

Carlos considered the suggestion carefully. "That's a fantastic idea, Dr. Harrow. A peer mentorship program could further enhance user engagement and help overcome the technology barrier. We could pilot this program in a few select regions to gauge its effectiveness before a wider rollout."

Elena, always keen to optimize marketing efforts, steered the conversation towards customer engagement. "With these operational improvements in place, we should also intensify our marketing efforts. Marina, can you update us on the current campaigns in Argentina?"

Marina, from Buenos Aires, detailed the marketing strategies. "Our recent campaigns have leveraged local success stories, which have resonated well with the market. We're seeing higher engagement on our platforms, and inquiries have increased by 15%. To build on this, we're planning a series of community outreach events to educate the public on the benefits of our technology."

Adrian nodded approvingly. "Good, let's ensure these events are well-integrated with our overall marketing strategy. Also, let's use the data from these campaigns to refine our approach continually."

The conversation then turned to future strategies. Elena asked, "Looking forward, how can we leverage the data from our operations and marketing to better anticipate market needs and adjust our strategies accordingly?"

Simon answered, "We are enhancing our data analytics capabilities to provide more predictive insights, which should help us anticipate market trends and adjust our inventory and marketing efforts more dynamically."

Adrian concluded the meeting with a call to action. "Let's proceed with these initiatives and meet again next quarter to review the progress. It's crucial that we maintain this momentum and continue to adapt our strategies to meet the evolving needs of the market."

As the meeting adjourned, Adrian and Elena lingered to discuss the finer points of the new initiatives, their conversation a blend of operational tactics and strategic foresight. They left the conference room with a clear plan for moving forward, each step echoing their commitment to not only expand their presence but also to profoundly impact healthcare standards across South America.

Late afternoon sunlight streamed through the large windows of the clinic's conference room, setting a serene backdrop as Dr. Adrian Harrow, Elena Markham, and their key team members convened for a crucial strategy session. The focus was to solidify the plans for the next quarter and to enhance collaboration across all teams to ensure the continued success of their operations in South America.

Adrian opened the meeting with a strategic focus. "As we move forward, it's essential that we not only consolidate our gains but also look for new opportunities to grow. Simon, can you provide an update on the operational efficiencies we discussed last time, particularly how the mentorship program is shaping up?"

Simon, well-prepared with his notes, began, "The mentorship program in Brazil has exceeded our expectations. The initial feedback has been overwhelmingly positive, with veteran users expressing high levels of satisfaction in aiding newer clinics. This has not only improved technology adoption rates but also fostered a sense of community among users."

Elena, clearly pleased with this outcome, added, "That's fantastic to hear. I think we should consider expanding this program to include Argentina as well. Marina, how do you think this would translate in the Argentine market?"

Marina, ready with her insights, responded, "I believe it would be very effective. There's a strong community spirit within the healthcare sector here, and leveraging that can significantly enhance our user engagement. I'll start laying the groundwork to introduce the program next quarter."

Adrian, noting the success, suggested, "Let's also look at integrating more advanced data analytics into the mentorship program to track its effectiveness more rigorously. Julia, could your team develop a framework for this?"

Julia was quick to affirm, "Absolutely, Adrian. We can set up a system to monitor key performance indicators related to the mentorship program, such as engagement levels, problem resolution times, and overall satisfaction. This will allow us to make data-driven decisions to enhance the program continuously."

Elena, shifting the focus, said, "Beyond operational strategies, we need to ensure our marketing efforts are aligned with these initiatives. Marina, what are the upcoming campaigns, and how can we integrate the success of the mentorship program into them?"

Marina detailed her plans, "Our next campaign will focus on 'Technology in Community,' highlighting how our systems and programs like mentorship are bringing healthcare providers together and improving patient care. We'll feature testimonials from participants and data points showing the program's success."

Adrian nodded, satisfied with the direction. "Excellent. Ensuring our marketing messages reflect our on-ground realities is crucial. Let's make sure these stories are told compellingly."

Simon, bringing up another point, asked, "Should we also consider any adjustments to our supply chain in light of the expansion of the mentorship program and other operational changes?"

Elena responded, "Yes, let's review our current logistics and supply chain setups to ensure they can support the expanded operations without hitches. We need a seamless flow of resources to support our growth."

Adrian wrapped up the meeting with a call to action. "Everyone, let's proceed with these plans and meet again in two weeks to review preliminary results and adjust our strategies as necessary. We're on a good path, and with your continued efforts, I'm confident we'll make even greater strides."

As the team members left the room, Adrian and Elena lingered to discuss some final thoughts on leadership and development strategies for their South American teams.

Their conversation continued as they walked down the now-quiet hallway, reflecting on the day's achievements and the tasks ahead. Each discussion was a stepping stone towards ensuring their initiatives not only succeeded but also set new standards in the industry, pushing forward their mission to revolutionize healthcare across continents.

Chapter 30
A Door Left Ajar

Under the warm glow of the early morning sun filtering through the windows of Dr. Adrian Harrow's office, he and Elena Markham were deep in preparation for a crucial strategic review meeting. Their focus was to assess the overall progress of their operations in South America and discuss potential expansion into other regions.

Adrian was reviewing a detailed report on the screen before him when Elena entered. "Good morning, Adrian. I've just finished the latest performance metrics, and they look promising. Our initiatives are not only taking hold, but they're also starting to influence broader market trends."

"That's excellent to hear," Adrian responded, turning away from his screen. "Let's ensure we capture these trends in today's presentation. The board will be interested to see how our strategies are translating into tangible outcomes."

Elena nodded, pulling up a chart on her tablet. "I've included a segment on user engagement and how the mentorship program has significantly boosted our user satisfaction scores. However, there are areas where we could improve, particularly in our supply chain responsiveness."

Adrian considered this, his expression contemplative. "Let's discuss potential solutions for the supply chain issues during the meeting. It's critical that we address these bottlenecks to maintain our service standards."

As they walked to the conference room, their conversation continued, focused on the upcoming discussion points. Upon arrival, they were greeted by the senior management team, all eager to contribute to the strategic planning.

The meeting began with Adrian addressing the team. "Thank you all for joining. Today, we're not only reviewing our progress but also exploring how we can leverage our success to expand further. Elena, please start us off with the performance overview."

Elena projected her charts onto the screen, pointing out key statistics. "As you can see, our market penetration in Brazil and Argentina has exceeded expectations. However, the success has stretched our logistic capabilities, leading to some delays."

Simon, head of operations, joined the discussion. "I've been working on potential solutions for our logistic challenges. Expanding our distribution centers in key locations could help. Additionally, partnering with local logistics firms might provide the flexibility we need to handle fluctuations in demand more effectively."

"That sounds like a viable strategy," Adrian said, nodding in approval. "Let's detail this approach and consider a pilot project to test these adjustments before a full-scale rollout."

Elena then shifted the focus to future opportunities. "Looking ahead, we have potential markets in Peru and Chile showing interest. Given our success in similar environments, I believe we're well-positioned to replicate our model there."

"The key will be adapting our approach to the unique challenges of these new markets," Adrian added. "Marina, what's your take on this based on the marketing perspective?"

Marina, always ready with market insights, responded, "Both Peru and Chile have burgeoning healthcare sectors with a growing acceptance of technology solutions. Our preliminary market research suggests high potential, especially if we tailor our marketing strategies to highlight local success stories from Brazil and Argentina."

Adrian concluded, "Excellent insights, everyone. Let's use the data we have to start formulating a detailed plan for potential expansion into Peru and Chile. Simon, coordinate with Marina and Elena to ensure all aspects are covered, from logistics to market entry strategies."

As the meeting wrapped up, the team felt a renewed sense of purpose and direction. Adrian and Elena lingered to discuss the next steps, their conversation a blend of strategic decisions and operational details.

They left the conference room with a clear action plan, ready to tackle the challenges and opportunities that lay ahead. Each discussion, each decision, was another step toward broadening their impact on global healthcare.

In a conference room filled with regional maps and demographic studies, Dr. Adrian Harrow and Elena Markham sat with their strategic planning team. The agenda for the day was clear: to craft a detailed entry strategy for Peru and Chile, integrating lessons learned from their experiences in Brazil and Argentina.

Elena opened the discussion with a focus on market readiness. "Based on our analysis, both Peru and Chile have shown significant growth in health tech adoption, but there are distinct differences in regulatory environments and healthcare infrastructure. We need to tailor our strategies accordingly."

Adrian, looking over the market data, added, "Let's start with regulatory strategies. Simon, what's the status of our applications for approval in these markets?"

Simon, flipping through his notes, replied, "We've initiated the regulatory processes in both countries. Peru seems to have a faster approval timeline, but Chile offers a more robust IP protection framework which is advantageous in the long run."

"Considering that," Adrian pondered, "should we prioritize one market over the other, or launch simultaneously?"

Elena weighed in, "I suggest a staggered approach. Start with Peru, given the quicker entry, and use our learnings there to smooth our subsequent entry into Chile."

"That's sensible," Adrian agreed. "What about our local partnership strategies? Have we identified potential partners?"

Marina, responsible for market partnerships, responded, "Yes, we've shortlisted several potential partners in both countries. In Peru, we're looking at partners who can help with distribution logistics given the challenging geography. For Chile, we're focusing on partners with strong governmental ties to navigate the regulatory landscape effectively."

Elena, considering operational tactics, asked, "How will we manage the supply chain complexities, especially with Peru's diverse terrain?"

Simon had a plan ready. "We're considering setting up a regional distribution hub in Lima, which can serve as a central point for both countries. This hub will manage inventories and ensure timely distribution to even the most remote areas."

Adrian, satisfied with the logistical planning, shifted the focus to marketing. "Marina, what are our marketing strategies for these markets? How do we ensure strong brand presence from the onset?"

Marina explained, "Our campaigns will emphasize the adaptability and effectiveness of our systems. For Peru, we'll focus on community health improvements, leveraging local success stories. In Chile, we'll highlight our technology's precision and compliance with stringent health standards to appeal to their more regulated environment."

"That's a strong differentiation," Adrian noted. "Lastly, let's talk about our post-launch support. It's crucial for customer retention."

Elena proposed, "Given the diverse healthcare landscapes, I recommend setting up dedicated support teams in each country. These teams will not only handle technical support but also gather ongoing user feedback to inform continuous product improvements."

Adrian concluded, "Excellent discussions, everyone. Let's finalize these plans and start implementation in phases. We'll meet again in two weeks to review progress and make any necessary adjustments."

As the team members began to leave, Adrian and Elena stayed behind to refine some of the finer points of their strategy. Their conversation continued as they walked toward their offices, discussing how to effectively communicate these plans to their stakeholders and ensure alignment across their global teams.

Each decision made in today's meeting was a step toward expanding their reach into new markets, driven by strategic foresight and a commitment to adapting their approach to meet local needs.

The early morning light filtered softly through the high windows of the clinic's strategic planning room where Dr. Adrian Harrow and Elena Markham were deeply engaged in implementing their carefully devised expansion strategy into Peru and Chile. The room was quiet except for the occasional shuffle of papers and the low hum of a projector displaying timelines and key performance indicators on the wall.

Adrian and Elena reviewed the detailed project timelines that outlined every step of the entry strategy for the new markets. They were focused on ensuring that each phase of the plan was executed flawlessly, aware that the success of their expansion heavily depended on the precision of their implementation.

Elena was particularly concerned with the setup of the regional distribution hub in Lima, which was a cornerstone of their logistical strategy for both Peru and Chile. She had been coordinating closely with Simon and local partners to ensure that the hub was operational ahead of schedule, which would enable smooth distribution of their systems across both countries.

Meanwhile, Adrian was overseeing the final touches on the regulatory submissions, ensuring that all documentation was compliant with local standards and ready for review. He had regular calls with their regulatory team and local consultants to track the progress and address any issues promptly.

The marketing team, led by Marina, was also in full swing, preparing for the launch campaigns tailored to each country's market. They were creating materials that highlighted the benefits of their technology, emphasizing its adaptability to different healthcare environments and its effectiveness in improving patient outcomes.

As the day progressed, Adrian and Elena took a moment to discuss the training programs for new users in Peru and Chile. They were determined to avoid the pitfalls they had encountered in earlier markets and had designed a comprehensive training program that included hands-on sessions, digital tutorials, and ongoing support.

Elena noted, "We need to ensure that the training is not just about how to use the technology, but also about understanding its benefits. This will help in achieving deeper integration into their daily operations and ultimately, better patient care."

Adrian agreed, adding, "Absolutely, and let's not forget the importance of gathering feedback. It's crucial that we set up a system to collect insights from day one. This will help us make real-time adjustments and improve user satisfaction."

They also planned a series of initial review meetings that would occur after the first month of operations in the new markets. These meetings would involve all key stakeholders and would focus on evaluating the effectiveness of the launch strategy and making necessary adjustments.

As the afternoon wore on, Adrian and Elena wrapped up their session, satisfied with the progress but aware of the challenges ahead. They had a brief conversation with the rest of the team to reiterate the importance of staying on schedule and maintaining open lines of communication across all departments.

Their conversation continued as they walked through the clinic, discussing future plans and potential strategies for sustaining long-term growth in the new markets. They were optimistic but cautious, knowing that the success of their venture depended on a multitude of factors, all intricately linked to how well they executed their current plans.

With a final review of their notes and a shared nod of confidence, they parted ways, each to their respective tasks, driven by the shared goal of transforming healthcare in new territories. Each step they took was a testament to their dedication to making a significant impact through innovation and careful strategic planning.

As the sun began to set, casting long shadows through the spacious windows of the clinic's operations center, Dr. Adrian Harrow and Elena Markham reviewed the first wave of operational data streaming in from their new expansions into Peru and Chile. The room was quiet, save for the soft clicking of keyboards and the occasional murmur of consultants discussing data points.

Adrian closely examined the user engagement statistics from the first month post-launch. He noted the uptake rates and the frequency of system usage, which were crucial indicators of initial acceptance and integration into daily healthcare practices. The numbers were promising but highlighted some areas for improvement, particularly in user retention and system utilization in remote areas.

Elena, meanwhile, was focused on the supply chain dynamics. She had set up an advanced logistics tracking system that monitored the movement of goods from their distribution hub in Lima to clinics across both countries. This system helped identify any bottlenecks in real time, allowing for swift adjustments. She noticed some delays in customs clearance which had caused temporary shortages at several clinics—a situation that needed immediate attention to avoid compromising service delivery.

The marketing feedback was also under scrutiny. Marina had initiated a comprehensive market feedback mechanism that collected responses from various advertising channels. The initial responses were overwhelmingly positive, with high engagement on digital platforms indicating successful outreach. However, there was a discrepancy in the expected versus actual turnout at some community health seminars, suggesting a need for better local community engagement strategies.

Adrian and Elena convened a small meeting with their core team to discuss these findings and plan the necessary adjustments. Adrian started, "The data gives us a clear indication of where we are succeeding and where we need to push harder. The supply chain issues, particularly the customs delays, are my immediate concern. Elena, could we expedite the resolution?"

Elena responded with a plan, "I'm already on it. We're increasing our on-ground support at customs to ensure faster clearance and considering alternative shipping routes to circumvent recurring delays."

Adrian nodded in approval and turned his attention to the marketing efforts. "Marina's efforts on the digital front are yielding excellent results. We need to replicate this success in our community outreach. Perhaps a more localized approach?"

"Yes," Elena agreed, jotting down a note. "I'll coordinate with Marina to integrate more local influencers and healthcare professionals who can resonate more with the community's specific needs and expectations."

The discussion then shifted towards ongoing training for the new systems. Feedback had shown that while initial training sessions were well-received, there was a demand for more in-depth follow-up training to ensure proficient usage of all system features.

"We should set up a series of advanced training webinars that address specific features and common user challenges," suggested Elena. "This could really help deepen the understanding and integration of our systems."

Adrian concluded, "Let's prioritize these webinars and make sure they are easily accessible. Also, keep monitoring the user feedback closely—it's our best tool for making real-time improvements."

As the meeting wrapped up, Adrian and Elena stayed behind to further discuss the strategic adjustments. They walked through the quiet, dimly lit corridors of the clinic, their conversation a mix of strategic deliberations and operational tactics, each focused on ensuring the success of their international expansions.

Their path through the clinic reflected their journey—meticulously planned, carefully executed, and continuously adjusted, all aimed at transforming healthcare practices in new markets with their innovative technology.

Conclusion

In the conclusion of the story, Dr. Adrian Harrow faces a profound reckoning with the unknown forces he has inadvertently unleashed through his mirror therapy. After numerous unsettling incidents and disturbing revelations about the mirrors' past, Harrow and his consultant on folklore, Elena, decide to confront the supernatural phenomena head-on. They conduct a series of experiments to understand and contain the entity they suspect is linked to the mirrors—referred to in ancient texts as "Mirrormask."

Their journey leads them deeper into a blend of science and the supernatural, challenging Harrow's rigid adherence to scientific methods. As they employ ancient rituals combined with modern psychological techniques, they begin to notice a significant reduction in the eerie manifestations. However, the true test comes when they attempt a final ritual to cleanse the mirrors during the peak of a lunar cycle, believed to enhance the ritual's power.

The ritual is tense and fraught with the unexpected, but ultimately, they observe a cessation of the disturbances. Harrow, profoundly changed by these events, decides to write about his experiences, blending his scientific observations with the folklore insights provided by Elena. This culminates in a published work that gains some attention in both academic and paranormal circles, leaving the door open for future explorations into the unknown.

The story closes with Harrow reflecting on the nature of belief, science, and the unseen world, acknowledging that the universe holds more mysteries than he ever imagined. His clinic continues to operate, but with a new-found respect and caution for the tools and methods he employs, forever mindful of the thin veil between the natural and the supernatural.